Demon's Sorrow

By
Linda M. Fields

PublishAmerica
Baltimore

© 2011 by Linda M. Fields
All rights reserved. No part of this book may be reproduced, stored in a retrieval system or transmitted in any form or by any means without the prior written permission of the publishers, except by a reviewer who may quote brief passages in a review to be printed in a newspaper, magazine or journal.

First printing

All characters in this book are fictitious, and any resemblance to real persons, living or dead, is coincidental.

PublishAmerica has allowed this work to remain exactly as the author intended, verbatim, without editorial input.

Hardcover 978-1-4560-6088-6
Softcover 978-1-4560-6089-3
PUBLISHED BY PUBLISHAMERICA, LLLP
www.publishamerica.com
Baltimore

Printed in the United States of America

January 18

If anyone had been traveling down the road that night, a sporadic flash of red against the solid white background of blowing snow would have been the only indication that a vehicle was parked in the small clearing at the side of the road. But no one was out that frigid winter night, so the car, the driver and the shivering teenage girl huddled fetus style in the trunk went unseen. The deadly arctic wind howled around the idling Ford but the girl no longer heard it as she sought to burrow deeper into the darkness, hiding from the bogeyman much as a small child hid from the monsters beneath the bed. Maybe, just maybe if she kept very quiet he would forget she was still there.

The thump-thump-thump of the man's heart danced with the bittersweet stench of tobacco seeping through the cracks around the car's back seat. She found little comfort in the thought that as long as his heartbeat and the cigarette smoke remained she was safe for a little longer. When his cigarette was done she was terrified that he would return to torment and torture her again, or, if she were lucky, take pity and end her suffering once and for all.

Lyndsay couldn't say why this was happening to her any more than she could identify the man that had done this horrible thing to her, though surely she knew him, as there were no strangers in Whitefields, and hadn't she willingly gotten into his car wearing only a thin nightgown and robe, assuming she'd be safe? Just after he'd raped her, a strange shocked sadness seemed to cover the man's face as Lyndsay cried out for her mommy, and at that moment she almost remembered who he was.

She'd stopped shivering minutes, or perhaps hours, earlier as a strange lethargic numbness embraced her bruised and abused body.

Shimmering gossamer-ice clung against her pale skin like frosting, as the wind-chill dipped into the double digits below zero, making the thin robe and nightgown worse than useless, and if not for the stiff smelly blanket she'd discovered in the cramped trunk earlier and covered her half frozen body with she was pretty sure she'd be frozen stiff by now.

Once, two or three cigarettes ago, a strangely haunting giggle had fluttered in the darkness startling the girl until a loud thud against the rear car seat, followed by a snarled curse, made her realize that the eerie sound had escaped her own cracked lips. That small sound was enough to send her soul tumbling into the blackest depths of Hell.

#

The first major snowfall began at dusk, and with the darkness the full fury of the storm descended upon the land. This storm would be talked about for years to come as the worst storm to hit Whitefields since the "Blizzard of '78".

Thousands of acres of virgin forest surround the small Michigan town, and when the snow fell, as it was doing this night, the town would be cut off from the rest of the world for days, or weeks, as drifts, high as a man, closed the only two roads into or out of town.

The weatherman in Lansing promised a slight chance of flurries, but the more knowledgeable residents of Whitefields knew from the signs that a big one was coming. In a larger city most people believed what they were told on television, not what they felt in their bones or what they saw in the land around them, but in Whitefields people believed in the signs, and they were ready.

Well before dusk most men, women, and children were tucked snugly in their warm secure homes. No one would venture from that safe haven unless their life or a loved ones life depended on it, and that night only a few people would be foolish enough to face the elements, and one wouldn't live to tell about it.

About eleven-thirty, a lone figure scurried erratically through the thick forest on the eastern side of town. Lyndsay stumbled and fell, then stiffly pulled herself up against the rough trunk of a maple tree, and tried to move forward, she had but one thought as she struggled to keep moving, she had to go home, home to the protective arms of her mom and dad, home where the nightmare would end, where bad things never happened to good girls because Mom and Dad would always protect her from the boogeyman.

Her tears had stopped long ago, and now the sixteen-years-old no longer felt the sting of snow pellets against her face. Lost and alone in the blinding white nightmare, Lyndsay mistakenly moved deeper into the forest.

Thankfully the numbing cold had eased the pain between her bloodied legs, and the side of her head didn't hurt any more either, and one word continually chased it's tail through her mind, nightmare.

"NIGHTMARE," Lyndsay screamed, then laughed hysterically as a broken tree branch clawed through the porcelain layer of flesh on her right leg. The seeping blood almost immediately stopped flowing, and then painlessly changed color from bright red-to-pink-to-frosty white. Content with this new source of proof that she was moving through a nightmare, Lyndsay pushed forward seeking the doorway to reality.

Stumbling, she seemed to move in slow motion as she slid down a huge old oak tree, leaving bits of flesh in the rough bark. Her body, as her mind had earlier, finally surrendered to the horror of the nightmare from which she could not awaken.

Thought of the anguish her parent's faced tugged Lyndsay's mind from its safe haven. "Mamma, I'm so sorry." A lone single tear slipped from her eye but almost instantly froze on the ice child's face, and then thankfully her mind once again withdrew into darkness.

A strange sound pursued her into the darkness and pulled her back. Slowly her eyes opened, then shut, and opened again in bewilderment.

"My God", she whispered. Standing before her was the most beautiful being she'd ever seen. A warm shimmering light radiated from the Native American woman, and her white buckskins shone brighter than the crystal snowflakes that swirled around, and through her.

The woman didn't speak but held her hand out to Lyndsay, as an encouraging smile danced in her eyes. When the girl tried to reach out the woman shook her head, then Lyndsay heard a beautiful soft voice in her mind, "Leave it, it's of no use."

Her frozen lips refused to work at first but finally Lyndsay managed to ask, "Leave what?"

"Leave the flesh."

"But…."

Stepping closer, the woman said, "No. Come now, your revenge shall be your reality."

Lyndsay's mind reeled back toward the abyss, "But I don't want revenge, I just have to go home."

"You can never go home again."

"Please!" She would have cried then but there were no tears left, just frozen flesh that looked like damaged porcelain on a beautiful china doll.

"No! They have taken it from you Lyndsay, and you'll know no peace until he who has wronged you has paid. It is the law. Search your soul and its memories, and you will know what I say is true. Come now, there is no reason for you to suffer any longer. The sin committed here this night is the responsibility of all your people because they have forgotten the law of this land, but soon you and I will remind them."

#

CHAPTER 1

April 10

Tommy Rogers raced along behind Bruiser barely able to keep up with his big buddy. After a long, especially cold winter it felt really good to be able to race through the woods again. Although, he admitted to himself, it had been much more fun last year when Bruiser was just a pup and really had to pump his little legs to keep up with Tommy. Now, Tommy suspected that, if the dog decided to, he could probably even beat Superman in a footrace, which meant Tommy wouldn't stand a chance of keeping up with the Siberian Husky.

By using his total body weight against the leash Tommy was able to bring the dog to a halt. Bent at the waist with his hands on his knees, Tommy sucked much needed oxygen into his lungs. When he glanced at Bruiser, he was sure the dog was smirking at him, but at the moment all Tommy wanted to do was rest against an inviting tree trunk and wait for a his strength to return. Reluctantly Bruiser settled down beside his little master and seemed content to rest his head in the boy's lap.

Tommy laughed at the expression on the dog's face. "Hey, don't look at me like that, I can't help I'm getting old, and can't run like I used to."

Bruiser grumbled a reply deep down in his throat.

"Yeah? Well I'm going to be ten next week, and that ain't no spring chicken," Tommy countered with one of his mother's favorite clichés.

Suddenly Bruiser stood, his nose pointing into the breeze. The hair down the middle of his back bristled and the noise coming from deep in his throat became a deep menacing rumble.

Goose bumps tightened the skin on Tommy's neck, "What? What's the matter, Boy?"

Never before had Tommy heard such a threatening sound. Bruiser would growl if a stranger got too close, but it never sounded like this, and he'd never seen the dog's hair stand straight up either.

"Bruiser, stop it, you're scaring me. Come here," Tommy, demanded trying to pull the dog to him, but Bruiser fought against the leash, and for the first time Tommy felt a twinge of fear towards his best friend and companion. The dog was stiff and unyielding, his growl lower, louder, and more threatening still. Cautiously Tommy touched the dog's stiff fur, sure that the hairs would be needle sharp.

Moving slowly so as not to alarm the dog Tommy stood, *If he's going to bite me I'd rather he bites me on the ass than have him eat my face.* Tommy giggled nervously.

Bruiser's afraid! Tommy suddenly realized, but that couldn't be right, the big dog wasn't afraid of anything!

Okay, if something out there's bad enough to make Bruiser afraid, then it's bad enough to make me afraid.

"Okay boy, you convinced me, let's get the hell out of here!"

Tommy was sure his arms were at least three inches longer because when he turned to run the dog decided to take off in the opposite direction. He almost let go of the leash, unwilling to face whatever was scary enough to frighten the bravest dog in the whole world. Out there in the thick green forest waited Frankenstein, or Dracula, or at the very least The Wolfman. "No Bruiser! Let's go home!"

When the dog turned his icy-blue stare on Tommy the boy felt more than just a hint of fear this time.

"Okay Bruiser, I'm not going to argue with you, because I know you can bite my arm right off if you wanted to, but please, let's go home, Boy. You're my best friend in the whole world, and I don't want nothing bad happenin' to you, so please…please come home with me."

Big wet tears streaked down Tommy's cheeks. Bruiser, only wanting to protect his little master from the bad smell coming from the forest, looked from Tommy to the deep woods then back to the boy again. Before either of them knew what was happening, Bruiser lifted his big head towards the heavens, and a long low howl floated out into the crisp spring air.

"Jesus Bruiser, you sound like a ghost! Let's get out of here!" Tommy turned and ran, and the dog quickly took the lead as though his eerie howl had frightened him as well.

When Tommy felt he'd put a safe distance between himself and whatever was back there, he slowed his pace enough for a quick peek over his shoulder. For a heart stopping second he was sure he saw a shimmering figure dart between the trees, but then it was gone, but Tommy knew he imagined the figure because there weren't any real Indians around anymore.

#

Anna Rogers poured another cup of coffee as she agonized over her current novel. *This use to be fun,* she thought scanning the page of uninspired script. Well, it definitely wasn't fun anymore. *Hell, it's too much like work to be fun.*

Rereading her hero's latest escapade, Anna sighed disgustedly. Just how many exciting adventures could a three-legged turtle have? At this point in her career Anna was ready to feed the soup-pot fugitive to a nice fat owl.

"Mom!" Tommy bellowed as he crashed through the kitchen door right behind her.

"Jesus Tommy, don't yell, I'm not deaf...yet."

"Can Bruiser come in the house, Mom? Please?"

Anna noticed the quiver in her son's voice and turned to look at him more closely. Ever since the trouble with Tommy's father, (she no longer thought of him as her husband) the boy was nervous and easily frightened. *If that worthless son-of-a-bitch is sneaking around again I'll kill him!*

"What's the matter, Honey? You look like you saw a ghost."

Tommy flinched. "A ghost? Why'dja say that?"

She was aware of him watching her, his little boy face etched with the fear she'd come to know and hate, " Just a figure of speech, Honey, now what's the matter?"

Tommy had just spent the last fifteen minutes as he ran home, trying to think of a way to explain to his mother what happened in the forest, and why Bruiser just had to stay in the house, even though the dog barely tolerated being inside even in the winter.

He reluctantly decided nothing he told Anna would make sense because it didn't make sense to him and he was there. What had really happened? Nothing, except Bruiser had growled and howled at something that could have been a rabbit, deer, or nothing at all. Maybe the silly dog was just singing his I'm-glad-it's-summer song. Of course Tommy didn't believe that because he'd never been scared of his own dog before, but nothing else made any sense either.

"Nothing's wrong, Mom, but can Bruiser come in for a while? We're kind of tired of playing outside, it's boring."

Anna almost gave in, but the manuscript beckoned.

"No."

"But Mom…"

"Tommy, its seventy-five degrees outside, and the last thing I need is buffalo dog leaving clumps of fur all over."

"But…"

"No! N—0. Fix yourself a sandwich and go outside and play with Bruiser, but you're not going to play in the house, either one of you, got it?"

Tommy grumbled under his breath, but Anna chose to ignore him. Tommy took bologna, pickles, Miracle whip, and cheese from the refrigerator, then reached back and grabbed the grape jelly. From the cabinet be brought out peanut butter, bread and a bag of chips. Anna watched, her stomach protesting as her son piled everything between the slices of bread even the chips.

"Silly sandwich, huh?" She asked, amazed at the boy's cast-iron stomach.

"Yeah, want one?"

"Ah, no, but thanks anyhow."

Tommy glanced thoughtfully out the window over the kitchen sink at the forest, and suddenly his face lit up. "Mom, are there bears in the woods?"

Anna's stomach flipped. "Bears? Why? Did you see a bear?"

Tommy's eyes brightened. "You mean there are bears around here?"

Are there bears around here? Hadn't she noticed more deer and rabbits lately? There seemed to be more raccoons and skunks, even a couple coyotes too, but bears, maybe, why not?

"I haven't heard of any bears around here, why, do you think you might have seen one?"

Tommy watched Bruiser through the window. The dog hadn't moved an inch. *I wish he wouldn't keep staring at the woods like that.*

"Tommy?"

"Huh?"

"Do you think you saw a bear?"

Tommy glanced at Bruiser again before turning back to his mother. "Nah, I didn't see anything, but Bruiser was acting really weird like maybe he saw something."

"Well, maybe he saw a deer, or smelled a skunk."

Tommy thought about this for a moment then shook his head. "Nah I don't think so 'cause he howled really weird, kind of spooky like."

"Howled, huh?"

"Yeah, you know like OOOOOOOHHHHHHHH." Tommy did his best to imitate the dog.

Anna laughed. "Huskies do that."

"They do?" Tommy frowned.

"Yeah, just like they kind of talk to you, you know how Bruiser does that. Well, other dogs don't talk to you like that, and they don't howl like Huskies do either."

"How come I never heard him do it before?"

"He usually does it late at night, after you're asleep. He does it really low too, like he knows if he's too loud he'll wake you up."

"You mean you've heard him do it?" Tommy asked skeptically.

Anna ruffled his hair. "Lots of times."

"Yeah?"

"Yeah."

#

Tommy woke sometime in the early hours of morning. An eerie sound pulled him from the comforting depths of sleep.

"Bruiser," he whispered into the night as a shiver crept up his spine. Tommy's first thought was of monsters in the forest, then his thoughts shifted to memories of another night not so long ago when his father crept up the stairs, the night his nightmare became real.

Tommy remembered his father's voice sounding especially loud that night. He'd tried to block the sound of their argument, but when Anna's cry of pain was cut short by a loud thump, Tommy was out of bed, and racing blindly to his parent's bedroom.

His mother was on the floor, knees drawn to protect her face and stomach from the blows his father rained upon her. Dad's face was red with rage as he drew his foot back to deliver yet another brutal gift, at that moment something in Tommy snapped and he attacked. His small hands beat air as his father held him by the hair at arm's length.

Tommy heard his mother's screams, but, before she could react, his father surprised them all by picking Tommy up and, screaming curses at the boy, threw him across the room into the bedroom wall.

Before darkness claimed him Tommy thought proudly, *at least I got him to stop hitting Mommy.*

Outside Bruiser continued to howl softly. Mom said it was because he was related to wolves, which Tommy thought was pretty cool, and everyone knows wolves howl at the moon. Turning his head slightly, Tommy saw the full moon shining through his bedroom window.

Cool or not, the sound was still a little scary, so he pulled the sheet over his head. Dad couldn't come back because Mom had something called a peace-of-bond on him, and he wasn't allowed near Tommy, or Mom, or even near the house 'cause the cops would put him in jail if he did. As he lay watching the shadows from the bright moonlight through the sheet the boy thought of monsters in the forest and realized that the scariest monster of all was the one that took possession of his father the night he'd beat and kicked Anna and threw Tommy into the wall.

#

CHAPTER 2

Alex Rogers threw the screwdriver against the garage wall. Six times he drove the screw into the hole, and six times it went in crooked. Damned thing has to be drilled crooked, he thought, twisting the cap off another Budweiser.

He kicked the scattered parts that, once together, would supposedly be a shiny new ten-speed bike for his son. Glaring at the bike parts scattered around the living room Alex decided that a person had to be a genius to assemble the damned thing, or at least have a degree in engineering. He swore again at the clerk at Lowe's for not letting him buy the bike they already had together on display, he swore stores did shit like this just to make a man feel incompetent.

The bike was suppose to be a peace offering for Tommy, for his tenth birthday, but at the rate he was going the kid would be forty years old before Alex got it together.

He drained half the beer in one gulp, thinking about that night a couple of months ago. Guilt over the incident drove him to buy the bike, but anger over the guilt kept him from getting it put together.

Then there was Anna. Getting her to let him see Tommy was something he wasn't looking forward to. A Peace Bond for God sake. He just hoped that she realized that if he *really* wanted to see her or the boy he'd by God see them, and no damned stupid piece of paper was going to keep him from away.

The problem with women today was their lack of respect for the husband and kids were even worse! Hell, if he'd ever tried to attack his own father the way Tommy had tried to attack him he would have ended up beaten to a bloody pulp. Anna and Tommy don't realize how lenient he was; instead of kicking him out of his own house they should have kissed his ass for not beating the shit out of both of them like his father used to do to him and his mother.

I work my ass off, and so what if I don't make as much money as she does with those stupid books, and so what if I stop occasionally with the boys for a couple of beers after work, does she appreciate me? No, all the bitch does is whine about being tired. What the hell does she have to be tired about, when all she does all day is sit around on her fat ass making up baby stories all day and night?

A man has to stand up for his rights, and that was all he'd been doing the night the little twerp lost control and attacked him. Shit, the kid deserved what he got, and more. "A whole lot more, and he sure as hell doesn't deserve this friggin bike, that's like rewarding him for being a disrespectful little pussy."

Since the night of the incident Alex had many nights of inner conflict. Once in a while he blamed himself for what happened, hence the bike, but most often the blame lay with his wife and son. What ever happened to a man being king of his castle? Damned bitch didn't respect him just because she made more money than he did, but he worked damned hard for his money.

Pushing newspapers to the floor Alex dropped down on the couch, and twisted open another beer. He thought about Anna. She was still a beautiful woman, as slim and desirable now as the day he'd married her. She was good in bed too. Too good, he thought, rubbing a hand roughly over his crotch. *She's she's still my wife, bond, or no bond. I could make her realize what she's missing. Sure, she might fight it at first just because she's so damned stubborn, but in the end she'd thank me. One more beer and maybe I'll take a little drive out to my house, and climb into the sack with my wife and I dare that little bastard son of mine to try to stop me again, he'll find out the meaning of respect if I have to beat it into him like my daddy beat it into me.*

#

Tommy woke hours later without remembering Bruiser's late-night howls. He faintly remembered having a bad dream in which Dad picked him up and threw him through the air with such force that Tommy sailed right out the window and far, far over the forest. The strangest part of the dream was the cold. It was so cold in the woods Tommy felt his fingers and toes turn into icicles. He just kept sailing through those old dark woods until he hit a big tree and slid right down its trunk and instantly went to sleep, which Tommy thought was kind of funny since he was already asleep.

"Hi, Honey", Anna, said over her second cup of coffee of the morning.

"Hi, Mom."

"You feel Ok?" She asked when she realized how tired and drawn he looked.

Tommy shrugged, "Guess so."

"Bruiser wake you with his howling last night?"

Tommy started. "Yeah, I think I remember hearing him. I was dreaming about Dad, and I got scared 'cause I thought he was coming back to get me."

Anna felt her heart climb to her throat. "Oh Baby, come here."

Tommy walked slowly to his mother. He didn't want to feel like a baby and wished he hadn't mentioned the dream.

Wrapping her arms around her son and pulling him close, Anna felt such hatred course through her body for her husband that if he walked through the door Anna was sure she wouldn't hesitate to pick up a knife and run it right through his heart without a second thought. How dare that monster cause all this pain to her son? Sometimes, Anna half wished Alex *would* come back to the house, because now she be waiting with a little surprise for him. As much as she hated having a gun in the house she now kept a loaded .38 hidden beneath the mattress on her bed. It was one thing for Alex to beat her, but by God he would never, ever, touch Tommy again

"Honey, I told you Dad can't come around here any more, the Judge told him he has to stay away, remember?"

Tommy nodded. "Yeah, you have a 'piece of bond' for him."

Anna laughed, "Peace Bond. It's a paper that says Dad has to stay away from us or go to jail, and your father doesn't want to go to jail."

"Yeah, he couldn't get all drunk if he did."

"Oh Honey, I'm so sorry."

Pulling away from his mother Tommy stated simply, "Dad should be sorry for hitting you all the time. You shouldn't be sorry, you never hit anyone."

"Sometimes your dad doesn't know what he's doing, Baby. He's sick."

Tommy considered this. "Then why doesn't he go to the doctor and get a shot so he'll get better?"

Tommy remembered his mother more than once begging his father to get help. She said they had places where he could go and they'd cure his demon. Tommy hadn't been sure what a demon was, but he thought it was something like a monster, because when Dad got drunk he acted like a monster. Tommy learned a long time ago that the only thing he had to be afraid of in the dark was the demon living inside his father.

One day his dad said, "I can quit drinking any time I want to," and to prove he was right he didn't drink for five days. It hadn't helped his father get rid of his demon though 'cause he was just as mean, as ever, the only difference was the demon kept its red eyes hidden. When Alex wasn't drinking he was home, and those turned out to be the longest days of Tommy's life. He was almost happy when Dad announced, "I'm running down the street", because that meant he was going to Jake's 1 – 4 The Road bar, and it would be quiet around the house for a few hours while Dad fed the demon.

Tommy wasn't sure exactly what his feelings for his father were. Sometimes he remembered playing ball, or going on hikes in the woods with his parents, and he missed his father. Mostly he remembered the bad times when the demon made Dad hit Anna over and over until blood covered her face. Those times Tommy hid in his closet, because if he saw any more blood his mind would just fly away and never come back, and then who would take care of Mom and Bruiser? Tommy figured he might love his father, but he hated the demon, and if that demon ever came around and tried to hurt his mother again he'd get the gun Mom had hid, and shoot his father right through the demon's eyes.

"He doesn't think he has a problem," Anna said softly.

Tommy replied coldly, "No, he just likes his demon better than he likes us."

Anna flinched at the venom in her son's voice. Not for the first time she realized the hatred he has for his father nearly equaled her own. Ok Anna, time to change the subject.

"Well Sport, what exciting plans do you and Bruiser have for the day?"

"Don't know, maybe we'll just hang around here today."

"Seems a shame to waste a beautiful sunny Sunday hanging around the house, especially since you've got school tomorrow."

Although he decided never to go into the woods again, Tommy soon gave way to boredom and curiosity. He'd been roaming the woods since he was old enough to walk, first with his parents, then last year it became just him and Bruiser. There was nothing there that would hurt him, especially with Bruiser at his side, Bruiser would protect him from any monsters, even the one that hid in his dad.

#

Karl and Sue Abbott returned home from church at 11:53. As Sue entered the kitchen door she felt the familiar emptiness of the house. It was almost as if the house itself died with their daughter, Lyndsay's, disappearance. Sue hated the feel of their home now it felt alien and foreboding. Used to be at least the house made noises, like houses were suppose to do, but for some reason Sue felt as if her home were holding it's breath, waiting for something to happen.

Karl stopped behind Sue, and, as one, their heads turned toward the answering machine on the kitchen counter. The light remained constant, no calls.

Right after Lyndsay's disappearance neither one of them would leave the house in case their daughter called. Then if one of them went out the other stayed home, just in case Lyndsay called. Finally they got the answering machine, not because Lyndsay might call, but because the police might call with information about Lyndsay. Although neither would admit it either out loud or to themselves, both had the same nagging little voice haunting their thoughts, Lyndsay's dead.

Neither said a word as Sue began a pot of coffee and Karl walked out to the road to get the Sunday newspaper. The day would pass like the day before and the one before that, each lost in his own thoughts, each wondering if perhaps there wasn't something they could do or should have done differently.

After lunch, as had become their custom, Karl retreated to his den, paper in hand. He read and reread every word, trying to see beyond the obvious, to read between the lines, in the hopes of finding any tiny clue to his little girl's whereabouts.

Sue washed and dried the lunch dishes then moved slowly through the house to Lyndsay's bedroom. There she would sit and stare into space until it was time to prepare dinner. Sitting in the rocking chair she relived Lyndsay's life from the moment of conception until the moment Cindy Milner called asking to speak to Lyndsay.

"Ah, Mrs. Abbott, could I please talk to Lyndsay?"

Somewhere deep in her heart something cried, some little voice, perhaps a premonition.

"Cindy, Lyndsay isn't home from your place yet. What time did she leave?"

(Silence.)

"Cindy? Are you still there?"

"Ah, yeah, I'm still here. Ah, Mrs. Abbott, Lyndsay left here last night, she didn't spend the night after all."

There it was, the words spoken, not simply fear now, but full-blown terror. A voice no longer whispering but screaming that their life was about to change, that a nightmare was moving in with them to occupy their daughter's room.

Gripping the towel tightly, Sue tried to remain in control. Lyndsay could be anywhere. She might have gone to Brenda's, or even to Jimmy's. Just because Lyndsay wasn't home didn't mean something bad happened to her, but in her heart and soul she knew that was exactly what it meant.

"Cindy, I'm going to hang up now. I'm going to call Jimmy's house and see if she's there."

"She...she's probably not there, Mrs. Abbott. That's what we had the fight about, and she was pretty upset with Jimmy...and me."

Of course Cindy was right Lyndsay wasn't at Jimmy's or Brenda's, or at any of the other places she could have been. Sixteen-years-old Lyndsay Abbott disappeared in a small town where the occasional families dispute was considered big crime.

Karl Abbott tried to remain calm those first few days. He drove around town for hours, claiming the police weren't really concerned. They hinted that Lyndsay, like so many young people, got on a bus and left town, a runaway. Karl knew his daughter, and, if Lyndsay had problems, she would have gone to her mother with them. Lyndsay and Sue shared everything, and, if Lyndsay had been upset with Jimmy, she would have come home to talk it out with Sue. That was the way it had always been.

Besides in a town this size no one went or did anything without most everyone in town seeing, or at least, knowing about it. The night Lyndsay disappeared it was snowing, a blizzard, and, if any one saw Lyndsay out in that kind of weather they would have either given her a ride home, or insisted she come into their home until the storm passed, that was the way of Whitefields. Lyndsay would have called home so her parent's didn't worry; she'd always been thoughtful like that, never wanting them to worry.

Someone in town knew what happened to their daughter; there was no doubt of that in Karl's mind. Someone he'd known his whole life, maybe even called friend, knew what had happened to his only child, and there was only one reason they wouldn't talk.

CHAPTER 3

"Come on, Bruiser, let's go over by the creek." Tommy pulled on Bruiser's leash to keep him from going any farther into the woods. Bruiser hadn't started acting crazy yet and Tommy didn't want to encourage him to start.

"Come on Boy, we'll just stay nice and close to the house," Tommy rubbed the dog's ear and Bruiser pressed his head against the boy's hand, enjoying the affection being offered.

Tommy kept Bruiser on a leash for several reasons. That it was the law wasn't one of them. If Bruiser met up with a porcupine he'd probably end up with a nose full of quills, and besides that, Tommy really hated to hear the sound small animals made when they died, like the rabbit Bruiser accidentally killed last summer. Tommy didn't think he could stand hearing that sound again; it'd given him nightmares for weeks.

"Wow, look at that?" Across the stream a mother raccoon and two kits played on the grassy bank. Bruiser tugged gently on the leash wanting to get closer. "No, Bruiser, you can't play with them. Their mother would get really mad and probably bite your nose off. We've got to stay here and be real quiet, and just watch."

Bruiser lay down in the tall grass next to Tommy. A gentle breeze blew from behind them, and suddenly the mother coon rose on her hind feet, nose in the air. Chattering madly she quickly herded the babies into the thick undergrowth in the forest behind her.

"Shoot, she must have smelled us, Bruiser. Well, come on, let's see if we can catch some tadpoles."

Tommy and Bruiser spent the next hour splashing through the shallow stream. Tommy waited patiently for the tadpoles to come out of hiding only to have Bruiser pounce on them.

"No, Bruiser!"

"Hi."

The voice startled Tommy so much that he lost his balance and flopped on his butt in the cold stream. Bruiser froze, staring at the stranger; a deep growl was rumbling deep in his chest, not quite as scary sounding as yesterday but scary enough to put Tommy's guard up.

"Hi," the girl said again, moving slowly toward Tommy.

"You better not come any closer, ah, my dog doesn't like strangers." Tommy got to his feet and moved to the opposite side of the narrow stream. He knew to keep the dog safely way from anyone he didn't know.

Tommy stopped and looked more closely at the girl. She looked familiar, but he couldn't remember where he'd seen her before.

"My name's Tommy, Tommy Rogers, and this is Bruiser."

The girl looked at the dog for a moment then back at Tommy. "Hi Tommy. Hi Bruiser."

Bruiser stopped growling, lowered his head, and whimpered. The whimper embarrassed Tommy. Sheesh, was the silly dog afraid of a girl?

The girl spoke from her side of the stream. "It's Ok Bruiser, it's Ok."

Bruiser looked at the girl again then did something that really scared Tommy. He raised his head and howled just like he had the day before when something in the forest had scared him.

Tommy knelt beside the dog and whispered, "It's OK Bruiser, it's only a girl."

The dog's muscles quivered beneath Tommy's arms. Bruiser was really scared, and that confused Tommy. When he glanced back at the girl he was surprised to see she'd started across the stream.

"Ah, I wouldn't come too close right now. My dog is acting really weird, and he might bite you."

The girl stopped, and Tommy thought she must have been standing on a rock just below the surface of the stream, because it looked like she was standing on top of the water.

"Tommy, I won't hurt you."

Tommy thought that was a funny thing for her to say, especially with Bruiser at his side howling that scary howl, but because she had said it Tommy began to worry. He slowly took a couple of steps backwards.

"Please," the girl whispered.

After another step back, Tommy thought he knew how the mother raccoon felt earlier because he wanted to run off and hide in the forest too. He didn't like the way this was going, and wouldn't Bruiser ever quit howling?

"I've...I've gotta go home now. Ah, my Mom's probably looking for me right now, so, ah, I guess we'll be going. Come on Bruiser."

Tommy glanced behind him; so he wouldn't trip stepping out of the stream, and then quickly back at the girl. She was standing back on the other side of the stream. How did she do that?

"How...?"

"Please Tommy, I need your help."

Tommy strained to hear over Bruiser's racket.

As if reading his thoughts the girl looked steadily at the dog and said, "Bruiser, stop!"

To Tommy's surprise, Bruiser stopped howling and actually wagged his tail.

"Tommy?"

She was talking to him again, and Tommy shook his head in amazement, "That's the weirdest thing I ever saw him do. He never wags his tail at strangers."

"It's because he trusts me, and I hope you will too, because I really need your help Tommy."

Tommy frowned, he was only ten-years-old, well, *almost* ten, and she was a big girl, probably from the high school, so how could he help her? The only way he'd be able to help her is if she was lost, he knew the woods as well as the inside of his own home.

The girl's eyes seemed to brighten. "Yes, yes Tommy, I'm lost and my Mom and Dad are really worried because I've been lost for a long time. Will you help me?"

Feeling important and proud for being able to help someone a lot older than himself, Tommy nodded happily. "Sure, come on, I'll take you to my house. You can call your Mom and Dad and they can come and get you. Come on, I know the way out!" Tommy turned and started away.

"Wait Tommy! I can't go with you!"

Tommy stopped, turned, and frowning at her asked, "Why not? If you're lost I'll take you to my house." Girls sure were dumb sometimes. Just like that silly Carrie in his class at school. She did some of the dumbest things sometimes. His friend Billy said it was because she liked Tommy, but he didn't think so, 'cause he wouldn't glue someone's gym shoes to the floor when they weren't looking if he liked them.

The girl seemed to be thinking about something, and Tommy sure hoped it was how stupid she was acting.

After several seconds she sighed, and said, "Tommy, you're going to have bring someone here, because I can't leave the forest right now. Won't you go get your mom or dad and have one of them come get me?"

Now Tommy was really confused, because if he was lost and someone wanted to take him to use his or her telephone he'd go. Unless it was a bad person, and then he wouldn't even talk to them, but he wasn't bad, he was just a kid, and she couldn't be afraid of his mom, not if she wanted him to bring Mom into the woods to get her. Tommy shook his head. Girls!

Maybe she was sick or something. She did look kind of pale, like she'd been sick a long time.

"Yes Tommy, real sick. Someone has to come here and get me."

"Hey! How'd you know I was thinking that?" Tommy asked wide-eyed.

"Please, will you help me?"

"I guess," Tommy shrugged. "You stay right there, and I'll go get my mom."

"No, not here! I'm not...I mean I won't be here."

Tommy was starting to get angry. "Well how am I going to bring my mom to help you if I don't know where you're gonna be?"

Suddenly the girl started to cry, and that got Bruiser howling again, and that caused Tommy feel like a real jerk for hollering at the girl.

"I'm sorry, please don't cry."

"Please Tommy, I just want to go home."

"Ok, I'll help you, but where will you be? How will we find you?"

The girl moved forward, and Tommy took two more steps backwards, because when she moved it didn't look like she was moving her legs, but sort of floating towards him.

Stopping, the girl said, "Remember yesterday when you were way back in the forest and Bruiser started howling and scared you?"

"Yeah," Tommy answered weakly, he didn't like thinking about that, about what might have been back there that scared Bruiser so badly.

"I'll be back there, just a little farther into the forest. You'll see a great big oak tree in a clearing; there's a clump on white birch next to the oak. I'll be by the oak tree, tell your mom to look for me, Ok Tommy?"

Tommy's eyes grew large. If there was anyplace he most definitely did not want to go it was that scary place in the forest. Something bad was there. He knew it, and so did Bruiser.

"Wh. . . why there?"

"Because that's where I am, ah, I mean where I'll be. Please Tommy, won't you do that for me? Nothing there will hurt you or Bruiser. It was me that Bruiser was afraid of yesterday, that's how I knew you were there, I saw you. I wanted to talk to you then, but you ran off."

Tommy thought about this bit of information. It made sense, especially considering the way Bruiser acted a bit ago when the girl first showed up. What made Bruiser howl like that? She was just a girl, and girls weren't anything to be scared of.

Finally, his mind made up, Tommy yanked the leash, and Bruiser moved to his side. "Ok, the big oak tree with the white birch by it. See ya in a little bit. Hey, what's your name?"

"Lyndsay. Please hurry Tommy."

"Ok, see ya in a little bit Lyndsay."

#

Sandy the three-legged turtle poked his head into the cold water. Where had Barney the Bass gone?

Anna sighed. "Where did Barney the Bass go? Sorry Sandy, he's probably in some fisherman's iron skillet right now turning a golden brown."

After twelve Sandy The Three-Legged Turtle books Anna was ready to boil the little troublemaker in a pot. What started out as a simple story for Tommy turned into a deadline for Anna. Never would she have believed that one of the stories she made up to entertain her son would end up being published and read to thousands of other women's children, but that's exactly what happened when seven years earlier Anna's sister, Donna, had talked her into sending one of the stories to a publishing house.

"You're nuts Donna. Why on earth would anyone want to read the stories I make up for Tommy? I'm sure if a mother wants a story for her children she'll just make up one of her own."

"Anna, Honey, people don't just make up stories for their kids, they buy them already made up. That way after a long hard day at the office they can pick up a book and read Junior to sleep without ever having to use their brains. Read the other day that publishers are begging for kid's stories. It's supposed to be one of the easiest areas of writing to get into."

It took Anna almost two years to actually get the first story written and mailed. She couldn't believe she'd actually done it. She knew they (whoever they were) were going to laugh at her. It was a stupid idea, a stupid story. Something to amuse her three-year-old son, and never meant to be read by anyone else. She fretted and worried for weeks, then began to relax after a month went by and she hadn't heard anything. Thank God, at least they hadn't sent her a nasty for wasting their time with such stupid nonsense.

After a couple of months passed Anna nearly forgot about it, except to wonder why her manuscript hadn't been returned in the self-addressed, stamped envelope she'd made sure to send with her story.

She would never forget the day the letter arrived. Instead of telling her how upset they were with her for wasting their time, the envelope contained a contract and a very nice letter asking for more. Now here she was, years later, trying to think of something new and adventurous for a three-legged turtle to do, and she had only two weeks left to finish the story. Not for the first time she wondered if it wasn't time to retire Sandy and try her hand with someone new, but fear of the unknown held her back. Right now she needed the income Sandy provided.

"Mom! Mom!" Tommy burst through the kitchen door. "Mom, there's a girl in the woods and she wants you to come and get her."

"Tommy, stop shouting, and slow down, I can't understand a word you're saying."

Tommy tried to contain his excitement. "A girl, in the woods. She wants you to come and find her."

Exasperated, Anna announced, "Tommy I don't have time to play with you and your friends now. I've got two weeks to finish this story and get it to the publishers, I'm sorry I can't stop now."

"But Mom, she's lost, and she wants you to come and find her."

"She's hiding?"

"No, she's lost."

"Tommy, if she's lost then why didn't she just come home with you?"

"She…she said she couldn't. She said we have to go find her by a big oak tree."

"Tommy, tell your little friend that I'm sorry, but I just don't have time to go looking for her right now. Maybe in a couple of weeks, after this is in the mail and I've got some extra time we'll play, but not now."

"But…"

"No buts. Out. Go get your friend and see if she wants to come back here and have lunch with you. You can make some Silly Sandwiches, and have a picnic in the backyard. But first go change those wet clothes. Go on right now."

"Mom, I told you, she can't come here."

Anna's temper neared the breaking point. "Then make your sandwiches and take them with you, have your picnic down by the stream." Anna watched as the words on the paper began to swim around the page. She could sense Tommy hovering behind her, "Go on Tommy, I've got work to do, and you know I can't concentrate with you hovering over my shoulder. Now scoot."

"But Mom."

"Thomas!"

"Sheesh."

#

"Lyndsay! Lyndsay where are you?" Tommy moved deeper into the forest. Bruiser, at his side, was more interested in what was in the brown bag that Tommy carried than where they were going.

"Lyndsay! My Mom can't come right now! Where is she, Bruiser? Girls! They're so weird sometimes. Lyndsay!"

"I'm here Tommy."

"Aghh! Don't do that!"

"Sorry, I didn't mean to scare you."

Tommy saw that Lyndsay looked like she was about to cry again. He hated to see girls cry, especially since he saw his mother cry so many times.

"Aw, you ain't gonna cry again, are ya?"

"I want to go home, Tommy. I need to go home. You said you'd help me."

"I tried, Lyndsay, but Mom's writing a story, and said she can't come right now because she has to get her work done. It's a story about this little turtle," Tommy hurried on, hoping to distract Lyndsay long enough to make her forget about crying again, "and he's only got three legs 'cause one got chewed off by this mean ol' red fox and…"

"Tommy, you're the only one who can help me. I've waited so long, you're the only person I've see, there is no one else. Won't you please try harder to convince your mother?"

Tommy sat on a large tree trunk that had fallen next to the path. "Here, have a sandwich while we try to figure out how I'm going to convince Mom that she has to come and get you. She thinks you want to play hide and seek."

Suddenly the girl giggled, "That's the most disgusting sandwich I've ever seen. What on earth do you have on it?"

If Mom hadn't said the exact same thing about Tommy's sandwiches many times before he might have been offended. Instead he proudly pulled off the top piece of bread so Lyndsay could get a better look.

"Well first you take a piece of bread, spread on some butter, and Miracle Whip, then peanut butter and some grape jelly, then baloney, cheese, pickles and crumble some chips on top, then butter the other piece of bread and tada, a Silly Sandwich."

"Gross."

"No it's not, it's good." Tommy was comfortable discussing something he'd become an expert on. "Don't you like peanut butter and jelly?"

"Sure."

"Baloney and cheese?"

"Yeah."

"Pickles and potato chips?"

"Of course."

"Well?"

"Not all together, yuck!"

"Why not? They all end up together in your stomach, don't they? And besides it tastes really good all together like this. My Grandma and Grandpa in Detroit let me make them when I was just a kid, they'd put everything they could find on the table and tell me to put anything on my sandwich that I wanted, I couldn't decided so I put everything on and it was really good, been eating them ever since."

Tommy felt pretty good now that he could talk to the girl about something that wouldn't make her cry.

"Here, just try a bite. I made us both one."

"Thanks anyhow Tommy, but I'm really not hungry."

"Why not? You said you've been lost out here in the woods for a long time. You probably haven't had anything to eat, have you?"

"No, but…"

"Well that's probably why you're sick. You haven't eaten anything. Mom always says that if you don't eat right you'll get sick, and I'll bet that's what's wrong with you."

Lyndsay laughed, "I don't think so Tommy."

Offended Tommy retorted, "Mom says that, and she's pretty smart. She writes books, and if she says you'll get sick because you don't eat right then that's the truth!"

"I believe you Tommy. I believe your mom, and I'll bet she is smart, and she really does know what's right, but I just can't eat, sorry."

Tommy frowned. "Will you throw-up?"

Lyndsay laughed again, "If I ate that I would!"

"Ah, it ain't that bad, besides it taste better than it looks."

"It'd have to," she giggled again.

Tommy chewed his sandwich thoughtfully a minute then asked, "How come a big girl like you got lost in the woods, Lyndsay?"

"It's a long story."

"You must not live around here, or you wouldn't get lost. Everyone in town knows these woods just as good as I do."

"I did live here Tommy." Tommy looked up, fearful of seeing tears in her diamond dust eyes.

As he tossed the last bite of sandwich to Bruiser, Tommy asked hesitantly, "You move away?"

The girl shook her head, and Tommy marveled at how the sun danced through her long golden hair.

"Then how come you don't know your way around?"

"I do know my way around."

Frowning Tommy said, "Then how come you're lost?"

"Not all of me is lost. This part of me knows where I am."

"Huh?"

"Bruiser understands, don't you boy?" The dog whimpered and Tommy wasn't sure he liked his dog understanding more than he did.

"Well I sure don't understand, just how many parts of you do you think there are?"

The girl sighed, and to Tommy it sounded just like the spring breeze rustling through the leaves.

"Can't you, please, try your mom again?"

"Nah, she was getting pretty mad at me for bothering her. When she's writing she doesn't like anyone to even talk to her."

"Ok look, this is our last chance. If this doesn't work I guess I'll just have to show you, and I sure don't want to do that, because I really like you, Tommy, and I wouldn't want to do anything to make you have any more nightmares. Go back home," she continued before Tommy could reply, "and tell your mother that my name's Lyndsay Abbott, and I've been missing since January 18th. Can you remember that Tommy?"

#

Tommy mumbled to himself as he trotted back to the fallen tree where he left Bruiser with Lyndsay. His mother hadn't given him a chance to tell her much of anything before swatting him on the butt and threatening to ground him until he was thirty-two if he didn't stop interrupting her, Mothers sure could be infuriating sometimes.

Lyndsay was sitting near the fallen tree where he left her. Bruiser lay near by, but not too close to Lyndsay, as though he liked her well enough, but didn't quite trust her enough to get too close. When he heard Tommy coming through the woods, he leaped to his feet and started grumbling excitedly in Husky talk.

"Hi boy! Hey Bruiser, you miss me?" Tommy called to the dog more to put off telling Lyndsay the bad news than anything else. He didn't want her to start crying again, but mostly he didn't want to find out what it was that she was going to show him that would give him nightmares. His dad gave him enough nightmares he didn't need any more.

"Didn't work, huh'?" Lyndsay asked, staring sadly into his eyes.

He shook his head, wrapping his arms tightly around Bruiser's thick neck. "Sorry, she threatened to ground me until I was an old man if I said one more word, and she almost made me go to my room and leave Bruiser out here with you. She thinks you're one of my 'little friends.'"

Tommy picked a piece of bark off the fallen tree. He didn't know what to do, or even what to say to help the girl. He even tried to sneak in the living room to call the police, but that's when Mom had cracked him hard across the butt. He really wanted to help Lyndsay get home to her mom and dad…her mom and dad!

"That's it!" he yelled suddenly, jumping up and down as he told her, "I'll call your mom and dad, and have them come and get you. They know you're lost, so they'll believe me, and all you have to do is give me your phone number so I can call them, and then they can come and get you!"

Lyndsay shook her head. "They won't believe you."

"Why not, because I'm a little kid?"

"Partly. Partly because I've been gone over three months."

"That long, huh?"

"You remember when Christmas was?" Lyndsay added, hoping to make the time period a little more understandable for a ten-year-old.

Tommy's eyes widened. "That was a long time ago."

"Yeah, well it was only about three weeks after Christmas when I…I got lost. Do you remember the night we had big snowstorm?"

"Yeah?" Tommy looked at her doubtfully. "And you been lost out here in the forest since then?"

"Yes."

"With just that funny sleep-thing on, in snow and freezing cold?"

"My nightgown, yes."

"How come you didn't freeze…never mind, I don't think I want to know."

"You have to know Tommy. It's the only way you're going to convince anyone you've found me. You have to know the truth. Come on, I want to show you something."

"I don't…"

"Come on Tommy, pleeeaase."

"Oh sheesh."

Tommy and Bruiser followed the pretty girl with the shiny golden hair and the funny nightdress through the forest, and Tommy tried not to think about the way the leaves beneath her feet never moved as she passed over them.

When Lyndsay stopped, Tommy and Bruiser stopped; keeping a safe distance from the strange girl whom was about to make him have more nightmares.

"I'm sorry Tommy. Go around to the other side of that big tree there, and you'll know the truth."

Tommy looked at the tree she indicated. It reminded him of a tree he'd seen in the spooky movie Poltergeist he'd seen last Halloween. In the movie that tree tried to eat the boy!

"Lyndsay," Tommy said looking towards Lyndsay, but she wasn't there. Tommy turned quickly one way then another. Where did she go? A horrible thought then, what if the tree ate Lyndsay!

"Lyndsay?" In the clearing around the massive oak, forest life continued as though nothing out of the ordinary was happening. The birds chirped happily, two squirrels chattered madly as they chased each other through the white branches of the birch clump. It was as though boys and their dogs came to the clearing every day searching for strange floating girls who disappear in the blink of an eye.

Tommy didn't like this at all, no-sir, no-way, and no-how. *I want to go home, and I don't care if Mom grounds me for a hundred years. Anything's better than walking around that tree, and I ain't gonna do it.*

"Bruiser!" Tommy yelped as the dog started dragging him toward the oak tree.

"No Bruiser, no!" He heard Lyndsay crying softly, and all his fear vanished. Lyndsay needed him. He alone could help her.

Like a sleepwalker, Tommy began to circle the tree.

#

CHAPTER 4

Anna stared into space. Sometimes it seemed as though a motion picture screen played the newest release of Sandy The Three-Legged Turtle. She'd watch with her inner eye as Sandy and his woodland friends scampered around from one adventure to another. Then there were other times when the inner screen played just old memories from Anna's past.

Today seemed to be one of those days as Anna tried repeatedly to erase the screen, the one showing her and Alex on their wedding day, and tune in Sandy. Sandy needed to be here now, and it frustrated Anna that she couldn't concentrate enough to picture him in her mind.

"Damn," she shouted at herself walking arm in arm down the long aisle with her father, her wedding gown trailing behind.

"Not today! I don't need to see that today. Today I need Sandy. Come on Sandy where are you, you little shit? Please?"

Suddenly the picture in her mind went blank, and there was Sandy staring out at her from beneath a large gnarled root. Anna sighed with relief as she watched the turtle's small-bullet shaped head poke out from his shell. Sandy looked one way then the other. His small body seemed to stiffen, and he quickly darted back into his shell.

"Come on Sandy. Don't be shy, come on out and play," she coaxed.

Slowly Sandy's head popped out again. This time he neither looked one way or the other but began climbing from his nest. Anna's fingers flew across the keys of her old typewriter, recording Sandy's every move.

The little turtle followed the instruction in his mind. Sometimes these voices in his head told him to move, to stop, to wake up and do something, to go to the stream and play with a fish. Today he heard two sets of sounds, the one inside his small head urging him out and the one from the forest beyond. The outside sounds frightened him. There was a quality to them that made him want to retreat to his hiding place beneath the gnarled root of the old oak tree, but the voice inside his head ordered him to advance into the adventure unfolding around him, so as always he obeyed the inner voice and moved forward.

#

Anna watched in her mind as the little turtle moved slowly through the leaves on the forest floor. Anna often cursed herself for imagining the turtle with only three legs. Sometimes waiting for the little beast to get into trouble took more time than the actual writing of the story.

Sandy stopped, raised his long neck as high as it would go rising on the toes of his two front feet. Something is coming Sandy-Anna knew, more than one something too. Before the turtle could duck safely into his shell a large black and white animal with icy blue eyes came into the clearing. A rope was hooked to the beast's neck, and attached to the end of the rope was a young human. Anna instantly recognized Tommy and Bruiser. *Strange*, she thought, *Tommy and Bruiser have never been in any of my stories before, but maybe it's a good idea. Maybe it's time for a change.*

Sandy-Anna watched as the boy and dog stopped just into the clearing. The boy turned and spoke to someone Sandy-Anna couldn't see. Then suddenly the dog pulled on the rope and Sandy-Anna thought he'd spotted the turtle, but the whimper of fear Tommy emitted convinced Sandy-Anna that it wasn't the turtle at all that held the boy's attention. The boy reluctantly followed as Bruiser pulled him toward the oak tree and Sandy.

Fear knotted its angry fist in Anna's stomach. This was her imagination working and it horrified her that she could even imagine of something so terrible as to put such a death-camp look on her son's face. Quickly Anna began thinking pleasant thoughts, picturing Tommy laughing with delight as he spots the three-legged turtle of his childhood waiting to be discovered. *Find Sandy!* She willed them. Sandy, hearing those thoughts tried to pull his head into his shell, but Anna held control of the little creature. Watch them, she demanded, and the turtle reluctantly obeyed.

As the boy and dog approached Sandy his little body stiffened. They're going to hurt Sandy, his little brain warned, but they passed without even noticing him. Anna willed the turtle to follow as quickly as he could, which even for a turtle was so slow Anna wanted to scream.

A new sound filled the forest one Sandy was familiar with, but not so Anna. It was two sounds in one, and it took her a moment to realize one sound was Bruiser howling like a crazed banshee, the other sound was coming from Tommy. Her son was shrieking louder than the dog.

"Tommy!" Anna shouted, pushing herself away from the typewriter, breaking the terrifying image.

Sandy felt immensely relieved and quickly pulled his little head and legs as far into his shell as he could get them. It didn't make the outside noises go away, but it muted them and thankfully the inside voice was gone now. Both those sounds at the same time made Sandy want to go find that mean ol' red fox and feed himself to it.

#

Anna poured herself some of the Black Velvet that Alex had forgotten to take when he left. She hated whiskey, but at this point just about anything that calmed her jangled nerves was welcomed.

"What the hell happened?" She asked the typewriter as though she'd find the answer miraculously written on the pages of her manuscript. Why did I see Tommy and Bruiser like that? What did it mean? A premonition? *No, that's dumb, there's no such thing. Tommy and Bruiser are fine; it's me who needs help for even imagining Tommy being so frightened. They're fine just playing in the forest with their little friend.* "What was her name?" *Tommy said they were playing hide-and-seek.* "No, he said she was lost. No, no, she couldn't be lost, because I told Tommy to bring the girl to the house, and he said the girl wouldn't, or couldn't come. So they were playing…" *and I'm talking to myself,* "but what did Tommy say her name was? Lori? Lisa...no, Lyndsay, that's it Lyndsay." Anna shivered, and gulped the whiskey, making her eyes tear as she gasped for breath.

What was it about that name that teased Anna's memory? "Lyndsay."

Anna sat down slowly, trying to pry into the depths of her mind for the meaning behind the illogical unease the child's name invoked. Her internal screen tried to show more of what was happening in the forest, but she couldn't stand to let her morbid imagination take over again. She didn't want to make-up any more scary things. *Tommy is fine, he's playing, and Bruiser is with him. Bruiser would never let anything happen to Tommy. But that name...Lyndsay.*

Anna shot to her feet. "Lyndsay...Lyndsay Abbott. The girl who disappeared a few months ago!"

Anna hit the back door at a run. Something was wrong. *Lyndsay Abbott, Lyndsay Abbott*, she kept thinking repeatedly. She stopped at the edge of the forest, and screamed her son's name into the still afternoon sunshine.

"TOMMY!" Please God let him answer!

Tommy knew he always had to be within shouting distance. That was the rule, and Tommy always obeyed the rules, so why doesn't he answer? Anna called again, still nothing. *Try Bruiser,* she thought. *Dogs have better hearing.* "BRUISER!"

She listened to the sounds of spring humming around her. Next door the sound of heavy footsteps crossing the wood deck let Anna know that at least someone had heard her calls.

"Anna? Is something wrong?"

Anna turned, only then realizing she was crying. She must look like someone just died. No, don't even think that!

The man stood several feet away as though he thought whatever upset Anna might be contagious. Her neighbors, Mr. and Mrs. Jenkins, were just past retirement age and spent most of their time working in, what seemed to Anna, acres and acres of flower beds, which was one of the reasons Bruiser was kept in his kennel when he wasn't with Tommy. They were a nice couple, and Anna knew they would become even closer if she hadn't kept it from happening. First because of Alex, she didn't want anyone to see the way he treated her and Tommy, then it just got to the point where being alone was easier.

As Anna took a step in Mr. (call me Ted) Jenkins' direction, the man took a step back, startled. "What is it Anna? What's wrong? Is it... Alex? Has he come back?"

"Alex?" Anna asked confused. "No, not Alex."

She took a deep breath, trying to control herself. The poor man probably thought she had finally gone off the deep end, and she couldn't blame him as she realized how she must reek of whiskey.

"Mr. Jenkins," she said slowly, trying to keep her voice from shaking. "Ted, do you remember anything about that girl, Lyndsay Abbott, who disappeared a few months ago?"

Ted stood staring at her so long Anna thought he'd forgotten the question, and was about to repeat it when he said, "No, just what I read in the paper. Why?"

"Well, Tommy came in a while ago and said there was a girl in the forest, and he wanted me to go with him to get her, he said her name was Lyndsay."

Mr. Jenkins cleared his throat and the sound embarrassed Lyndsay, made her feel foolish. "Well Anna, I'm sure there must be other children around here with that name, unless Tommy specifically said Lyndsay Abbott. Did he?"

Anna thought back, and then shook her head. "No, maybe, oh, I can't remember, I didn't pay much attention, I was working on my book, but I think he just said Lyndsay."

"Well, there you are." Ted smiled, looking out toward the forest, his thin face etched with concern. "Maybe you shouldn't let him play in the woods by himself. You never know what might happen."

In spite of her inner fears Anna laughed. "Yeah, you're probably right about the girl's name, I jumped to conclusions, and Tommy's been playing in those woods all of his life. Nothing will happen to him, especially with Bruiser with him." She mentally crossed her fingers to ward off a jinx.

Far off in the distance a dog barked. The sound evaded Anna until it turned into a long eerie howl.

"Oh my God!" Anna screamed as she turned and raced into the woods.

Her neighbor stood watching after her, maybe I should go with her. *Ah, to hell with it. Kids are always looking for trouble, and they usually find it.* With a shrug of his scrawny shoulders Ted returned to his begonias. "Well, how are Daddy's pretty little girls today?"

Bruiser met up with Anna about a quarter of a mile into the forest. Her voice was little more than a raspy whisper from screaming for her son as she called to the frantic dog. "Bruiser, come," she croaked as the dog began pulling away from her towards the heart of the forest. He seemed unable to move and Anna approached carefully, not sure of his strange behavior. She realized then that his leash had caught on a fallen tree trunk, and the dog was staining with every ounce of strength he possessed to get free. When he realized Anna was there Bruiser whimpered, his tail battering not only saplings growing near by but also Anna's bare legs as well.

"Easy Boy, I'm here now. Come on Bruiser settle down. That's a good boy, hold still so I can get you untangled."

The dog quieted slightly, enough so Anna could work the lead from around the gnarled split tree trunk. "Ok Bruiser, now where's Tommy. Go to Tommy," she commanded, holding tightly as the dog bound through the thick underbrush.

She held tightly to the leash because she'd never been this far into the forest before and didn't want to lose track of the dog for fear she not only wouldn't find her son, but also be unable to find her way back home.

Bruiser didn't have to be told to find Tommy, and was pulling Anna towards her son even before she'd finished the command. Bruiser knew exactly where Tommy was and was just as anxious to get to the boy as Anna.

The dog ran so fast Anna had a hard time holding the leash and once actually tripped and dropped it, but Bruiser came back to her and whined impatiently as he waited for her to regained her footing and retrieve the leash.

A thousand thoughts went through Anna's mind as she hurried behind the dog. Tommy, something bad happened to Tommy. She pictured him ripped apart by the big black bear she'd asked him if he'd seen, she saw him buried beneath quicksand with only his little hands sticking out. She saw him dead in a hundred different ways and each time had to scream at herself to stop before she drove herself crazy. She had to keep in control, for Tommy's sake she had to remain calm, no matter what.

Her breath came in ragged burning gasps, and she briefly wished Alex was there for her and Tommy, but quickly dismissed the idea as totally ridiculous. Alex's answer for any crisis was always the same, drink until he was too numb to care.

Bruiser stopped just inside a clearing. Anna's shocked gaze scanned the clearing as in a slow motion dream. A large oak tree dominated the center of the clearing, and off to one side stood a large clump of white birch. Tommy was sitting facing the oak tree. On his lap a three-legged turtle poked its small bullet-shaped head out and twisting around looked knowingly at Anna.

Tommy neither moved nor made a sound, and his eyes were glassy and unseeing. Bruiser, his leash finally free of Anna's grasp, moved to Tommy, he sniffed the boy's face, then satisfied that Tommy was safe laid down next to him.

An eternity seemed to pass. No one moved, and no sound penetrated the silence. Anna stared at her son, who stared at something on the other side of the tree. The turtle stared at Anna as if waiting for her to tell it what to do next, and Bruiser slowly raised his head toward the heavens and sang his mournful song.

#

The call came at 3:05 p.m. Karl was standing at the window looking out at the street where several of the neighborhood kids were playing some game of cops-and-robbers. He remembered when Lyndsay and her friends used to play the same kind of games.

Sue stood staring into the freezer, trying to decide what to fix for supper. Neither she nor Karl ate much these days, but it gave her something to do.

When the phone rang neither Karl nor Sue moved to answer it. On most days the ringing phone brought them racing, but today something deep inside told them that this time the news wouldn't be good.

Slowly, as walking in a dream, Sue crossed the kitchen to the phone. Karl stood in the doorway, watching her.

A tear rolled down the side of her cheek as her hand grasped the receiver and lifted it slowly to her ear. "Yes." just that one word, nothing more, but Karl knew. In his heart, he knew. Someone had found Lyndsay.

#

CHAPTER 5

After finding Tommy, Anna's only thought was to get her son out of the forest and tucked into his nice safe bed. She didn't want to leave Tommy alone with that...that dead thing, but, to her dismay, her son had grown, and carrying him as she had when he was a baby was unrealistic. Finally Anna gave up and ran from the forest to call for help. Bruiser watched her leave and moved closer to Tommy, his large body adding warmth to the boy's. Slowly Tommy began to rock back and forth, and a sound almost like a faraway lullaby escaped his parted lips. Bruiser whined softly and laid his head across the boy's legs.

To Anna the trip back to the house then the endless wait for the police and paramedics seemed to drag on forever although only twenty minutes passed before Chief Morman's squad car shot into her driveway.

Later Anna remembered the shocked look on Ted Jenkins's face as she stumbled, scratched and bruised, from the forest. She would laugh until she cried at the way he threw his stick-thin arms out to protect his precious flowers, as if she were some flora-eating monster descending on his pretty little babies. But that would be later, much later. At that very moment only one thought dominated her thoughts: Get help for Tommy!

After regaining his composure from the initial shock, Ted Jenkins forced himself to hurry towards Anna. "What is it? What's the matter? Is it Alex?"

Alex? Alex? The man has Alex on the brain.

Mr. Jenkins reached out and grabbed Anna's arm, trying to get her to stop long enough to tell him what was wrong. Anna yanked away and continued hurrying toward her house.

Running behind to keep up, her neighbor again reached out to once again grab her arm, but Anna stopped him with a hissed, "Get the hell away from me!"

Mr. Jenkins froze, his eyes bulging. "Well I...I...well." He didn't stop following her though, even when she ran through her kitchen door, and he stayed long after the ambulance took the body away. He even stayed when the evil Alex appeared.

God only knew how Alex found out about it so soon. He was supposed to be at work, but Anna knew only too well how his one drink at lunch could last well into the night. When Alex came shouting and staggering up the front sidewalk Anna's heart shot up into her throat. The last thing Tommy needed right now was to see his father, and it was sure as hell low on her list of desirables also.

Hurrying down the walk Anna cried out, "What are you doing here? You're not supposed to be here. Go away!"

"Yeah, right. I'm not going anywhere until you tell me what you did to my son!"

Anna saw the Chief out of the corner of her eye, moving in towards her. "Alex, get out of here right now! You're not supposed to be here!"

Morman quickened his step when he saw the other man reach out and grab Mrs. Rogers's arm, nearly jerking her off her feet.

"I want to see my son. I have a right you...you ignorant..."

Before he could finish formulating the insult in his slowly functioning brain, Morman had him by the arm. "Buddy, I don't know who you think you are or what business you think you have here, but I'd say without a doubt that you're not welcome."

Alex's face turned flaming red, "You stupid ass-wipe I live here! That piece of shit," he spit toward Anna, "is my wife, and the kid's my son. Now take your stinking hand off of me before I make you sorry!"

Morman glanced at Anna, his bright blue eyes full of questions.

Anna shrugged, embarrassed. "I have a Peace Bond on him. We're separated. He's not supposed to be here. He. . . he hurt Tommy."

Alex exploded, swinging at Anna he screamed, "You rotten, lying BITCH!"

Ted Jenkins, who Anna hadn't even realized was standing behind her, grabbed her around the waist and pulled her out of the way just before Alex's fist connected. Morman subdued Alex quickly by throwing him to the ground, placing his knee in the middle of Alex's back, and twisting his arm behind him hard enough that Alex cried out in pain. The Chief barely contained a contented smile at the drunk's pain.

Panting, Morman looked at Anna. "You want, we can throw his butt in the can?"

Anna shook her head. That would just make him madder the next time he came around. "No, I just want him to stay away from us, especially away from Tommy."

Anna could swear that Morman pushed a little harder on Alex's arm. Part of her shouted, Yes! Break it off! Another part of her was appalled. This was her husband after all.

Morman called to another officer standing near the corner of the house apparently taking notes for the paperwork to be prepared later. "Hey Ben, when you get a minute I want you to find out where this piece of garbage lives and take it home. Oh, and Ben, have someone from Pete's gas station tow his car to the impound yard." Smiling up at Anna he added, "We wouldn't want him driving in his condition, he might get a ticket."

Alex's cheek was pressed into the dirt in the flowerbed, and mud caked around his mouth and nose, and, when he looked up at Anna with his bloodshot eyes, she could easily see the demon that frightened Tommy so badly. Her skin crawled and she quickly looked away. She had never in her life seen such hatred as that now in her husband's eyes.

Anna watched as the officer dragged Alex to the squad car. His drinking had gotten worse, and she could only thank God she'd had the nerve to kick him out before now.

Doctor Klein came up to her. "I want to take Tommy to the clinic. I'm sure he'll be all right but I'd like to run a couple of tests on him. He's not responding as quickly as he should."

Anna felt her legs go to rubber. "Oh my God."

Klein took her arm. "Come on Anna, he's a strong boy, and he'll pull through just fine. He's had a bad shock, and, on top of everything else he's been through these past few months," he glanced at Alex being pushed into the squad car, "I'd be more worried if he weren't in a bit of a tizzy right now."

Morman touched her arm. "You go ahead with your son, Mrs. Rogers, I can talk to you tomorrow about," he nodded toward the forest, "the other thing."

Anna nodded, her stomach churning. She didn't want to remember the body, or the craziness surrounding its discovery, right now the only thing that mattered was Tommy.

After gathering a few necessities Anna, with Tommy silently staring through the car window followed Doc. Klein to his small clinic in town. The doctor had called ahead and told them to prepare a room for Tommy and Anna so she could be with her son through the night.

It was close to midnight when Tommy was through with the tests the doctor ordered and a bit of Anna's fears lifted when Tommy smiled sleepily and whispering "Good night". Anna sat in a fairly comfortable chair next to the bed, a guardian through the long night in case her son was plagued with bad dreams. She hoped his sleep was dream-free, prayed that neither of their dreams would be plagued by the decomposing corpse of a teenage girl named Lyndsay Abbott.

#

CHAPTER 6

Anna moved through the house double-checking all the new locks. In the kitchen she stopped to look into the aquarium where Sandy, The Three-Legged Turtle, now huddled deep within his shell. The poor thing had been gripped so tightly in Tommy's hands, Anna was sure he'd be dead when the paramedic finally pried him loose. To her surprise when finally free the turtle poked his little head out and gave her a look that sent chills up her spine, it seemed to say, I know you.

"Silly, huh, Sandy? You're just a dumb little turtle that happened to get caught up in a nightmare. It was just an eerie coincidence that I saw what I thought I saw yesterday afternoon. You aren't Sandy, not really even if that's what Tommy calls you, and you do have only three legs. No, if I thought that were true I'd probably go totally nuts."

The turtle crawled over to the glass where Anna stood and stretched his head towards her. *Why does he look at me like that?*

"You'll be free again, I promise, just as soon as Tommy is back to normal I'll talk him into letting you go."

As if satisfied by her promise Sandy turned and moved back to the clump of grass in the corner. There he settled down and pulled his head back into the dark comfort of his shell.

#

After checking on Tommy, Anna relaxed in a hot bubble bath. She felt the tension leave her body if only for a short time. The day seemed endless with all the police questions, even if she did think Chief Morman was cute. The last thing she needed or wanted was an involvement. Men weren't to be trusted, at least not with her heart. Somehow they always managed to trick her into believing they were something they weren't. Look at Alex, the first time she ever saw him she felt a tingle race through her body. Oh yes, he was so charming and so sweet, and there wasn't ever a mean word between them, at least not one that couldn't be forgotten with a kiss. Life back then was so very, very good.

He wined her and dined her and, in three short months, convinced her he was her Prince Charming. On their wedding day he showed up at the church still drunk from the bachelor party the night before and that was the first time she saw him drunk. Unfortunately it wasn't the last. At the time she convinced herself it was just a fluke, and that his buddies had gotten him drunk on purpose. Wasn't that what bachelor parties were for, one last night of drunken camaraderie? At least he showed up for the wedding. *I would have been better off it he hadn't,* she thought. *No, I wouldn't have Tommy now if weren't for Alex.*

The really sad part is that even after all the beatings and arguments a part of me still loves the bastard. Not him really but whom he could have been, who he was suppose to be.

The bath water turned cool, and, with a sigh, Anna pulled herself up. The night was quiet. For once Bruiser wasn't howling, as though even the dog needed peaceful silence.

When she brought Tommy home from the clinic Bruiser was waiting. Tommy went to the kennel, and the two of them spent most of the day sitting in the yard staring off into the trees. If Tommy got up to go in to use the bathroom Bruiser was at his side, the dog and boy had made a special bond in the forest, a horrifying experience that none the less seemed to bring the two even closer together. This evening after Anna had Tommy put the Bruiser in the kennel, every time she'd look out the dog was staring up towards Tommy's bedroom window. It made her nervous, yet at the same time comforted her to know how devoted the dog was to her son.

Anna looked forward to Tommy's tenth birthday Saturday. If anything would snap him out of his black funk it would be the party with all his school chums. Even the girls were invited, which got a bit of the old Tommy riled up. At his age girls were still icky, which was just fine with Anna, since Tommy seemed to be growing up too fast as it was.

Someday Tommy would find a girl, fall in love, get married and Anna would be alone. She planned to enjoy every precious moment she had with her son so she'd at least have lots of fond memories to keep her company in her old age.

#

CHAPTER 7

Tony Morman checked his watch again. Bill Padgett was supposed to call him back with the results of the autopsy on the Abbott girl. Tony knew that the body was so badly decomposed that there wouldn't be any way to tell exactly how the girl died, but an autopsy was standard procedure in any unexplained death. Bill wasn't the fastest man around, but when it came to finding the exact cause of death he was one of the best in Michigan. Lyndsay's body was sent to Bill's office in Detroit when it was found, and Tony was waiting anxiously for the report. Bill didn't have to tell Tony that Detroit's morgue was a busy place; Tony's known his friend for years and on more then one occasion visited Bill at work while waiting for an autopsy relating to a particular case he was working on. He admired Bill, knew there was no way he could do Bill's job, he shuddered just thinking about the gruesome details of Bills job.

Because he was born and raised in Detroit, Tony understood the pressure his friend tolerated day in, and day out. It was exactly that kind of pressure that ruined Tony's marriage and sent him scurrying to the peace and quiet the small town of Whitefields promised.

He often thought if only Shelia could have kept her pants on long enough to make the move with him they could have made their marriage work. Yet in his heart he knew Shelia would have hated Whitefields. A native Detroiter herself, she thrived on the excitement of the big city. The last he'd heard she was singing in a small dive on the northeast side of town, and was shacked-up with some small-time hood. But she was happy; at least the friend who informed Tony of his ex's where about declared. Shelia wouldn't have lasted six month in Whitefields;

it was hard adjusting to a small town after living your whole life in a big city, one that took time, even for him.

His mind wandered from Shelia to Anna Rogers. Anna belonged in this town, would probably go crazy if she had to live in a big city where she had to lock her front door if she were in the back yard because if she didn't she might go in and find the place cleaned out. Anna knew about locking doors though, and it wasn't to keep out robbers. Tony shook his head when he thought of Alex Rogers. How could a man treat a beautiful woman, and Anna was a beautiful woman, she just didn't know it, the way Alex did? And that kid, Tony would have given anything to have a kid like that, a little cutie, and such manners. Shelia didn't believe in having kids, said it was cruel bringing kids into this shitty world, and some of the things Tony has seen made him wonder if maybe she was right.

Tony sighed when he thought of Anna, her narrow waist, appearing even smaller because of her full breast and hips that were made for childbearing. She hid her figure beneath baggy tops, which was probably some of her husband's doing. He'd probably been telling her for years that she was too fat or too skinny, that she was homely, until she finally gave up and started believing his lies. Tony had seen it a hundred times before, beautiful women beaten down by the men who were suppose to love them. Anna would be surprised if she could see herself through Tony's eyes.

He'd done some checking on the husband. The man was a real creep, and Tony would like nothing more than to find a way to get him out of Whitefields and out of Anna's life.

Thinking of Anna made his skin feel tight. He needed to talk to her, to see how she and Tommy were doing. He needed to be close to them, and that was as good of an excuse as any to call her. Just as his hand dropped to the phone it rang, startling him.

"Morman."

"Hey Tony, Bill here. What's up, my man?"

"Same ol', same ol'." Tony leaned back, propping his feet on the edge of his battered old desk.

"Well I hope that's the same ol' that was going on before this little girl you sent me. Man, I thought you told me you was living in a nice little place with no crime."

Tony sighed. "Shit. "

"Yep, 'fraid so. Not only was your girl raped, she was pretty badly beaten. She wasn't attacked where you found her either. I'd say she stumbled around the forest for some time before the cold finally got her. But hey, don't feel too bad; if we didn't have at least three bodies in the same shape every week I'd think something was wrong. Like maybe people were actually getting civilized or something."

Tony was trying to think of a gentle way to tell the parent's. They definitely weren't taking this well, not that he could blame them. Then even if he had searched for her body when they first came to him, he would never have found her clear out there in the middle of the forest. How had she gotten way out there anyhow? Could anyone walk that far in a blinding blizzard with nothing on but a nightgown and slippers? Why wasn't she found closer to the road?

He felt bad for the parents. They seemed like really nice people, and losing their only child was hitting them hard, but not being a parent himself Tony could only guess at the depth of their grief.

"Shit," he hissed again, wishing the body had never been found. That way at least there would be some hope left for the parents, if only a little.

"Tony? Tony, you OK man? Hey, you got to be used to this shit by now. You've been a cop how long, ten, twelve years? You've got to know how to face it, or it'll do you in. You've been a cop long enough to know that."

"It's different here Bill. These people don't know what crime is. If they hear a siren they run outside to see who got a speeding ticket, or to see whose house is on fire. They're innocents, babes in the woods when it comes to shit like this.

You know what's funny? After all this shit happened I checked back in the files to see what the worst crime committed around here was. Know what I came up with?"

"Nope."

"Back in 1953 a certain Mr. Warrington built a garage. The garage was on his neighbor, a Mr. Redman's, property by three inches. Three inches! Redman, a seventy-eight-year-old man by the way, didn't want a garage on his property, so he waited until Warrington was gone."

"And burned it down," Bill interrupted.

Tony laughed. "Not this seventy-eight-year-old man. He went out, measured off exactly three inches, then took an old saw and cut off the wall that was on his property! Do you know how long, and how much work that would be, and we're not even seventy-fuckin'-eight-years old!"

Bill laughed, "You're really in your element out there, my friend. Those people are as crazy as you."

"I know this is a stupid question but there wasn't any chance you found semen so we can ID the bastard, is there?"

"You're right, it is a stupid question. Tony, that kid was frozen for probably a couple of months, then thawed and slowly rotted as the days turned warmer, do you have any idea how badly she was decomposing?"

Tony nodded, then realized Bill was waiting for a verbal reply, "Yeah Bill, I was on the scene when she was brought in. Wasn't a pretty sight, you'd never know that he was once a beautiful young woman." He sighed and added, "Two years of peace and quiet, I should have known it was too good to last."

"Shit Tony, no matter how blue the sky, sooner or later some rain's gotta fall. Makes you appreciate the quiet times more, know what I'm sayin'?"

"I suppose, but to tell you the truth, I wasn't having any trouble appreciating the quiet times before she was found. Well, guess I'd better go out and talk to the kid's parents. Take it easy Bill, and I'll talk at ya later. Oh, and thanks for getting back to me so quickly on this."

#

CHAPTER 8

Tending bar wasn't exactly the job that twenty-three-year-old Dee Clark would have chosen for herself if there had been another choice. Unfortunately in Whitefields a girl had to take what she could get, or she got out of town, which was exactly what Dee planned to do just as soon as the opportunity arose. Every time the job started getting to her too badly Dee just reminded herself that she could be working at the K-Mart, or the 7-11 over in Ashton making minimum wage and still have to put up with obnoxious customers. At least here even on a bad night she could make over ten dollars an hour, but the worst part of the job was Jake, boss and owner of Jake's 1—4 The Road Bar and Grill.

Using her index finger and thumb, Dee gently lifted Jake's arm from across her bare chest. With great effort she resisted the urge to pinch the bastard black and blue, but knew better so she very carefully, so as not to wake the fat little cockroach, took his arm and draped it across his gray E.T. chest. She absolutely loathed this part of her job but knew it came with the territory when she hired on. If she refused Jake it would be hello K-Mart and good-bye Florida.

It was common knowledge in town that if you worked for Jake you were expected to do more than just tend bar and wait tables. Everyone in town seemed to know what was going on except Peggy, Jake's bible-thumping-turkey-throated-string bean of a wife. Dee suspected that Peggy knew what was going on but preferred to look the other way most of the time. There had been a few times when Peggy showed up just after close. Dee was pretty sure she was trying to catch the old pervert in the act, unfortunately Peggy always arrived too soon because Jake insisted Dee have all the cleaning and stocking done before he'd honor her with his advances. One of these nights though Peggy was going to get her timing right, and Dee hoped she was still working for Jake when that happened. She'd love nothing more than seeing bird-woman rip off limp-dick's head, both of them.

Slipping quietly off the soiled couch, Dee tiptoed into the bathroom, easing the door closed behind her before turning on the light. The old wash cloth and towel she'd brought from home hung from a nail inside the cleaning cabinet, and Dee quickly put them to good use scrubbing the stink of Jake from her goose bumped flesh.

Alex Rogers had been taking her home at night, but for some reason he hadn't come in tonight. That bothered Dee, she hoped he hadn't gone back to his wife. Alex wasn't much better than Jake, especially when he was drunk, which was most of the time, but he looked better, smelled better, and, most of the time, made love better, but, most importantly, Alex promised to take her to Florida in June. Once she got that far she wasn't coming back. She didn't tell Alex that, because he'd probably beat the hell out of her if he thought she was just using him as a one-way ticket. Alex had a bad habit of using his fists to make his point and nothing she said or did could make him stop once he started pounding on her. She learned a long time ago you never criticized Alex, talked about his wife or son, or disagreed with him; even the tiniest thing could set him off.

Dee didn't blame Anna for kicking his ass out; especially after the stunt he pulled with the kid a couple of months ago. If that would have been her kid he slammed against the wall she would have done more to the bastard than kick him out of the house, but of course that was one of the things she could never say to Alex. Instead she had to sympathize and tell him how Anna was wrong, (yeah, right, wrong for not shooting the creep).

The Lava soap Jake kept in the bathroom did nothing for Dee's skin, but it did make her feel clean, as though she'd just scrubbed off the top layer of flesh. She glanced at her watch, and shuddered, she had to hurry in case crazy Peggy chose tonight to catch Jake in a compromising situation. She wanted Jake to get caught, but she didn't want to be in the room when he did. Slipping quickly into her clothes, Dee thought about Jake's Golden Rule: "If I fall asleep you make sure I'm awake before you leave the bar, understand?"

Dee, a nasty grin pulling up one corner of her full lips looked down at her boss and thought, Now how can I possibly wake him when he looks so content lying there with his little limp pecker clutched in his paw like it's his favorite teddy bear? Barely able to contain a giggle, Dee pulled the door closed as she slipped from the office.

Whistling happily as she hurried down the deserted street to her apartment three blocks away, Dee drank in the warm spring night. Nighttime was her favorite time, when all the world seemed locked away and the earth belonged to her alone. She always thought she could live very happily as a vampire, but then she thought of Florida and bright warm sunny skies and her heartbeat increased with excitement.

She heard the car engine before she saw the lights, and quickly ducked into the dark doorway to her apartment building, as the headlights grew brighter.

As a gray, rusty Ford raced past Dee clamped her hand her mouth to muffle the sound of her laughter. She would have given fifty dollars of her hard-earned Florida money right then to have a hidden camera in Jake's office. One of these nights Peggy was going to come hunting for Jake with one of the guns he always bragged about owning.

Upstairs in her apartment the little red light on the answering machine was flashing, and Dee knew if could only be Alex calling and didn't want to listen, didn't want Alex ruining her good mood, but finally habit and curiosity got the best of her. It was Alex, and he was drunk as usual, and mad, as usual, and suddenly Dee was positive that this was, without a doubt, the best night of her life. Alex wouldn't be coming by tonight, because he'd gotten cocky with a cop and was spending some time behind bars. She laughed out loud and said to the answering machine, Jake's going to get caught and Alex already did, it just don't get any better than this."

Peggy would be watching Jake's every move, which would keep him away from her, and Alex would spend at least a night in jail so he wouldn't be apt to be coming around soon. Peace and quiet, "There is a God after all."

#

Tommy opened his eyes to darkness. Something woke him, but he wasn't sure what. He listened, heard nothing out of the ordinary, and propped himself up to look out the bedroom window. The night was black, and even by straining his eyes he was unable to even make out Bruiser's kennel. Sweat appeared on this forehead as he imagined Bruiser gone, kennel and all. Then his stomach grumbled at a sudden bout of diarrhea coming on, because not only were Bruiser and his kennel gone, but also the whole world was gone! Holding his breath to block any noise, he concentrated trying to hear the dog's heavy paws crunch over the fresh straw he'd put in the kennel this evening. Then suddenly Bruiser howled, and as suddenly as they appeared, the stomach cramps disappeared.

Tommy had pretty much gotten used to the sound of Bruiser howling, but for some reason tonight the howl sounded different. He was pretty sure the howling wasn't what woke him though. It had to be something unusual to pull him from his dreams because Tommy was known to even sleep through the worse thunderstorms with out even flinching.

"Tommy," the voice whispered.

Tommy whipped the covers over his head. "Shit!"

"Tommy, I need your help again."

I'm dreaming.

"Please Tommy, you're the only one."

If I ignore her she'll go away. I'll pretend I'm sleeping, and she'll go away.

"Tommy, I won't go away, and I know you're not sleeping."

Flushed with anger, Tommy yanked the covers from his head, and snapped, "Quit doing that! Quit knowing what I'm thinking! And you, you go away 'cause you're dead!"

"Tommy, I can't stay."

"Good!"

"Meet me in the forest tomorrow."

"Ha, ain't no way!"

"More people are going to die if you don't help me Tommy."

"Dum-dee-dum, I can't hear you...what?" Tommy shuddered as he reached out and turned on the bedside lamp. In the glare of the lamp it didn't take long to see that the room was empty.

"I was dreaming, I knew it!"

"Tomorrow, Tommy, in the forest. I'll be waiting by the oak tree."

"Shit!"

The bedroom door opened and Tommy almost wet his pants until he realized it was his mother standing there.

"Oops."

"I guess oops, Thomas. Are you all right, it's almost two-thirty in the morning?"

Grasping the only logical thought that came to mind, Tommy lowered his voice and replied sadly, "Sorry Mom, I was having a dream, ah, a bad dream." If Anna thought he was talking to dead people she'd make him go back to Doc. Klein's clinic, and Tommy didn't much care for playing like a dartboard while everyone stuck needles into him, (and what did they do with all that blood they kept stealing from him?)

As he hoped Anna's face softened, she crossed the room, sat on the edge of his bed and she pulled him to her, holding him tightly in her arms, "Oh Baby, I can certainly understand that, because I have bad dreams sometimes too." In fact it was a nightmare that awakened Anna just minutes earlier sending her scurrying to her son's room.

In her dream Lyndsay Abbott's ghost was standing next to Tommy's bed trying to lure him back into the forest. Just thinking about it sent shivers up and down Anna's back. Anna leaned against the headboard, Tommy safe in her embrace. She held him tightly, unwilling to leave even after his eyes closed and his breathing told her he was sleeping peacefully, and her arms ached from holding him.

#

Karl Abbott moaned in his sleep, as his body jerked and stiffened. He just identified Lyndsay's body, again. Over, and over, all through the night Karl watched as Chief Morman pulled back the sheet covering his baby's face. In the dream he'd cry out as Lyndsay's sunken eyes snapped open, and she'd keep asking, "Why Daddy? Why did you let him kill me? Why didn't you save me? You promised you'd always protect me but you didn't, you let me die.'"

Karl sobbed the only reply he could, "I didn't know, Baby, honest to God, I didn't know. I'm sorry; I'd give anything if it were me."

The dream became really bad then when Lyndsay asked, "Anything Daddy?" And her face began to melt, shifting and swirling until it became so horrible he had to turn away. When he looked back his daughter had vanished and where Lyndsay had been laying was a beautiful Native American woman in shimmering white buckskins.

He turned to ask Morman where Lyndsay was, but the Chief didn't have a face any more. Instead there was a gaping hole where maggots and beetles circled in a bazaar dance.

"Daddy, look at me."

Turning slowly, dreading what would appear before him next, Karl looked at the stranger. "You're not my daughter, who are you?"

As though not having heard, the stranger said, "You can right the wrong."

Trembling, Karl asked, "How?"

"You must find the man responsible and with your own hands take his life as he took you're daughters", then the stranger was gone and Lyndsay, as she used to be when she was so very much alive, said, "It's the only way I can find peace. It hurts so much! Please make the pain stop, Daddy! Look at what he did to me!" She cried, pulling the blanket aside to revel a bloody gaping hole between her legs that reached all the way to her navel.

When she turned to him it was the dead thing from the forest that raised decomposing arms and whispered, "Give your baby a good night kiss, Daddy." A long black bloated tongue snaked between her shrunken lips, wiggling obscenely.

Karl screamed, but the sound was lost in her laughter. Shooting up in bed, a hand over his mouth to muffle the terror, Karl tried to slow his breathing.

He heard Sue stifle a sob. She'd given up asking him about the nightmare. He was sure she had enough of her own, and didn't want her to suffer any more than she already was.

Thank God she hadn't gone to the morgue with me to identify what was left of Lyndsay. The sight that awaited him would probably have killed Sue, God only knew it almost killed him. The dream he kept having was going to finish the job, and even though he knew it was probably spurred on by the guilt of not being able to save his daughter, he knew in his heart that he'd know no peace as long as the murdering bastard went unpunished. His salvation would come when he choked the life from the monster with his own two hands. "An eye for an eye."

#

Ted Jenkins pulled the bedroom curtains back in place after watching the light go out in the kid's bedroom. Earlier, just after the light in Tommy's bedroom came on, Ted watched Anna moved past the window, and he waited patiently, hoping to catch another glimpse of his beautiful neighbor.

He wondered if the kid was having nightmares, and couldn't blame him if he were after seeing what was left of the Abbott girl. Lyndsay was always such a pretty young thing, a bit too sexy for her age, though. Girls who looked and acted like that were destined for trouble. You could tell the girl was oversexed just by the way she walked and dressed. To bad, Ted thought, because there sure wasn't anything sexy about what they put in back of the ambulance yesterday.

His wife, Betty, stirred on the bed so Ted hurried back before she realized he was up again, she tended to nag about his not sleeping. He tried to tell her that insomnia often came with age, but she kept insisting he go see Doc. Klein.

He even had to give up his late-night drives and walks, because if she caught him she'd start nagging again. Most nights he lay in bed staring at the ceiling waiting for daybreak so he could get up without Betty carrying on.

The way she treats me, you'd think I were ninety-eight instead of sixty-eight.

Though a bit on the thin side Ted thought he looked pretty damned good, and he felt twenty years younger than he was. He was sure that Betty was just jealous because he looked and acted so much younger than she did.

He glanced sideways at her sleeping form beneath the light sheet. Too bad it was so late, but if he woke her now for a little slap-and-tickle she'd start nagging him about being awake. Turning his back to her, Ted stared out the window at the night sky. Rats, he thought. I can't sleep now, with the boner I've got.

He wished he could see into Anna's bedroom window, but since that wasn't possible, he crept from the bed and hurried into the bathroom. Closing the door as quietly as possible Ted tiptoed to the toilet, and carefully lifted the corner of the flooring, gently pulling out his brand-new Penthouse magazine. I'm going to have to replace the tile in here pretty soon, before Betty notices the way that it's curling.

#

Jimmy Russo immediately regretted slamming the phone back onto its base, not because he was worried about hurting Cindy's feelings, but because he was afraid of waking his parents. He wasn't concerned about disturbing his parents sleep, because concern for another wasn't high on his list of priorities, he just couldn't stand the thought of his mother's sad-puppy-dog-eyes as she fussed over him, asking for the twenty thousandth time if he was all right. Whatever small pain and guilt he felt, he knew he deserved it, and probably a whole lot more. If only I hadn't let that stupid bitch Cindy talk me into screwing her. I should have known she'd tell Lyndsay. He'd only done Cindy so he could laugh in her face and tell her that she wasn't even good, let alone the best he'd ever have. Yet, he hated to admit it, even to himself, but Cindy had been pretty damned good. More than once he fantasized about her, but he'd go to his grave before he told her that. The conceited bitch!

Cindy used Lyndsay's death as an excuse to call him. She called day and night, never caring about the time. She cried to him how it had been her fault that Lyndsay was dead, as if he didn't already know that. She never meant to tell Lyndsay, it had just slipped out. Yeah, right. Like he believed that!

It wasn't fair that Lyndsay was dead and he had to feel guilty just because he'd loved her.

Sure you loved her, you loved her so much you screwed her best friend. Oh yes Mister, you really loved her a whole lot, didn't you?

"I did love her. I swear I did, I was just stupid."

Yeah, you were stupid, and now she's dead. Not a very fair trade, is it?

Jimmy wasn't surprised to find he was talking to himself. He had these conversations frequently with himself since the day after Lyndsay's disappearance. He tried to convince himself it wasn't his fault, it wasn't like they'd been engaged or anything. Actually they never really talked about their relationship. They never actually said they wouldn't see other people.

He knew Lyndsay thought they would get married one day, but that was something he hadn't wanted to think about. If someone asked them if or when they were getting married he made a joke out of it or ignored the question. Marriage was the farthest thing from his mind, and he hadn't wanted Lyndsay thinking about it either. The only thing he had planned for his future was playing football, and getting out of Whitefields.

He spent too many years perfecting his skills on the field to let anything or anyone stand in his way. Michigan State already offered him a scholarship, and he couldn't wait until June and graduation, because he was history in this shit-can of a town.

Besides it wouldn't have been fair to Lyndsay if he married her. He was good looking, and the groupies were bound to be hanging on him all the time. What kind of life would that have been for Lyndsay?

Lying back on his pillow, he began his favorite pastime, fantasizing. He loved to think about all the twisted, kinky things those young beauties would do to, and for him. He was drifting into sleep; a beautiful, big-busted, redhead whispered what she could do for him with her long, long tongue, and endless throat.

Beside his bed, the telephone rang. "Shit!" There was only one person who would call this time of the night. He toyed with not answering it, but knew that sooner or later one of his parents would hear the damned thing and he'd catch hell, even though it wasn't his fault.

Snatching up the receiver Jimmy hissed, "What?"

"Jimmy."

His first thought was that he'd finally lost his mind. His second was that he was asleep and dreaming. The voice on the phone couldn't belong to Lyndsay. Lyndsay was dead!

"Jimmy? You there?"

He tried to be mad, but he was so relieved to hear it really was Cindy that he actually chuckled.

"It's not funny Jimmy. My best friend's dead and its all your fault."

Instantly Jimmy sobered. "My fault? Listen you stupid. . ."

"Ah, ah, ah, be nice Jimmy."

"What do you want Cindy?"

"Only what's right, Jimmy boy."

"What's wrong with your voice, you sound funny?"

"Oh no Jimmy my love, there's absolutely nothing at all funny about the sound of a human voice fighting to be heard through all those squishy old maggots and bugs that eat away at a decomposing body. Know what I mean, Lover Boy? No? Well trust me Sweetheart, you will. Poor Baby, looks like the kinky sex with your imaginary redhead will have to wait, you've got more important things in store for you this night."

Jimmy dropped the phone as though he had accidentally picked up a hot ember. He opened his mouth to scream, but instead of screaming he gagged. There was something in the back of his throat, cutting of his oxygen. Desperate for air, Jimmy coughed, and a huge bloated maggot squirmed from between his lips, and flopped onto the bedspread. Horrified Jimmy gagged again, and moaned when several more maggots and three ugly little black and green beetles dropped from his mouth.

His stomach churned violently and he knew he was going to vomit, but he did not want to throw-up, because he could feel them down there in his stomach wiggling and scuttling around looking for a way out.

Laughter sang from the telephone receiver lying at his side. Lyndsay, and suddenly Jimmy remembered her favorite saying: "I don't get mad, I get even," and she laughed louder.

With a head pounding clunk Jimmy clamped his teeth together, but it was too late, the insects were gushing out by the thousands, and there were more, millions more, in his stomach, and throat, and even crawling into his nasal passage, they were suffocating him!

One particularly large maggot wiggled away from the rest, and, when he looked at it, he tried to scream again but couldn't, because the rest of the insects had finally found their way out. The large maggot, the one with Lyndsay's face, stuck it's tongue out at Jimmy before scooting to the edge of the bed and dropping quickly out of sight.

Just before everything went black Jimmy heard Lyndsay laugh, "See you in hell, Love of my life."

#

CHAPTER 9

Tommy woke early, and sneaked out of the house before Anna was awake. He knew his mother wouldn't let him go back into the forest by himself, not after finding Lyndsay. He didn't want to go, but, frightened as he was, Tommy was more afraid not to obey the persistent ghost.

Bruiser paced Tommy step for step as though even he was reluctant to be back in the forest. The sun was warm on his face, and all around them thousands of birds chirped happily, yet the magic of the forest was lost to him. He didn't understand the meaning of the words 'bad vibes', but, if he had, he'd say he was having them now.

The bad feelings he was having were familiar though, because sometimes when Dad's demon got out, Tommy had these same jittery feelings right before something bad happened.

He thought maybe his mother got the feelings too, because sometimes just before Alex came home Anna started pacing. She'd become nervous and agitated, constantly rubbing her hands up and down her arms. If she and Tommy were eating dinner when she got the feelings she'd suddenly push her plate away and look like she was about to throw-up. Most of the time she told Tommy to go to his room and play or watch television, and she'd get a strange look on her face, because Tommy would have just told her that he was going to his room. He was never sure if he knew what she was thinking, or if she knew his thoughts, or if they were both reading the thoughts of Dad's demon.

Tommy had those feelings now, and his stomach was rumbling way down deep like it did when he had stomach flu and got the runs.

A raccoon and three kits darted across the path in front of Tommy and Bruiser, but neither seemed to notice.

In the clearing near the oak tree, Tommy stopped, and swallowed rapidly several times to keep down his churning stomach. The clearing was empty, and with a start, Tommy realized even the birds had stopped their racket. The only sound was a low, deep growl coming from way down in Bruiser's chest.

Tommy wrapped his arms around the dog's neck as sudden anger welled up in him. "I'm only nine years old! I'm not supposed to do this; I'm just a little kid! Why don't you pick on someone your own size?"

"Hi Tommy."

"AHH! Shit!"

Lyndsay laughed softly. "You say that a lot, don't you?"

Tommy ignored the reprimand. If anyone had the right to say shit he figured he did. "Why don't you leave me alone? You asked me to help you get out of the forest, and I did, not go away!"

"Well Tommy, I wish I could leave you alone, but unfortunately you're the only one I've got to help me."

"What'd you mean last night when you said someone would die if I didn't come here today?"

The girl drifted closer. "Someone did die, Tommy."

"Yeah, I know. You died, and I don't think that was very nice of you doing that to me either. I think it was shitty of you."

Shaking her head Lyndsay said, "No, someone else died, last night, and someone else is going to die tonight, maybe a lot of people, if you don't help me." Seeing the stubborn set to the boy's face, Lyndsay added, "Maybe even your own mother. She saw your mother the day you found me here."

A loud belch escaped Tommy's taunt lips. His stomach was boiling away, ready to erupt, and he thought, you better watch out, Lyndsay, you're gonna look pretty silly trying to scare people with puke all over you.

"You leave my mom out of this! You hear me, you leave my mother alone!"

"No, it's not me, Tommy. I wouldn't hurt your mother, or anyone else. All I want is to go on to wherever I'm supposed to go. I don't want revenge. It's the Indian woman, she's keeping me here, and she's making people die, and she'll keep making people die until I find out who killed me."

"Well I didn't kill you, and my mom didn't kill you, so leave us alone!"

Her head shaking sadly, Lyndsay continued, "I can't leave you alone Tommy. I like you, and I'm really thankful that you helped me, but Tommy she's killing people who knew me, people who I was close to."

"We weren't close to you, I didn't know you before."

"I know, but you helped me after."

"Shit, if this is what happens when you help someone remind me not to become a Boy Scout."

Lyndsay laughed. "That's funny, Tommy."

"It ain't either," Tommy snapped. "What do I have to do this time?" He was embarrassed that his voice sounded whiny instead of mad. Clearing his throat he tried to sound brave, "Who is the Indian woman you keep talking about? I ain't never seen any Indians around here."

"Well that's kind of hard to explain. She came to me when I was dying and told me to leave my body because I hurt so bad. She said if I would leave my body that I wouldn't hurt any more, and I didn't. She told me I have to stay here until the man who…ah, who hurt me was punished. After you found me she came back. She said someone's going to die every day until I remember who…who I can't remember."

"That don't make any sense, why would she kill people who didn't do anything just because you can't remember who did?"

"She said I have to be avenged."

"Huh?" Tommy, still squatting next to Bruiser, slowly stood. The dog pressed his huge body next to the boy, almost knocking Tommy over. Tommy reached out and patted the dog absently on the head.

Lyndsay looked confused, "Oh! The person who killed me has to be killed. An eye for an eye, that kind of stuff."

"An eye for an eye?" Tommy exclaimed. "Gross!"

Lyndsay smiled. "It just means if someone does something bad to you they get the same thing done to them."

Tommy considered this new bit of information. Actually it sounded pretty good, that way the next time Bryan Herman beat Tommy up and stole his lunch money, someone else would beat up Bryan and take his lunch money. Yeah, it was definitely a good plan.

Then, his curiosity peeked, Tommy asked, "What did happen to you?"

For the first time Tommy noticed Lyndsay was starting to fade. *Just reminding me that she's a ghost, for Pete's sake!*

Lyndsay reply was cold and sharp, "That's none of your business, besides you wouldn't understand even if I told you."

Hurt by the tone of her voice, Tommy rebutted, "Well fine, but just how am I suppose to do it to him, if I don't even know what it is?"

When the girl laughed and, much to Tommy's relief, she became more solid, "Tommy, I'm sorry for snapping at you. You don't have to do anything to him, just help me find out who he is. Besides, ah, you couldn't do to him what he did to me."

His hurt feelings somewhat appeased Tommy boasted, "Oh yeah? Well I'm stronger than I look, and Bruiser could help."

This time Lyndsay laughed so hard that she floated right up off the ground a couple of inches. Tommy didn't like that one bit, 'cause it scared him and that made him mad. "It ain't funny!"

"Someday, when you're grown-up, you'll think so."

"How come big people always say 'you'll understand when you're grown-up?' I ain't stupid you know. Mr. Parks says I'm the smartest fifth grader he ever saw. He says if it weren't for my, huh, emotional problems that I'd already be in the sixth grade!"

"Poor Tommy, I sure got you in a mess didn't I? I promise I'll protect you from the Guardian if you promise to help me."

"What about Mom and Bruiser?"

"Oh, I don't think she'll hurt Bruiser, and if you help me I'll try to protect your mom too, deal?"

Shifting from foot to foot and rubbing his hands up and down his arms, Tommy looked a lot like Anna waiting for Alex to storm through the door.

"Tell me some more about the Indian lady, huh, the Guardian?"

Lyndsay glanced over her shoulder, causing Tommy to sneak a peek also. "She's bad, Tommy, even though she's beautiful, she's meaner than you could ever imagine!"

"I can imagine pretty good," Tommy said glancing again in the direction Lyndsay had looked before. "I saw Nightmare on Elm Street and Freddie's pretty darned mean, and scary, too. I think he's the scariest thing there is. Mom doesn't know I saw Nightmare on Elm Street, though, 'cause I saw it over at my friend Billy's house one night. The Indian couldn't be worse than Freddie, no one could be!"

Again Lyndsay nervously glanced over her shoulder. "She is, because she's real, and real is always worse."

Tommy, who'd been looking where Lyndsay kept glancing, suddenly noticed a weird dark area between two trees. An area about the size and shape of a doorway was moving around in circles the same way water in the pond in Billy's backyard did when he threw rocks into it and they made little circles of waves. Unconsciously his butt cheeks squeezed together as he whispered, "Lyndsay?"

Lyndsay knew what was happening and pressed Tommy for an answer, "Will you help me?"

"How?" At that moment he would have promised her the world just to be away from the weird black area that was getting closer and closer.

"Just ask questions, and listen, that's all. Now run Tommy and don't stop until you're out of the forest!"

His feet barely touching the ground, Tommy moved from the clearing even before Lyndsay finished warning him. He slowed long enough to glance back as someone, or something tried to pull Lyndsay into the swirling blackness. Bruiser jerked and suddenly Tommy was practically flying out of the forest behind the big dog.

#

Ted watched as Tommy and Bruiser broke breathlessly from the woods behind the kid's house. Damned kids were always poking around looking for trouble.

"What are you looking at, Ted?"

With a guilty flinch Ted turned and snapped at his wife, "Christ woman, don't go sneaking up on me like that!"

Barely able to contain a smirk, Betty apologized. "Sorry, didn't mean to scare you. What are you looking at?"

Turning back to the window he replied, "Just watching the kid and his dog. You'd think with all the trouble they ran into last time they'd stay the hell out of the woods."

Betty moved to her husband's side, and watched as Tommy quickly put Bruiser in the kennel. "Kids will be kids. You know how they like to go exploring."

"No, I don't know."

Stung by the rebuttal, Betty turned away and started out of the room. At the door she stopped and said softly, "I forgot, you never were a kid."

She knew that wasn't what he'd meant. He never let her forget the reason they couldn't have children of their own. A botched abortion, which almost took her life, ended any chance of her ever having children of her own. What hurt the most was that it had been his child, and his idea for the abortion. Ted set everything up for her to have 'the problem' taken care of', even though the doctor he'd arranged for her to see looked like a refugee from a defunct meatpacking house. She'd begged and pleaded with him, promising anything, if he wouldn't make her go through with the abortion. He was worried about what his family would say; afraid he wouldn't be permitted to finish college, never once considering what having a baby at sixteen would do to her reputation. It was a choice she was willing to accept for the sake of the tiny life growing inside her.

"A baby now would ruin everything, you don't ever think of me," he told her, his face red with anger. "We can have ten kids later after I'm done with college, but not now. We can't afford a kid now. You're so selfish, always thinking of yourself and what you want, and to hell with everyone else."

His words stung, and although she knew in her heart that he was manipulating her as he always did, she finally relented, feeling as selfish as he claimed her to be.

True to his word though, after he finished college the following year, they'd gotten married, but there weren't ten babies in their house as he'd promised, there were none, ever. She was pretty sure the only reason he married her was because their parent's had forced the issue after she almost died. When she ended up in the hospital, hemorrhaging and in a coma for three days, there really hadn't been any way for Ted to keep the abortion secret, especially from her parent's, although he'd tried his damnedest.

They were frantic when Betty hadn't come home, and the logical place for them to look for her was at Ted's. From there it wasn't long before her father had the whole truth from the frightened young man. She learned later that Ted at first denied knowing where Betty was, claiming he hadn't seen her for several days. It ripped her heart out when, after they were married, Betty's sister told her that Ted was going to let her lay in that hospital all alone. Thank God Daddy hadn't believed him.

In the bathroom Betty stared back at her reflection. So many years ago, why can't he let it be? She often wondered why she'd stayed married to him all these years. He very seldom wanted to make love to her, and when he did, he never said her name, or that he loved her. She couldn't remember the last time that he said he loved her. Once several years ago she came right out and asked him if he still loved her, he ignored the question, but Betty persisted until Ted snapped, "I married your ass, didn't I?"

It hadn't been the answer she wanted to hear, so she never asked him again.

The tile behind the toilet was pulled up again, and Betty chuckled to herself, his hiding place, as though he never suspected that she mopped the bathroom floor. Damned old fool probably thinks it cleans itself. She wondered if, on those rare occasions when he had sex with her if it were she, or one of the staple-in-the-navel girls he held when his eyes were closed. Once, feeling mischievous, Betty had glued a staple just above her belly button, but he didn't notice, or if he had, didn't think it worth mentioning. The only thing that little stunt had accomplished was a whole lot of pain for her, Super Glue sticks for keeps!

For the most part Betty had a comfortable life, at least until Ted retired from the Ford plant in Detroit last year. Now he was home all the time, and that was something she was having trouble adjusting to. Before she had the house to herself most of the day, because with the hours he worked and the travel time, he was gone at least twelve hours a day. Now he was moping around the house, working in his flowerbeds, or spying on that nice family next door. At least Anna and Tommy were nice, but she was greatly relieved that Alex Rogers finally moved out.

With a sad shake of her head Betty left the bathroom. Men, they never realized how good they have it until they loose it.

At the kitchen window, Betty watched as Anna and Tommy got into their Taurus and, at the end of the drive, turned toward town. My child would be about Anna's age right now, and Tommy could be the age of the grandchild I'll never know. Betty sighed, blinking back a lifetime of unshed tears.

#

CHAPTER 10

Anna pulled up in front of Willie's, Whitefields' only grocery store. Because it was the only grocery store in town the prices were outrageous, and Anna knew that most people in the area preferred to make the hour drive to Mt. Clemens to shop in the large Kroger store where, not only were the prices cheaper, the selection was considerably larger. Today though Anna wasn't up to the long drive, maybe next week. She'd pick up what she needed for Tommy's party, and enough groceries to last them until one day next week when, hopefully, Tommy was back in school. She hated for him to miss so much class this close to the end of the school year, but Doc. Klein had insisted Tommy have as much time as be needed getting over the shock of finding Lyndsay Abbott's decomposed body. Anna shuddered, and wondered if the young girl would ever stop haunting their dreams. How does anyone ever get over a discovery like that?

Anna yawned, and Tommy, looking so small and fragile, smiled sadly. "Gee," Anna smiled back, "I don't know why I'm so tired, I haven't slept as late as I did this morning in years, probably not since I was a teenager."

Tommy nodded; he had a feeling maybe Anna had help sleeping so late this morning. More than likely a certain girl-ghost wanted to make sure Anna didn't keep Tommy from his rendezvous in the forbidden forest.

Checking her purse to make sure she had her money and coupons, Anna started to open the car door. When Tommy made no move to get out Anna asked, "Aren't you coming in?"

Tommy loved shopping with Anna, and never missed an opportunity to play their favorite game where Tommy tried to sneak goodies into the cart without Anna catching him, and then distract her at the checkout counter until the snacks were paid for. He wasn't really getting away with anything, because there were times when he'd cross the line and Anna would make him put some of the snacks back, but the game was a lot more fun than her just telling him to pick out what he wanted.

What he really wanted to do right now was sit quietly and think about what Lyndsay had said, and about the thing, the Indian demon, that was wrestling with

Lyndsay in that weird black swirly air, but he knew he had to go with his mother because the last thing he wanted was for Anna to worry about him any more than she already was.

He did wonder if the Demon took Lyndsay away for good? Or was she just mad because Lyndsay told him about her?

"Yeah, I'm coming. Just trying to think of what I'm really hungry for that I'm not suppose to have," he said, trying to laugh.

Relief washed over Anna like a spring rain as Tommy slipped from the car and walked beside her into the store.

#

Tony Morman slowed when he saw Anna and Tommy go into Willie's. He smiled a little feeling like a teenager suffering his first crush. He had all the symptoms, rapid heart rate, and sweaty palms, not to mention the little beads of sweat that had popped up on his upper lip when he realized the object of his affection was so close.

Turning the wheel sharply Tony made a quick U-turn and pulled up behind Anna's car. He wanted an excuse to see her again, and now he had it.

"When opportunity knocks", he chuckled heading for the store.

#

Captain Robbins pulled around the corner and turned off the ignition. Morman took him by surprise with that sudden U-turn.

"Jesus, he gets that excited just seeing a pretty face, I'd hate to see what he'd do if he actually thought he was going to get lucky." Robbins chuckled. He'd been following Morman almost twenty-four hours, and the policeman still hadn't spotted him. He found it hard to believe a Detroit cop would let himself be tailed that long without spotting the tail. Strange.

Robbins, having been born and raised in Whitefields, was very interested in the Abbott case. Things like that never happened here, it was unheard of. That was the main reason he joined the State Police instead the local force, the town was too damned boring.

He wanted to see just how good the big city cop really was. Things like murder and rape were taboo in Whitefields, and unless Morman did something really fast Robbins had a feeling his peaceful little town was going to be turned up side down. Yep, and I wouldn't miss seeing that smart-ass get knocked down a notch or two. Smiling to himself, Robbins lit a cigarette as he prepared to wait for his quarry to emerge.

#

They were halfway down the first aisle when Anna noticed Tommy stiffen. Glancing over her shoulder she saw the object of Tommy's concern headed their way. Anna felt a tightening in her stomach and wondered briefly if it was Morman's good looks, or the possibility of more bad news that caused the reaction.

Tommy continued down the aisle, pretending to be interested in the different types breads that Willie carried. Actually he wanted to be as far away from the policeman as possible, because if the Chief asked Tommy anything about Lyndsay he didn't know what he was suppose to say. Lyndsay hadn't told him not to tell anyone, yet he knew in his heart the cop wouldn't believe a thing Tommy told him about Lyndsay being a ghost, or the demon lady either. Best to just keep his distance, so he didn't accidentally say something to make anyone mad.

"Chief," Anna nodded as he approached, her hand unconsciously going to the lock of hair draping her forehead.

"Morning Mrs. Rogers." Looking down the aisle where the boy hurried along, he included her son, "Tommy."

Tommy ignored him as he disappeared around the corner. Just as well the boy didn't hear what he was going to say to Anna. He shouldn't be saying anything at all, but it was the only thing he could think of to talk to her about.

Taking off his hat, Tony moved closer, and breathed deeply of her scent, which made him lightheaded. Noting Anna's anxiety Tony lowered his voice to a near whisper. "I wanted to let you know, I got the results of the autopsy. She was beaten, raped, and left for dead." He didn't know why he blurted out the bit about rape, as he'd had no intention of telling her that much.

Anna feared she was going to pass out, but to her relief the dizzy spell passed, "My God!"

"The news hasn't been publicized yet, so I'd appreciate it if…out of respect to the parent's."

Nodding rapidly, Anna agreed, "Yes, yes. Oh, those poor, poor people. Do you know who…who could have done such a vile thing? You don't think it was anyone from around here, do you? People around here don't do things like that. That's one of the reasons I let my husband talk me into moving here when we got married. My husband was born here, you know? You don't think it could be someone from here do you? It must have been someone passing through, yes that's it, they were passing through and they're long gone by now! Oh, my God!" Anna knew she was babbling but just couldn't seem to stop. The image of the poor child huddled all alone against the trunk of that oak tree flooded Anna's mind. So alone! The horror the poor girl must have gone through before she mercifully slipped away!

Anguish washed over Tony, he hadn't meant for her to get that upset. He had no reason for telling her anything at all except for his selfish need to be near her. He had an idea she would react, would be drawn to him as a protector, but he never thought she would react so strongly. He tended to forget that the average person wasn't use to the harsh realities of life. Murder and rape became common everyday occurrences in large cities, well maybe not everyday, but often enough that a cop learned to think of the victims not as people but as statistics. He also realized belatedly that her being a parent probably had a lot to do with her reaction.

"I'm sorry, I shouldn't have told you so much about this, maybe I shouldn't have told you at all, but I didn't want you finding out about it from anyone else. I, ah, I wanted you to be prepared."

Anna rubbed her arms, not from the chilled air in the store but from the thoughts tormenting her. "I'm glad you told me, it's just that Tommy plays in those woods by himself all the time. Well he's not really by himself, I mean he has Bruiser with him, and I know the dog wouldn't let anyone hurt Tommy. Still…"

She didn't need to finish the sentence Tony knew what she was thinking. If someone murdered a young girl, what was to keep him from doing the same thing to an even younger boy, dog, or no dog?

"I think she was killed accidentally, I mean I don't think the murder meant to kill her, things probably just got out of control." He wanted her to be concerned, but not paranoid, "Just to be on the safe side though, I'd not let the boy play in the forest by himself for a while, or until I've got this solved." He hoped that daily life in Whitefields would return to normal soon. He liked Whitefields being quiet and peaceful, and it upset him that peace was shattered by a mindless fortuitous murder.

"Oh, I don't think we have to worry about that. I have a feeling it's going to be a long time before Tommy's willing to go back in there alone," she hesitated, thinking about something, then added, "but just the same, since kids usually do exactly the opposite of what we think they'll do, maybe I'd better talk to him."

#

Tommy was one aisle over listening. He already knew Lyndsay had been murdered, so unlike Anna, he hadn't been shocked by the news, except the rape part shocked him. No wonder Lyndsay got weird when he offered to do to the person what they'd done to her! He wasn't exactly clear on the subject of rape, but be had a pretty good idea what it meant. Some of the bigger boys at school laughed and told dirty jokes about rape. He never was sure what they thought was so funny about making a girl do something she didn't want to do, but he'd shrugged it off figuring that when he was bigger he'd see the humor in it. Now, knowing that rape and murder could be used in the same breath, Tommy hoped he never got dumb enough to think it was funny.

Listening quietly, Tommy heard his mother tell the Chief how he'd not be going into the forest by himself for quite a while. Boy, if they knew what I know they'd shit!

Then it hit him. Someone right here in this town is a murderer. It could be anyone. Willie, there behind the counter, watching Mom and the Chief talk and pretending he's not paying any attention. The murderer is a man; it could be my teacher, Mr. Parks, or Reverend Kent from Sunday school, or even Dad, he thought with a shiver. Maybe Dad's demon is doing more than beating up on Mom and me?

He turned away and walked slowly down the isle. What was he supposed to do? How was a nine (almost ten)-years-old kid suppose to find out something that even the Chief of Police couldn't find out? When he first started eavesdropping he'd been hoping the Chief was going to tell Mom that he'd caught the murderer, but that hope died a quick death, as he learned the cop didn't know any more than he did. He bet even a grown-up would have trouble knowing what he knew. How many grown-ups could handle having a ghost tell them that a demon was going to hurt their mother?

His teacher, Mr. Parks, said Tommy was very smart for his age, but he didn't think he was smart enough to handle this all by himself!

Anna poked her head around the corner surprising him. "Here he is now." She smiled as she dragged him around the end of the isle and almost into the Chief's arms.

"Hello Tommy, how you doing?" Chief Morman asked, a sympathetic smile tugging the corners of his mouth.

Tommy hadn't told the policeman any of the details about finding Lyndsay just that he and Bruiser accidentally found the body, and Mom never told him about Tommy coming home and trying to get her to come into the forest with him to find his "little friend" earlier that day, so Chief Mormon only knew that him and Bruiser found the body, nothing more, and for now that suited Tommy just fine. He just wanted this to be all over with so he could forget about it.

"I'm okay, Sir."

Sir. The kid had actually called him Sir. It's been a long time since I heard a kid call a cop Sir.

Tony smiled, "I hear you're having a birthday party Saturday." Tony wanted this boy to like him, to trust him, for some reason he felt it was very important, and not just because he wanted to get close to the mother. No, there was something more to it he just couldn't grasp what.

Tommy nodded. "Yes Sir."

"How old will you be?"

"Ten."

"Ten, huh? That's a really good age to be. If I could be any age I wanted, I'd have to pick ten."

Frowning, Tommy wanted to know, "Why?"

"Oh, I guess because when I was ten I didn't have a worry in the world. I chummed around all summer with my friends, and pretty much did what I wanted to do. Don't you feel like that, Tommy? Like you don't have a care in the world, I mean?"

"No, sir."

Confused, Tony inquired, "No, you don't have a care in the world, or, no you don't feel like that."

"No, Sir, I don't feel like that."

"But why? What are you worried about?"

Glancing quickly at Anna, Tommy sighed, "I worry about demons."

Tony shot a glance at Anna, and her cheeks suddenly felt inflamed. Clearing her throat, Anna tried to explain, "Tommy thinks that when his father gets drunk he becomes possessed by a demon. He overheard me make a remark to Alex years ago about getting his demon cured, and it stuck in his mind because ever since that day he's insisted that a demon lives in his father. A child psychologist told me it's his way of exonerating his father. No child wants to think badly of a parent."

Tony looked at Tommy for a couple of seconds. The kid looked terrified, and it infuriated Tony that a child should have to live with that kind of fear. If Alex Rogers was a piece of shit in Tony's mind before, the bastard was quickly becoming the worse kind of slug Tony could imagine.

"You know what? I think you're right, I've seen some super nice people get really mean and nasty when they've had too much to drink. Now that I think about it, it is like there's a demon in them."

A small smiled tugged at Tommy's lips as he nodded, "Yeah, and Dad even looks different! His eyes get real red, and everything!"

Next to him Tony felt Anna's discomfort. She probably felt like a traitor even though Alex abused both her and her son. At least Tony was relieved that Alex no longer lived with Anna and the boy. Who knows what a man like that is capable of?

Suddenly Tommy had an idea, a great idea! "Would you come to my birthday party, Chief Morman?"

"Well I..." The question coming unexpectedly threw Tony and he glanced helplessly toward Anna, who shrugged, and nodded. So Tony, silently thanking the kid for his chance, replied "Sure, I'd love to come to your party, Tommy, thank you for asking. What time?"

Anna said, "It starts at two, but, if you'd like to come early, before all the kids get there, you're more than welcome."

After they said their good-byes Anna looked closely at her son. What was he up to? Why on earth had he asked the chief of police to his party? And why had she held her breath, like a schoolgirl, until he said yes?

Tommy just smiled as he hurried down the aisle ahead of Anna, remembering to throw snacks into the cart every time her back was turned. He knew what he was doing all right.

Neither Lyndsay nor the Indian would dare come near Tommy or his mother with a policeman there to protect them. Maybe being smart for his age was going to help after all.

#

Doctor Klein was waiting when Tony returned to his office. The doctor looked pale and tired, and more than a little upset. Not a good sign, Tony thought with a sinking feeling in the pit of his stomach.

"What's up, Doc?" Sounding, but not feeling much like Bugs Bunny, Tony dropped to the old wooden chair behind his desk.

The doctor sighed, rubbing the bridge of his nose between his index finger and thumb. "I'm not really sure, Tony, but I figured I'd better fill you in just the same."

Taking the cup of coffee Tony handed him, Klein leaned forward on his chair, looking a decade older than the last time Tony saw him. "You know Jimmy Russo? The kid that was dating Lyndsay Abbott?"

Tony shrugged.

"It's OK, there really isn't any reason you should know him, 'cause he was a pretty good kid, never in any major trouble."

Tony's ears perked. "Was?"

Nodding, the doctor went on. "Yeah, was. I got a call early this morning from Jimmy's mother. She was hysterical, said her boy wasn't breathing. I hurried over, and sure enough, the kid was dead. Seventeen years old, top health, not a mark on him, but stone-cold-dead just the same."

"How?" Tony tapped a chewed-on pencil nervously against the side of his coffee mug.

"I'm getting a second opinion before I say for sure."

"You send the body to Bill?"

Klein nodded. "Didn't know what else to do. I checked him out as well as I could. Checked for drug use, any trauma to the body that would account for his death, that sort of thing, but other than that I figured Bill's the expert." The doctor sipped his coffee slowly, a frown playing between his eyes. "The thing that really gets me on this one was the look on the kid's face. I'll tell you what Tony, that kid looked like he was scared to death. If I live to be a hundred, I'll never forget the look of pure horror on his face. If someone told me he'd seen the demons of hell I'd believe it."

The Rogers boy's voice whispered In Tony's mind, "I worry about demons."

CHAPTER 11

Cindy brushed past several of her friends without even acknowledging them. She had more important things on her mind that afternoon. Things like where the hell was Jimmy? She wanted to give him a piece of her mind for hanging up on her last night. How rude! Who did he think he was anyway? She was busy going over possible paybacks when someone grabbed her arm, startling her.

"Shit Judy, don't do that!" Cindy snapped, jerking her arm away from the scrawny hand that held it.

Her eyes gleaming with excitement, Judy asked, "Did you hear?"

Cindy sighed. Judy was the biggest gossip in school, and if anyone wanted something known, all they had to do was tell Judy, then tell her not to repeat it, before the end of the next period half the school would know whatever it was that Judy wasn't supposed to repeat.

"I really don't have time for this right now, Judy."

Barely able to contain herself, Judy almost jumped up and down. "You haven't heard! You don't know about Jimmy!"

I don't think I want to hear this, Cindy thought with a sudden intuitive shiver.

"He's dead. Jimmy Russo is dead. I think they said it was drugs or maybe AIDS? I can't remember. I've heard so many different versions that I'm having trouble keeping up. Didn't you and him kind of have a thing going after Lyndsay disappeared, or was it before?"

Cindy just stared. Jimmy dead? Jimmy dead? Lyndsay dead. Jimmy dead. What the hells going on here?

"Cindy? I asked you a question. Didn't you hear me?" Judy asked impatiently. After all she'd just given Cindy some juicy information.

The least Cindy could do was give Judy something in return. Everyone heard how Cindy was throwing herself all over Jimmy now that Lyndsay was dead. Some were saying that Cindy screwed Jimmy before, and that's why Lyndsay ran out in the blizzard last January. Come on you little slut, give me proof!

Cindy looked at the other girl. Judy reminded her of an ugly dog begging for a bone. Jesus, she's practically drooling. So why not, why not give her what she wants to hear? A little attention and sympathy couldn't hurt right about now.

"I'm sorry Judy, what did you ask me? I'm just so shocked and upset that I'm not thinking straight. It's just, my God, my poor Jimmy. First Lyndsay and now Jimmy, what am I going to do?" With little effort she managed to squeeze out a couple of fair-size tears. She glanced at Judy through lowered lashes. The nosy bitch was eating it up.

#

Alex turned on his side and braced his chin with his hand as he watched Dee checking herself in the mirror. She was going to be late for work again, but Alex didn't care. He knew Jake wouldn't dare say anything to her about it, after the story she told him about leaving Jake naked as a jay bird when she sipped out of the bar the other night. At first he'd been pissed, but then the more he thought about that slob Jake getting caught by that nutty wife of his, the funnier it became. He'd known Dee was sleeping with Jake, hell everyone in town knew that was one of the job requirements, it just pissed him off at first having her throw it in his face.

He thought maybe he was getting a little weird because when he thought about Dee doing it with Jake he actually got a hard on. That's why Dee was late for work, and if he kept thinking about it she was going to be even later.

"Tell me again," he coaxed.

Putting down her eyeliner Dee turned to him, "Not now, Babe. You know I have to go in early so Jake can drive to Detroit to get beer since the stupid delivery guy never came in yesterday. But if you're here when I get off I'll tell you every juicy little detail."

Lately keeping Alex in a good mood was harder than getting Jake to keep his filthy hands off her. Ever since his night in jail Alex was a worse pain-in-the-ass than usual, constantly bitching about everything from his wife and son, to the Chief of Police, to what Dee wore to work the day before. He showed up today looking for a fight, a reason to slap her around, and it'd taken quite a bit of imagination on her part to get him in a halfway descent mood. She'd never known anyone before who got turned on by listening to details of her sex life, but if that were what it took to keep Alex happy she would take full advantage of his quirk until June when they left for Florida. If she had to she'd make up stories to entertain her lover, she had a good imagination.

Alex chuckled again. "You're right, I would have given anything to had a hidden camera in his office that night. Has he said anything to you about it? I mean about what happened when Peggy found him like that?"

Loosening another button on her blouse so more cleavage showed, she replied, "All he said to me was, 'I owe you one, bitch.' I just laughed, and went about my job. One of guys heard him though, and asked what was going on, but Jake told him to mind his own business. You know, now that I think about it, Jake was walking kind of funny, you don't suppose Peggy kicked him in the gonads, do you?"

Alex burst out laughing. "God, I hope SO!"

"So you going to be here when I get off, or what?" She asked, bending down to kiss him.

Instantly Alex sobered. "Maybe. I have the kid's bike together, finally, and wanted to take it out to him, but I don't know if 'she' will let me give it to him. His birthday is Saturday. 'She' should let me give it to him for his birthday, don't you think?"

Dee was always amazed at the difference in Alex sober and Alex drunk. She could actually like the sober Alex; he could be a really sweet guy.

"I would think so, since Tommy is your son too, and it's his birthday. Well Honey, gotta run. Hope to see you later for a little more show-

and-tell." She wiggled her fanny on the way out the door, and Alex chuckled. She was no Anna, but the kid definitely had a nice ass. Scrub off a pound and a half of make-up, and do something with that awful mop of frizzy bleached hair, and Dee would be able to turn heads on any beach.

#

Cindy drove home from school slowly, her mind whirling. She'd planned on making Jimmy take her to Lyndsay's funeral, but now Jimmy was dead too. This was all too weird.

Some of the kids at school told her they were sorry to hear about Jimmy, but most of them had just given her dirty looks. She wondered if Jimmy had been telling them things about her. In his warped little mind he probably thought she'd been chasing after him. Hell, she'd been stupid enough to let him seduce her once, and it was definitely no big deal. She still didn't know why Lyndsay had gotten all upset. The guy was a jerk, and instead of being pissed at her, Lyndsay should have thanked her for showing her what a cheating creep Jimmy really was. Try to do a good deed and look what happens.

"Oh well, no big loss." She shrugged off the boy dumb enough to turn her down.

Her main concern was buying two new black dresses, and finding someone to take her to both funerals since stupid Jimmy went and got himself dead. Luckily she had time because Lyndsay's body was still in Detroit, and she'd heard that Doc Klein had sent Jimmy's there too. Lyndsay and Jimmy, together again, she thought with a chuckle, when shivered and wondered, what the hell are they doing with the bodies anyhow?

Cindy's purse fell over on the seat next to her, spilling most of its contents on the floor. "Shit," she swore bending over to grab as much as she could reach. As she straightened up she caught movement out of the corner of her eye. At first it looked like something was pacing the car on the driver's side. The forest loomed deep and dark behind the white blur, she could see it just fine, but couldn't focus on whatever the white thing was.

Looking straight ahead and catching the suggestion of movement in her peripheral vision was the only way she could see whatever was racing along beside her. Every time Cindy turned her head to get a better look the object disappeared. She rubbed her eyes in case there was something in them, but the only thing that accomplished was making her vision blurred even more. Whatever the cause, Cindy was becoming more nervous by the second. Her foot plunged down, accelerating in the hopes of out running it, whatever 'it' was, but the apparition continued to dance just out of sight.

Finally, more than a little irritated, Cindy pulled onto the shoulder of the road. Maybe something was stuck on the window, or on the roof of the car. That would explain why it seemed to keep pace with her.

Before getting out of the car though, just to be on the safe side, Cindy looked through all the windows, and then slowly opened the door to check the roof. Tiny fingers of ice danced along her spine. Silly, she thought, it's the middle of the afternoon, and I'm on a public, if deserted road in Whitefields, nothing will happen to me here. Still her mouth was so dry she couldn't have spit if she'd been on fire. Bogeymen only come out at night, and never in Whitefields. Well, almost never, she conceded, remembering Jimmy and Lyndsay.

Knowing that Lyndsay had probably been abducted right along this very stretch of highway did little to calm her jitters nerves.

Finally, skewering up her courage, Cindy opened the car door, emerging into warm spring sunshine. As the bright sun warmed her face, Cindy felt silly for her childish fears.

She checked the side of the car, then roof in case something had gotten stuck to the outside of the car and was blowing in the wind within her line of vision as she drove. Quickly scanning the car proved this hopeful idea to be false, the car was clean, but for some highway dust. Whatever she saw pacing the car was either in her head or…she shivered, not wanting to think about it any more, because now she knew someone, or something was watching her.

Bent forward, keeping her eyes riveted to the ground, Cindy walked around the car towards the open door on the driver's side. Unseen eyes bore into the back of her head, watching her from the dark forest across the road. Don't look, she whispered to herself like a mantra. Just get in the car and drive! Her hand snaked out longingly to the open door just inches away. Just another step and I can go home. I never meant for anyone to get hurt. I'm sorry! She wasn't quite sure why these thoughts were dancing in her brain, they just seemed appropriate, sort of like saying the Lord's Prayer in church, the words were always in her head, just in case He really was listening, and keeping score, "Hey, look, Cindy's at the Pearly Gates", St. Peter would chuckle, and "she's been a real little bitch." But then the Big Man would speak up and reply, "Yeah, but she thought the words to the Lord's Prayer 32,936 times, so let her in." Cindy long ago decided it probably wouldn't work that way, but what the hell it was worth a try. Now the apology thought to Lyndsay seemed as unlikely to work, as did her prayers to God, but as with God, she figured it couldn't hurt to try.

From miles away her fingertips touched the hot metal of the car door. Almost there!

Out of nowhere an iron vice clamp around the back of her neck, squeezing icy finger deeper and deeper into the tender flesh. Cindy's mouth opened, lips pulled back in a scream that only she heard along with her apologies. Cindy so badly needed to scream, scream so loud everyone in Whitefields would hear.

Her neck burned where the numbing hand clamped tightly, preventing her from moving to the safety of the car. Then a body moved up close, pressing tight against her back. An icy blue fire penetrated the thin material of her skirt and blouse. Gasping frantically for breath, Cindy finally managed a small pitiful yelp.

A rancid chuckle fogged the air near her ear. "Hi best friend, do ya miss me?"

When the icy grip on her neck loosened, Cindy dropped to the ground, her legs no longer able to hold her. Still she refused to look at whoever, no whatever, stood laughing above her.

It was important not to acknowledge the thing. To acknowledge it would be to give it life. Cindy reached for the car door, only inches away. If she could just get inside the car she could lock the door and go home. She refused to give credibility to her nightmare.

Grabbing the door handle, the chrome blistering against her half-frozen fingers, Cindy attempted to throw herself into the car. When had the day turned so cold? What happened to the warm summer sun, and why was something warm running down her legs, and suddenly she was horrified, because she realized she'd wet her panties.

The thing Cindy wouldn't give recognition to laugh tauntingly, "Baby peed her pants. Baby, baby, baby, stick your face in gravy."

What a stupid rhyme, it doesn't even make sense, Cindy thought.

Mad that Lyndsay dared laugh at her, Cindy turned without a second thought to tell her best friend exactly that. "That's really a stupid saying, Lynds, and it doesn't even make any sense. None of this makes any sense. You're just a figment of my imagination. I know it because not only is the rhyme illogical, it's impossible that you're standing here right now looking just like you always did when I know for a fact that you are dead and rotting in some autopsy room down in Detroit. It doesn't make sense that I'm standing here with piss running down my leg either, ruining my last pair of good pantyhose. What do you want from me? You want me to say I'm sorry that you're dead? Well I am sorry you're dead, and I'm sorry I screwed Jimmy, but I only did it so you'd realize what a cheating jerk he really was. But now Jimmy's dead too, and I'm pretty sure I'll be dead before this conversation is done, and still none of it makes any goddamned SENSE!" Cindy finally managed the scream she'd hoped for, and she continued to scream as Lyndsay dragged her, kicking and struggling from the car, across the road towards the forest beyond.

Lyndsay screamed into Cindy's face, "You like screwing don't you Cindy? You'll screw anyone, anytime. Sometimes I think you'd screw a tree if you could figure out a way. Well, girlfriend, I'm here to let you know that I found you a way!"

#

CHAPTER 12

Alex was traveling along Forest Drive towards home, more accurately his ex-home, thinking about Anna and Tommy. He couldn't believe Anna was actually going to let him see the kid. He'd been prepared to beg if need be, but Anna saved him that humiliation by saying it was okay if he brought the bike out, and wish the boy a happy birthday. Of course she'd asked the kid first, but Tommy only hesitated a couple of minutes before agreeing! Maybe if I straightened up my act they'll let be back in, he hoped. No more drinking, I have to quit altogether, and I have to stay stopped this time. I can do it, I know I can, if I have something to stop for, and nothing is as important as my family.

Alex wouldn't admit that he had this very same conversation with himself many times before. I just want to go home and be with my family, he thought, not realizing he wasn't the first person in town to have the same thoughts in the past few months, and he wouldn't be the last.

The sun was low in the afternoon sky, turning the western horizon bright crimson and purple. The trees on the eastern side of the car were deep in shadow, and he almost passed by without noticing the thing near the top of one small dead tree. When what he was looking at finally registered in his mind Alex hit the brakes hard, throwing the car into a perilous spin.

"No way! No f'n way," Alex swore in stunned disbelief. It had to be someone's idea of a sick joke; it's just a dummy or something, he thought, but it doesn't look like a dummy, it looks to friggin real, too bloody and gross not to be real. He managed to put the car in park, then just sat staring, trying to convince himself that what he was seeing was not real, just a hallucination caused from not having had anything to drink. Unfortunately no matter how many times Alex blinked, or rubbed his eyes, the aberration remained.

In the cool golden hue of dusk, Alex Rogers emptied the contents of his stomach on the still warm asphalt. The heated stench of vomit made him puke until only dry heaves racked his abused diaphragm. Slowly, by refusing to look at thing at the top of the tree, he was able to control his urges and regain some semblance of order in his addled brain.

Don't look at it, don't think about it, just start up the car, oh please God, please let the car. Got to see Anna, she'll know what to do.

#

Tony sat at his desk; the only sign of his irritation was the steady strumming of his fingers across the scared wood top. He thought about Cindy Milner, Jimmy Russo, Lyndsay Abbott, Anna and Tommy, and especially he thought of Alex Rogers.

It bothered him that Alex called from Anna's house to report the discovery of the Milner girl. Tony tried to convince Alex to go back to the spot where he supposedly saw a body so they could find it, but Alex refused. He was acting like a lunatic, and said there was no way in Hell he would go anywhere near that body. All he'd say was that it was about halfway between town and Anna's house, near the top of a small tree. "Use your spotlights, that's what you have them for, just look for the puke in the road, that's where you'll find her."

They found her all right, exactly where Alex said she'd be. Her car was parked across the road, and, from the look of it, if Alex had pulled off the road up a little further up he would have crashed into Cindy's car. Tony couldn't blame him for tossing his cookies. Of the six men at the scene only one managed not to lose his supper, and that was one of State boys, and Tony figured the only reason he hadn't was because he never left his squad car.

Tony called in the State Police after checking out the situation; this was one he definitely didn't mind admitting he needed help with.

He would love to figure out a way to lay blame on Alex Rogers, unfortunately he couldn't think of any way for Rogers to have gotten the girl up there. Actually he was at a loss to figure out how anyone could have gotten her up there without at least having help, and some very heavy machinery, if then.

After carefully cutting down the tree, it was sent, intact, to Bill Padgett's office in Detroit. Bill was going to love him for this one. They'd cut the tree off just below the bottom of the girl's feet, the top; narrower section came out of her mouth. There were small branches on the top section of the tree complete with some dried leaves still attached. What they sent to Bill was impossible, yet they all saw it. They all agreed it would be like trying to put a Christmas tree through a car window bottom end first. The branches would break off, yet the branches on the top of the tree weren't broken. It was as if her body had grown around the tree, or the tree had grown up through her body. Totally impossible, yet it had happened. Somehow the impossible had happened.

Tony picked up the phone and punched out Anna's number. Three hours should be plenty of time for Alex to calm down enough to leave, he hoped. It'd taken every ounce of willpower to wait that long before calling, but somehow he had managed.

"Anna, it's Chief Mormon, you okay? Is Alex still there?"

"Oh, hi Chief. Yeah, he's here, said he's not leaving until the body's removed. He's been ranting something about some girl skewered to a tree. Says she looked like an animal on a spit ready for roasting. He's pretty upset, and I'm not even sure I understood most of what he was saying."

Tony felt a need to protect Anna from the horror he'd witnessed, so he neither confirmed or denied Alex's statement, "He's leaving tonight?"

Anna laughed softly, "He sure is, I told him I don't have anything stronger than coffee in the house. He's been pacing for hours, waiting to hear you cleared the road so he can hightail it to Jake's and drink himself oblivious."

"Good, ah, I mean tell him the road is clear and I'll need to talk to him in the morning. I'll need his statement. You all right?"

"Yeah, I guess so. Hold on a second so I can give him your message," she put her hand over the mouthpiece on the phone, then a couple of seconds later she spoke to Tony, "OK, I'm back. Ah, Chief, what he told me…what Alex said about the girl? Was it true, or just more of his drunken babbling?"

He didn't want to lie to her, but was uneasy about her reaction. "Unfortunately he gave a pretty accurate description."

He listened to several seconds of silence before Anna finally said, "Yeah, I was afraid of that because I didn't smell any booze on his breath." She laughed tightly, "Funny though, it's the only time I can ever remember wanting to smell whiskey on his breath."

Thinking Anna was worried about her safety, Tony quickly offered, "I can come out there and talk to Alex tonight and make sure he leaves you alone, it you'd like."

"What? Oh, no, don't worry about Alex he's leaving right now as a matter of fact." There was a moment of muted conversation, and then Anna said, "OK, he just left. Chief, do you have any idea who might be doing these horrible things?"

Tony thought, if you'd seen her on that tree you wouldn't be asking who, but what! "I'm afraid not. At least we have no leads at the moment, but we're working on it. Look, Anna, do me a favor will you? While I'm still on the line I want you to go and lock all your doors and windows, OK?"

"Sure, hold on."

A few minutes later Anna was back, "All done. Thanks Chief."

"Don't mention it."

"I even made Bruiser stay in Tommy's room tonight. He usually doesn't want to stay in the house very long, but tonight for some reason he seems perfectly content up there on the floor next to Tommy's bed."

"Dogs are pretty smart. Bruiser probably feels more comfortable next to Tommy where he can protect him. Animals sense fear and nervousness in the people around them. I'm glad you have him, makes me feel a little better with you and Tommy living clear out there all alone."

"We're not completely alone. The Jenkins live next door, and I'm sure if I screamed loud enough they'd hear me."

I'm sure they've heard screams coming from your house before, but they've never done anything to help, Tony wanted to say but didn't. Instead he said goodnight and hung up.

That had been last night. Now at almost noon Tony knew no more than he had then. The Abbott girl was a case he could deal with, rape and murder, but nothing fancy, just like thousands of other cases. That kind of crime, if unsolved, would be filed away with hundreds of other cases, and as new cases came in no one would ever give it another thought, except the family. But this! This was something he'd never seen before, couldn't even start to explain. How in hell had someone gotten the girl up there? She'd been at least ten feet off the ground, and the strength it would take to force her down on the tree like that, if that's how she was impaled on it, was a force Tony hoped he never came up against.

If something didn't break soon he'd have the mild mannered residents of Whitefields running around killing anyone who looked at their kids wrong. He'd already seen Karl Abbott several times, driving aimlessly around town with a shotgun mounted behind him in his pickup truck. Several complaints had already come in about Karl asking weird questions and acting crazy. Tony knew the story behind the Abbott girl's death, how she'd run from her best friend's house the night she was murdered because the friend, none other than the recently departed Cindy Milner, blurted out that she'd slept with Lyndsay's boyfriend, now also among the dearly departed. Some best friend, he thought, but even at that she sure didn't deserve to die the way she had. Karl Abbott could be a prime candidate for the latest murders. At least he could be if Tony ever figured out how anyone, even a crazy man, could ram a tree through a person without stripping limbs and leaves. Of course anyone with any knowledge of drugs could have caused the Russo kid's heart attack, if that's what Bill concludes the cause of death to be, and Tony was checking into Karl's background for any medical training. One thing Tony did know, Karl hadn't murdered his own daughter, but revenge was a strong motivation for the other two.

The Abbott girl was murdered the night of the big snowstorm. There hadn't been many people out on the roads that night. With the exception of Jake's 1—4 The Road, every place closed up early, and no one remembered seeing any strangers around, but that didn't mean someone couldn't have passed through without being seen. Tony tried convincing the townspeople that there was a good chance that an outsider, someone just passing through had killed the Abbott girl that cold winter night, but the word on the street was that there was a murderer was in their mist that whomever had murdered Lyndsay Abbott and now Cindy Milner was from right here in Whitefields. That made everyone nervous, and suspicious of his or her neighbor, and Tony noticed tension in the air everywhere he went.

Pulling a sheet of paper from his pocket, Tony again went over the list of people who had been at Jake's that night: Jon Black, owner of the Texaco station, two of his employees, Bryan North and Jimmy Johnson. Also on the list were Pete Noble, undertaker and owner of the funeral home, Pete Miller, Mayor of Whitefields, then, of course Jake himself and his bartender, Dee, and, last but not least, none other than Mr. Alex Rogers.

The ringing of the phone brought Tony from his ruminations. Sally, the woman who answered the phones and manned the radio during the day, poked her head around the corner, "Chief, Bill's on three."

"Thanks Sally." Grabbing the phone, Tony continued, "Bill, old friend, what have you got for me?"

"Don't you old friend me, Anthony, just what the hell is going on out there? I've never in all my years seen anything like the stiff you sent me last night. If that's your idea of a joke I can tell you right now I don't think it's the least bit funny."

"Hey, take it easy, even I don't have a sense of humor that sick! Tell me what you got."

"Just what you saw. You want the cause of death? I'll tell you, she had a fucking tree rammed into her vagina, through her body, and out her mouth. Wouldn't that just about kill anyone, for Christ sake?"

"OK, sorry, you're right it's obvious, whatcha got on the other one, the kid, Jimmy, ah, Russo?"

"Russo, hold on a minute. Yeah, here it is, bugs."

"What?"

"Bugs. The inside of the mouth, nasal passage, ears, esophagus, stomach, intestines, bowels, bugs everywhere."

"Bugs?"

"Yep."

"What the hell kind of bugs?"

"Well mostly maggots, but there were a few green and black beetles too. I sent those to a friend of mine to identify. Maggots I know, I've seen enough in my life not to need an expert's help, although these were some of the biggest mothers I've ever seen."

"That's disgusting!" Tony tried not to gag.

"You think it's bad, just think how that kid felt when they started coming out of him."

"Aw, Bill, you're not going to tell me he knew they were in him, are you? Please say you're not."

"Sure he knew, Christ they suffocated him. You obviously didn't see the look on his face or you wouldn't have asked. Oh, he knew all right, no doubt about it. Do me a favor Tony, old buddy, please, no more surprises, OK?"

"I sure as hell hope not!"

Bill chuckled, "You know, you sure have those State boys shaking in their boots. Want to know what they're calling your peaceful little town?"

"I'm afraid to ask."

"Demon's Hollow only instead of Hollow they're pronouncing it Howler,

H-o-w-l-e-r. Cute, don'tcha think?"

"Bill, eat shit and die."

Demons again. What is it with demons all of a sudden? Tommy's afraid of demons, because he thinks that one possesses his father when he drinks, and now the State Police are calling us Demon's Hollow. Shit.

#

Tommy sat at the kitchen table eating a bowl of cereal. He was still tired after laying awake for what seemed to be hours last night waiting for his father to leave. He felt safe enough because he had Bruiser, but Mom was downstairs with a potentially dangerous man. Tommy wasn't sure if his father was drunk or not, he ranted and raved like he did when the Demon took over, yet somehow Tommy thought his father was more frightened than anything else. Bruiser was listening to Dad, too, because every time Alex raised his voice the dog growled. Tommy was prepared to throw open the bedroom door and let the dog eat his father's face if he laid one finger on his mother.

The only reason Tommy agreed to see his father was to find out where Alex was the night of the snowstorm, the night Lyndsay died. He remembered the night of the big snowstorm because they'd said that school was cancelled the next day and Mom had let him stay up late watching movies with her. He remembered how nice it'd been sitting there, just him and Mom eating popcorn and watching movies. The last movie they watched was Stephen King's Dream Catcher and it was a longer movie than Mom thought, so it was after midnight when the movie ended and Mom finally told Tommy he had to go to bed, and Dad still wasn't home when Tommy had gone upstairs.

Unfortunately when his father arrived last night he was screaming and talking all crazy about a body in the woods. Before Tommy could understand much of what Alex was saying Anna sent him to his bedroom, he supposed in case Dad got crazy again. He tried to listen from the top of the stairs but, because his parent's went into the kitchen, he couldn't make out what they were saying.

Shortly after that his mother brought Bruiser upstairs to stay with him. That frightened him, because Mom never let Bruiser stay in his room at night. Maybe she was afraid something bad was going to get him during the night while he was sleeping. She'd told him it was just so he'd have company, but Tommy knew better.

When he asked about seeing his father Anna just said, "He's not feeling well right now, so maybe you can thank him for the bike another time."

Tommy hadn't even seen the bike yet, and wondered if Alex remembered to leave it. He hoped so, because it would be neat to have a bike to ride. He wouldn't be able to take Bruiser with him when he went riding, but at least he'd have something fun to do now that the forest had lost its attraction.

Lyndsay needed his help, and the only way to do that was to snoop around where people were so he could overhear what was being said. The only way he could do that was if Dad left the bike, 'cause it was too far to walk to town. After rinsing out his cereal bowl and putting it in the rack on the counter, Tommy hurried out the kitchen door in search of his birthday present.

Disappointment clouded his face; the bike wasn't by the back door. Alex must have been drunk after all, he had a bad habit of forgetting all sort of things when the Demon came to visit. Now what was he going to do? He couldn't walk to town, it was at least five miles, and Mom wouldn't let him out of her sight that long.

"Shoot," he mumbled as he walked around the end of the garage. The garage! Sure that's where Dad would put the bike if he remembered to leave it! Tommy's face split into a beaming grin. A brand-new, shiny, red ten-speed sat balanced on its kickstand right where Alex's car used to sit. The bike even had a big white bow taped to the handlebars. Dad sure can be nice when the demon lets him, Tommy thought as tears welled up in his eyes. Before the tiny drops of salt water could spill down his cheeks Tommy had the bow off and was running down the driveway, ready to sling his leg over the crossbar.

He pedaled to the end of the drive and back, testing his ability to handle his new freedom. He'd ridden his friend Billy's bike a lot of times, so he was familiar with the gears and brakes. Now all he had to do was think up something to tell Anna so she wouldn't worry if he were gone a couple of hours.

"Hey Sport, see you found the birthday present from your dad," Anna called from the front porch where she'd been watching her son test his biking skills. Any apprehension she had vanished the moment she saw how easily he handled the big two-wheeler.

Beaming, Tommy called back over his shoulder, not even swerving, "Sure did, and isn't it magnificent?"

Magnificent? "Yep, don't forget to call and thank him later."

Tommy, bringing the bike to a stop by the porch steps, asked, "How far can I go? Can I take it over to Billy's when he gets home from school?"

"Well," Anna replied hesitantly, "until things settle down I don't think you should be going too far from the house."

Frowning, Tommy asked, "What things?"

Anna didn't know whether or not to tell Tommy about the other girl. She didn't want to scare him, but she wanted him to know to be on the watch for anyone acting strangely.

Alex does something right, and it's still wrong. Why did he have to give Tommy the bike now of all times?

"Mom? Hey Mom!"

Shit! "Look Honey, remember when your father came in last night, and how he was all upset?"

"Yeah?"

"Well that was because he'd seen a dead person beside the road on his way out here."

Tommy's eyes widened. "Really? Who? Where?"

"I'm not exactly sure where, just someplace between here and town, and I don't know who either except it was another girl from town."

Another girl? She means another girl like Lyndsay. Did that mean that whoever killed Lyndsay killed this other girl too? Now were there going to be two ghosts pestering him instead of just one? If Dad found her maybe he knew where she was 'cause his demon killed her, and where was he when Lyndsay was killed?

He needed time to think about this new turn of events, so it was no problem promising Anna that he would stay very close to home.

He tried to take all parts of the puzzle that he had and piece them together, but unfortunately there were more questions he needed answers to first, like had the second girl died the same way as Lyndsay?

If she had, then the same person probably killed her too, but if she hadn't then maybe the demon lady was at it again. Chief Morman would know, and maybe he should tell the Chief about Dad not coming home until late the night Lyndsay was murdered, but then maybe he wouldn't tell, because he'd feel like a big shit 'cause Dad just bought him the shiny ten-speed. Yet he had to do something because each time someone else died he felt like it was his fault for not doing something. Tommy wondered if he'd feel better being a big shit and squealing on his father, or not telling what he knew and having some other girl die? He looked at the bike and knew he couldn't tattle on his father, but he prayed it didn't turn out that Dad's demon was the murderer, because then he'd feel worse than shit, and Lyndsay might even sic the Indian Lady on him, and then he'd be dead shit!

Tommy pumped the pedals harder, mumbling under his breath as he streaked down the road, "Sure Chief Morman, I'd like to be ten years old and not have a worry in the world! Yes Sir that would be fine as butterfly shit!"

#

CHAPTER 13

Alex awoke with a taste like dirty socks in his mouth. When he groaned his head felt as though someone had detonated an impressive sized explosive. Thank God, he had the kind of job where he didn't punch a time clock, nor did he have some demigod to answer to if he didn't make it to work, which he hadn't more times than he cared to remember. The only draw back to a no show was no money, which he really could use at this time, but what the hell, if he didn't have it Anna couldn't take it away.

Sales wasn't a job for everyone, but for Alex it was an easy living, embarrassingly so at times. Long ago Alex had found out that the general public was an extremely gullible lot. Alex could sell insurance to Lloyds of London if he so desired. He had that special gift which empowered him to sell rings around ninety-nine percent of other insurance salesmen.

Without a sound, he slipped out from under Dee, and padded across the tiny, cluttered, bedroom. He desperately needed a cup of strong black coffee, and a shower, and then maybe he'd feel human again.

In the bathroom he shuddered at the reflection gazing back from the mirrored cabinet above the sink. For a man not yet forty he knew he could easily pass for fifty. He didn't know most people thought he looked closer to sixty. Better stop drinking, or people are going to think I'm Tommy's grandfather, for Christ sake, he thought with disgust at the image glaring back at him.

Thoughts of taking Tommy his birthday present brought memories he'd managed to drown in a bottle of scotch the night before. Memories he'd hoped to destroy along with the brain cells the booze eradicated. There was no way in hell he really saw a girl skewered to a treetop. She must have been tied up there, and he just hadn't looked close enough to see the ropes. The image of her hanging there flashed through his mind, making him gag. Unfortunately no matter how hard he tried to convince himself otherwise, he really did see what his brain so frantically tried to deny. Somehow that poor girl had managed to have a tree grow right up through her body. Eyes clenched, Alex gagged again, but then his eyes snapped open, because with them closed her image was too real, too vivid. Getting passing out drunk hadn't helped either, because the image was still there, perhaps burned into his brain forever, and that hopeless thought darkened Alex Rogers mood even more.

Perhaps what he really needed to so was get his fat-ass on the road and sell some insurance. With his mind occupied with mundane bullshit maybe the girl would stay out of his head, at least for a while.

"Shit", he swore, remembering his first priority of the day was to stop by and give Mormon a statement. So much for keeping my mind occupied on other things, he thought with a groan.

OK, so he'd tell the pain-in-the-ass-cop what he knew, then he'd hit the pavement. He had to keep busy if he wanted to keep his sanity. Busy, or drunk, either way, hopefully, in time the image would fade completely.

#

Chief Mormon wasn't the only person in town looking to speak to Alex Rogers; Karl Abbott also had a few questions for the man. Karl found out that 1—4 The Road was the only place in town open the night Lyndsay was murdered. He'd already talked to Jake, and the other men who were there that night. Jake told him Alex left sometime between ten and eleven, and he'd been drunk, as usual.

Karl never did have much use for Alex, although he'd been quite fond of Joan and Will Rogers, Alex's parents. They'd been quiet, hard-working farm people who never had a bad thing to say about anyone. They considered Alex their miracle baby, born when Joan was going through menopause, the child they never believed God would grant them. The only miraculous thing Karl saw about Alex was that the little bastard hadn't gotten himself shot years ago. As a kid Alex was constantly in trouble, causing his parents one heartache after another. When he got into high school he discovered booze, and as far as Karl could tell Alex Rogers hadn't been out of the bottle since he took his first drink at age thirteen. From there it was down hill, and by the time Alex turned twenty-one both parents were dead, Will of a heart attack only two months after Joan died of brain cancer. Alex couldn't wait to sell off the farm, and drink away the profits.

When Alex brought that pretty little wife of his home to Whitefields everyone hoped maybe the boy was finally going to settle down and become a respectable member of the community. Unfortunately, even after he became a daddy, Alex didn't change, and Karl heard more than enough rumors to wonder why Anna hadn't kicked the bastard out long before now.

In Karl's mind if there was anyone in Whitefields capable of rape and murder, it was Alex Rogers.

Karl drove slowly through town searching for Alex's car.

#

"So, you got all you need? I've got more important things to do than hanging around here chatting with you," Alex complained after giving his statement to the tall, cocky, cop.

Tony leaned back in his chair, watching the other man closely. Tommy was right about one thing; Alex Rogers had the reddest, most bloodshot eyes Tony had ever seen. "Yeah, that's all the questions I have for you on the Milner girl, for now, but believe me, we're just starting on the list of questions I have for you."

Alex, instantly on the defensive, snapped, "Now look here…"

"No, you look here? I'm investigating more than one murder here today, and I want to know where you were on the night of January 18, last winter, between nine at night, and one o'clock in the morning.

Crossing his legs, Alex began bouncing his foot rapidly. "I was probably at home. At home with my wife, and my son."

"No…you weren't. At least not all of the time in question."

"You know so much, you tell me where I was." Alex uncrossed his legs then crossed the opposite side and began bouncing his foot again. Tony made a mental note of the man's obvious agitation. "January 18th was a long time ago. How the hell am I suppose to remember where I was?"

"OK, I'll make it easier for you. It was the night of the big snowstorm, remember now?"

"The blizzard, oh yeah. Let's see, where was I that night?" He hated the way Morman watched his every move, making him feel guilty and nervous as hell. "I think I probably stopped at 1—4 The Road for a couple of beers to help me relax, yeah, I remember now, I had to drive out to Lapeer to meet a client. It began snowing when I was on my way back, and the roads were slick as greased owl shit. I stopped for a couple of beers, like I said to help me unwind, no law against that, as far as I know."

"What time did you get to 1—4 The Road, and what time was it when you left?"

"Christ, I don't remember what time it was when I got there, early though, because I don't think Dee was on duty yet, and she starts at seven. I guess it must have been around, shit I don't know, maybe ten-thirty, eleven o'clock when I left."

"What time did you arrive home"

Alex was getting mad. "I don't remember. I don't sit around staring at my watch every minute of the day. All I remember was that Anna and Tommy were already in bed. It took me a lot longer than usual to get home because of the shitty road conditions. Now, are you accusing me of something, or what?"

Tony smiled because he could almost feel Alex's anger as the man bit his tongue to keep from saying something he'd later regret. "Nope, not yet. Thank you for your time, Mr. Rogers, you can go now."

#

Alex slammed out of the police station right into Karl Abbott, almost knocking the older man down.

Disgust and hatred radiated so strongly from Karl's glare that Alex flinched as though he'd been physically assaulted, "So what's your problem old man?"

Taking a step back, Karl looked Alex over from head to foot. "Who you calling old man? You look older than I do."

Turning to walk away, Alex shot back, "Go to hell!" He stopped when he realized Karl was following him. "What the hell do you want?"

In a low threatening snarl, Karl asked, "You murder my little girl, Alex Rogers?"

Alex glared, unable to believe that a day, which started as shitty as this one, had still managed to go down hill. "You're as crazy as that asshole Cop," he snapped, nodding toward the police station. "Get away from me, and leave me alone, do you understand, old man? I'm not going to tell you again, and that's a promise!"

Karl stood watching several minutes after Alex's car disappeared around the corner. Karl looked like a man in troubled thought as he turned and went into the police station. Had anyone been brave enough to look into Karl Abbott's eyes at that moment they would have sworn they saw the brimstone fires of Hell.

#

Tony stepped out into the humid spring air. The sky was overcast yet no rain was predicted, but Tony knew that didn't mean a thing. It could be pouring like a S.O.B.. in Whitefields, and the weatherman would swear it was clear and sunny across the entire state. Just like the night of the blizzard, Tony remembered, according to every weather report there had been no snowfall anywhere in the state of Michigan on January 18th. Tony chuckled to himself, if there wasn't any snow in Whitefields that night then the whole town suffered from the most amazing, not to mention coldest, mass hallucination in history.

Turning right, Tony headed for the Golden Goose Diner two doors down. Not only did just about everyone in town end up there at least two or three times a week, it was the only place to get a decent cup of coffee. Tony's reason for heading there was to gather information.

Every gossip in town was usually seated at the worn lunch counter between noon and one. It was now twelve-thirty, prime gossip time.

As he walked through the door, Tony swore under his breath. Seated at the counter between Bea Goode and Art Simmons, two of the biggest gossips around, was that busybody Robbins, "Captain Douglas Robbins of The Michigan State Police, whoopee", Tony mumbled sarcastically, as he tried to force the corners of his mouth into a semblance of a smile.

"Hey Tony." Robbins smiled, and it irked Tony because Robbins' smile looked like the genuine article. "We were just talking about you. Come and join us."

Art moved down a seat making room for the two lawmen to sit next to each other. Even at eighty-three Art enjoyed a good fight, and these two men had the atmosphere in the diner thick with tension. Sneaking a peek toward Bea to see if she'd picked up on what was going on, Art almost laughed, the old gal looked ready to wet her panties.

"Captain Robbins, what brings you to our fair town?" Tony asked, pouring on the charm so thick he wanted to puke.

Turning to Bea, Robbins confided, "These small town boys always get so defensive whenever we drop in for a little visit."

Bea blushed, tickled that Robbins had turned to her as a confidant, she continued to smile at Robbins while she addressed the new boy in town, "Now Chief, don't go being snippy to Doug, huh, Captain Robbins. It ain't polite."

Gritting his teeth, Tony tried harder to smile. "No offense meant, Miss Goode. It's just that these boys don't normally bother with a little burg like Whitefields unless they think something big is in the works." Still smiling, Tony looked Robbins right in the eye and said, "No offense."

Robbins laughed, enjoying the little sparing match more than he would have thought. "None taken. Actually I was curious, and, since this is my hometown, I thought I'd take a look-see. You have to admit we've had more excitement in the past few days than we've had in the past two hundred years put together.

Since you moved out here in the boonies after being a cop in Detroit, I thought maybe you could use a little help, you know, understanding the ways of my people. No offense meant towards your police abilities I assure you."

Tony's ears burned. Your people my ass, if you're so concerned about your people why did you leave, you lying ass-wipe?

"So what are you doing here, if I might ask?"

Robbins shrugged. "Just what I said, visiting. I'm sure you don't mind me visiting my family and friends for a few days, do you? Besides all the excitement interests me, I'm curious to see how a big city cop handles crime in rural America."

Turning to Bea, he added with a wink, "Besides all my favorite people in the whole world are right here."

"Are you saying you're taking an active interest in my cases?"

"No, actually I don't believe I said that at all."

Tony threw a dollar on the counter unable to endure Robbins sugarcoated sarcasm any longer. As he stood to leave Tony glared at Robbins, "Do us both a favor and stay out of my business."

Robbins chuckled as Tony stormed from the diner. "Touchy, ain't he?"

Art shrugged. "You know how them outsiders are, Doug. Plain fact is you have to be born here to be one of us."

Slapping Art on the shoulder, Robbins smiled. "How right you are Arty, how right you are. Now what was it you were telling me about Alex Rogers?"

#

Holding the little turtle close to her face, Anna felt a twinge of guilt. The poor little thing hasn't eaten a thing since he became an unwilling houseguest, and Anna was afraid he was going to starve to death sitting all alone in his terrarium.

"OK little guy, we're going to take you back to the forest today. Right after lunch, promise."

The turtle pulled his head in farther, making Anna feel even worse. Tommy hardly paid any attention to the animal since the day the paramedics pried it from his hands. It wasn't right to keep it caged up.

It was a wild creature, born to roam free, and that's exactly where it belonged, in the wild, not some glass prison starving to death

."Maybe with you back in the forest I'll be able to write again. God only knows I haven't been able to come up with anything since you've been cooped up in there." She convinced herself the turtle wasn't really Sandy, yet she felt he was somehow her good luck charm, and, as long as he was out there creeping around in the forest, she'd be able to come up with new stories. Her agent called twice last week wanting to know where the pages were that she'd promised. She explained about all the trouble, not about Sandy though because she didn't want him to think she'd gone completely over the edge, and he was sympathetic, but still wanted the promised pages as soon as possible.

Tommy came through the kitchen door, his cheeks red and hair wind blown from riding his new bike up and down the drive. Anna felt bad she wouldn't let him take it to Billy's, but she couldn't stand the thought of not being near if he needed her.

"How are you're legs holding up?"

"OK, they don't bother me at all. Maybe if I could ride a long way they would." Tommy said, flopping down on a chair at the kitchen table.

"I know, and I'm really sorry, Tommy, but I promise that as soon as Chief Morman catches the bad guy you can ride over to Billy's house, OK?"

Shrugging as though he doubted he would ever be able to go further than the road in front of the house, Tommy asked, "What if he never finds out who did it?"

What a terrible thought! "He will," she said without much enthusiasm, "I have an idea, after lunch why don't you and I take Sandy back to the forest and set him free? He hasn't eaten anything since we got him, and I'm afraid he's going to starve to death. What do you say?" She wanted Tommy to be able to walk in the forest without being afraid, but, for now, she didn't want him in there alone. Like falling off a horse, Tommy had to get up and go back into the forest, and this would be the first, and hardest step in that direction. She had no idea that Tommy had already taken that first step without her.

"Back to where I found him?" Tommy asked, his face drained of color.

"No, I was thinking more like over by the stream," Anna replied quickly. "Turtles like water, and he'll probably be happier there." *I know I'll be happier with him over there instead where he was.* She had no desire whatsoever to see that section of the forest again, ever.

Tommy, feeling somewhat better, laughed. "Yeah, maybe he can play with Barney the Bass."

"Benny!"

"I know that," he giggled.

"Brat," Anna said, feeling good about Sandy's immediate future, and how Tommy seemed to be getting more like his old self.

Tommy was just finishing his sandwich when someone knocked on the front door. "I'll get it." He jumped from his chair before Anna could move.

A couple of minutes later Tommy came back into the kitchen, smiling broadly, "Look who's here, and only a couple of days early."

Stepping into the room behind the boy, the Chief laughed, "I'm sorry I interrupted your lunch. I'll wait out back while you finish."

"No, please," Anna said, then asked, getting up to clear away the lunch dishes. "Have you eaten? Tommy would be more than happy to make you one of his special sandwiches, wouldn't you Tommy?" Anna smiled, flashing Tommy a conspiratorial wink.

"Sure! You never had a sandwich like the ones I make."

"Thanks, but I very seldom eat lunch."

"Oh, come on, one little sandwich won't kill you, maybe." Anna coaxed.

"Yeah, you eat one of my special sandwiches, and you'll never skip lunch again," Tommy boasted.

"Tell you what, while Tommy makes you a sandwich, we'll have coffee on the back deck, deal?" Anna suspected that Morman wasn't here on a social visit.

Tony looked from mother to son. They were definitely scheming up something, but he wasn't quite sure what, just that the sandwich he was about to eat would be memorable, it nothing else.

"OK, but remember," he told Tommy, "cops don't have very good medical insurance."

Blushing, Tommy chided, "Ah, you'll like it, you'll see. Just remember not to look at it before you take a bite, OK?"

"Oh, that's encouraging," Tony laughed as he took the cup of coffee from Anna, and then followed her out onto the back deck.

Anna turned to Tony when they reached the far side where she was sure Tommy wouldn't overhear, "I know you didn't come early for the party, and you sure didn't come out for one of Tommy's world-famous sandwiches so that could only mean you've come about the murder. Am I right?"

Glancing back toward the kitchen door, Tony nodded. He didn't want the kid coming out while he was asking questions about the boy's father.

Anna smiled, "Oh, don't worry about Tommy. It takes a good five minutes for him to make The Sandwich.'"

"Well, yeah, five minutes, huh?"

Anna nodded, and Tony stated his business, "I'm, ah, checking the whereabouts of everyone the night the Abbott girl was murdered."

"Everyone?"

"Well not everyone, just men, because obviously a woman couldn't have done what was done. What I need to know is if you remember what time Alex got home that night? I talked to him earlier, but he wasn't sure of the exact time, and I was hoping you could help shed some light on the subject."

Anna was stunned, "You think Alex…?"

"This is just routine, Anna. Anyone who was out that night has to have their whereabouts verified."

"Well let's see, that was the night of the snowstorm, right? Tommy and I stayed up and watched television until midnight then I sent Tommy went to bed. I started watching another movie, but I kept nodding off, so I went to bed. Let's see that was about one, or so. I heard Alex come in about half an hour or forty-five minutes later, so he must have gotten home around two."

"You're sure?"

"Yes, I'm sure, because of the storm and all. I know how drunk he gets, and I was afraid he'd get in an accident, so I couldn't really go completely to sleep until I heard him come in."

Tommy came out the door holding something on a plate that looked like it came right out of a Blondie comic strip.

"That's a sandwich?" Tony asked, causing Anna to burst out laughing. Tommy had gone overboard, the Silly Sandwich was at least six inches high. She pitied Tony, hoping he had a cast iron stomach.

"Now just remember what I told you, don't look at it, just eat it. I'll bet you never tasted anything like it before," Tommy boasted, handing the heavy plate to the Chief.

"That's what I'm afraid of," Tony whispered to Anna.

It was a job, and Tony knew he'd spend the rest of the day chewing on antacids, but he finally managed to swallow the last of Tommy's creation. Feeling full to the point of exploding, Tony volunteered to go with them to set the turtle free, in the hope of not only walking off some of his lunch, but also continuing his earlier conversation with Anna.

Bruiser was ready. He missed his runs in the woods with Tommy, and now spent most of his time in the kennel while Tommy pedaled his new bike up and down the driveway.

The day was warm, and birds chirped by the thousands as the small caravan made its way through the forest. Wildflowers grew in abundance, in every shade imaginable, and the smell of spring was everywhere. In a way it made Tommy feel sad, this walk in the woods with his mother and Chief Morman. It reminded him of some of the walks he'd taken with his father on those rare occasions when he was little and the demon wasn't in control.

Bruiser wanted to run, and Tommy had his hands full keeping him under control. Actually Tommy wanted to run, too, but he was sure his mother and Chief Morman were too old for that, so he contented himself with walking and trying to hold Bruiser back. He wasn't really sure why it was so important to his mother that Sandy be put back in the forest. If it were up to him he would have just turned the turtle loose at the end of their yard and let him find his own way back. He wouldn't stay where they put him anyway, so why bother? Oh well, moms were weird sometimes. Tommy watched a lot of the forest animals, and he knew that if he spotted them one place this week, next week they wouldn't be there but someplace altogether different. They didn't like it when other creatures found their hiding place.

Tommy and Bruiser were a little ahead of Anna and Tony, but he still heard them talking softly, like they didn't want him to know what they were saying, so he knew they weren't too far behind. It was hard keeping Bruiser from running, and he knew the stream wasn't far ahead, so finally he gave in, and together boy and dog shot through the forest as a blur.

Tommy was laughing as he tried to catch his breath when they reached the stream, "Man, that really felt good, didn't it boy?"

The dog wagged his tail, and Tommy knew Bruiser thought the run was way too short, as the Husky was hardly panting at all. Tommy thought so too, but didn't want to make Mom mad by getting any farther ahead than they already were.

"Hi Tommy, I'm glad you finally came to see me. I've missed you and Bruiser."

"Lyndsay!" Tommy exclaimed. "You shouldn't be here. Mom and Chief Morman are coming right behind us!"

"I know, and I won't stay long. I just want to know if you've found out anything yet?"

Feeling guilty, Tommy shook his head. Here he was out running in the forest with Bruiser having all kinds of fun and poor Lyndsay was dead, and would never have fun like this again, and he wasn't even helping her. "No, only that another girl was murdered last night."

"I know. That was Cindy, I thought she was my best friend but she wasn't really. The Demon killed her."

Tommy stood staring, his mouth agape. Lyndsay sounded so strange when she told him about Cindy, like she didn't even care the Demon killed her best friend.

Tommy managed to say, "Oh."

Lyndsay looked over Tommy's shoulder. "Got to go, but before I do, don't forget what I told you. More people are going to die until we find out who murdered me. 'Bye Tommy, 'bye Bruiser." And just like that she was gone.

"Thomas Andrew Rogers!"

Jumping, Tommy turned toward his mother; he knew by her tone that he was in trouble. "What?"

Anna didn't say anything, but he knew by the look that she gave him that he'd definitely hear about it later when they were alone.

#

CHAPTER 14

Ted Jenkins watched as his neighbors and the Chief of police disappeared into the forest behind the house. Now what was going on? He heard there'd been another murder the night before, but so far he knew none of the details. He was still waiting for the pipeline to come through, namely Betty's friends. There wasn't much that happened, if anything, in town that they missed. In a town the size of Whitefields Ted figured that anyone in town could tell him exactly what he'd had for breakfast, and whether he came to the table in his underpants. At times this lack of privacy irked the hell out of him, this however wasn't one of those times.

Betty came out in the yard where Ted was tending his flowers. She'd just gotten off the phone with her best friend Thelma Wilson, who was Sally's husband's aunt, and now had the complete story on the latest murder, thanks to Sally and her job at the police station.

Ted looked up expectantly. "Well?" He noticed his wife looked kind of pale and thought; This must be a good one.

When she finished the story, Betty went back into the house, and Ted sat looking thoughtfully towards the forest. No wonder Alex had been driving like a madman last night when he pulled in next door. Imagine finding something like that! Imagine something like that going up inside the girl! Sometimes the pipeline turned up some very interesting shit.

Several minutes later Ted got up and headed for the house, the warm spring day had suddenly taken on a weird chill that crept into his bones.

#

Sandy sat for a long time where Anna placed him beside the stream, without moving. He hadn't heard any human sounds in quite a while, and, finally getting his courage up slowly poked his head out to have a look around.

Sitting cross-legged on the ground in front of him was a being who wasn't like the others. There was something about this one that frightened Sandy even more than the others had. Quickly he sought the safety of his shell, but other forces stopped him before he could complete his escape.

"No you don't," the being spoke softly. "You come right back out here where I can see you."

Reluctantly Sandy's head reappeared. All of his animal instincts told him this being was dangerous, yet he felt no threat. It was almost like the times when the Anna-being got into his head, and made him do silly and dangerous things. He stretched his neck to look at the creature above.

"That's right, I'm not going to hurt you," She laughed lightly. "I've got a very important job for you, little one."

#

CHAPTER 15

After putting Sandy next to the stream, Anna, Tommy, and Tony stood for several minutes to see if the turtle would come out of his shell and check out his new home. When it became evident that he wasn't going to move as long as they remained, Tony announced he had to get back to the office. He still had questions for Anna, but with the kid so near by he'd hesitated asking any more, yet he didn't want to go back to town without accomplishing the task he come for.

So far Alex looked like Tony's best bet. He was surprised how many of the townspeople really disliked Alex Rogers. Dislike was really putting it mildly in some cases.

If it hadn't been for Dee insisting that Alex took her home because of the storm that night, Tony would already have Alex locked up. Unfortunately, no matter how much he questioned her, Dee stuck to her story. He had to talk to Jake and find out if Dee had left early that night, and if she was in fact in the company of Alex Rogers. If he could get Dee to say that Alex didn't take her home that night he could close the case on Lyndsay Abbott, and make a lot of people in town happy.

Tommy, asking and receiving permission this time, ran back to the house ahead of Anna and Tony. This was the chance Tony had been hoping for. The questions he had for Anna wasn't going to earn him any Brownie points, and he didn't want the kid hating his guts if he upset his mother.

"Do you know a woman named Dee Clark?" Tony asked, breaking the silence that settled comfortably over them as they walked through a shower of soft, white dogwood blossoms.

He could see the question embarrassed Anna as she answered, "Yes."

"What do you know about her?"

Anna stopped walking, and turned to face him. "I know my husband is having an affair with her. Why?"

"I'm sorry I have to ask you these questions, Anna. Believe me if there were any other way, I wouldn't. Do you know how long they've been seeing each other?"

Anna couldn't bring herself to look him in the eye as she answered, and her gaze scanned the forest behind him. "I don't know for sure, just that since we've been separated he sees a lot of her." She'd been looking at a white shape that sort of wavered in and out of focus, but hadn't really given it much thought because of Tony's line of questions.

"Dee claims Alex was with her the night the Abbott girl was killed, and she said it was twelve-thirty, or one o'clock, when she decided Alex was sober enough to drive home. In your opinion, do you think her statement is true? Is it possible Alex's been seeing her that long?"

Anna's tongue felt welded to the roof of her mouth. Possible? She thought about all the nights that Alex came staggering in long after the bars were closed. When she asked him where he'd been he'd say he went for breakfast at Denny's over in Howel, or he'd start ranting at her about something totally unrelated, and they'd end up fighting about something she had or hadn't done, never getting back to her question.

"Possible? Yeah, I guess with men anything is possible, isn't it?" She was cool, calm, and proud of herself when she answered, unfortunately it was short lived, "That rotten bastard," she hissed.

Tony moved close to her, carefully laying his hand on her shoulder. She was mad, and he knew she might strike out at him. Not that he had done anything wrong, but just because he was a man, and he was pretty sure he could tell her that the sky was blue, and, at this moment, she wouldn't believe him. He knew the feeling, had felt the same way about women, thanks to Sheila, but he got over it, and so would Anna. It had taken him a long time, and for a while he'd gone a little crazy, but then he met Anna.

Suddenly the silence was broken as Anna snapped, "What the hell is that?"

Startled by her language as well as the venom behind the words, Tony spun around to see what she was looking at, but saw nothing unusual in the lush forest behind him.

"What?"

Anna looked at him as if just realizing he was still there, and with a jerk of her shoulder shook off the hand still resting there. "Nothing. I thought I saw something, but I guess I was wrong…again." Fire danced in her eyes and Tony watched helplessly as she turned abruptly and headed out of the forest, still mumbling as she went. "Wrong about a lot of things. I have to go home, I've got work to do. I hope you're done asking questions, because I don't have any more answers."

Tony followed silently as Anna crashed through the heavy foliage, snapping off any tender branch unlucky enough to get to get in her way.

#

Tommy paced, wanting to talk to Chief Morman alone but not knowing how he was going to get the opportunity with his mother always nearby. He had to tell the Chief that whoever killed Lyndsay hadn't killed the other girl, Cindy. He knew he wouldn't be able to explain who did, or even how he knew, but he had to do something or the policeman might spend all his time looking for the new girl's murderer and not Lyndsay's. Lyndsay was the important one, because the killing wouldn't stop until her killer was found. Chief Morman would probably laugh at him when he told the policeman his story, but he was out of ideas, and out of time.

Suddenly Bruiser looked toward the forest and started wagging his tail. A couple of seconds later Anna emerged, and she looked mad. Tommy wondered if she was still mad at him for running ahead of them earlier, but she seemed to have gotten over that before they left the stream. A couple of seconds later Chief Morman came walking down the path, and Tommy thought he looked just like Tommy felt when Mom scolded him for something. *Gee, I wonder what Chief Morman did to make Mom that mad at him?*

It looked as though Tommy was going to get his chance to talk to the policeman in private after all. Mom acted like she didn't even see Tommy sitting on the deck, as though he was the ghost, as she stomped past in into the house. Tommy felt sorry for Chief Morman. He knew how bad Mom could make him feel when she was really mad at him about something stupid that he said or did.

Morman stopped beside Tommy, and stood staring towards the kitchen door.

"She's really mad at you, huh?" Tommy asked, staring at the kitchen window.

Tony smiled slightly as he looked down at the boy. "I guess so, and I'm really sorry, because I didn't mean to upset her."

"Aw, it's OK. She doesn't stay mad very long. I'll bet by the time you get here Saturday she won't even be mad at you any more."

"Think so?" Morman, still staring at the kitchen door, asked hopefully.

"Sure. Um, could I talk to you for a minute, please?"

Tony looked at the boy. He sounded so serious. "Let's walk around the house to my car, OK?"

As they walked Tommy's mind circled around and around. How to begin? Finally he just asked, "Do you know yet who killed Lyndsay?"

Morman was surprised to hear Tommy use the girl's first name. He hadn't thought the boy knew her. "Not yet, but I hope to have something real soon. Why?"

They reached the squad car, and Tony leaned against the fender watching the boy closely.

"Well, I…ah, I…shoot, I don't know how to tell you this without you thinking I'm just making it up, but I'm not, honest! Cross my heart, hope to die, stick a needle in my eye."

Tony laughed, the poor kid was hopping around like he had a bee in his skivvies, "I believe you Tommy, just say whatever you're thinking."

Nodding at the brilliant suggestion, Tommy replied, "Yeah, OK. I don't know who killed Lyndsay, but I know who killed Cindy."

Of all the things the kid could have said this was so astounding Tony could only stare.

Before he could chicken out Tommy continued, "It was the demon. The demon killed her."

They looked at each other silently for several seconds. Blood pumped through Tony's veins like a runaway locomotive. He closed his mouth, took a deep breath through his nose and asked as calmly as possible, "The demon in your dad?"

Tommy blinked twice, glanced back at the house, and then moved a step closer to the cop, "No Sir, it was the Indian demon that killed the girl Dad found. The girl that used to be Lyndsay's best friend but isn't any more."

Disappointment dripped from Tony's brow, "I'm sorry Tommy, but I don't have any idea what you're talking about. Why don't you start from the beginning, OK?"

Tommy took another step forward, close enough now that Morman could smell lingering traces of peanut butter and dill pickle on the kid's breath. Before he spoke Tommy scanned the surrounding landscape, he couldn't shake the eerie feeling of being watched. But there was no one except Mr. Jenkins out back working in his flowerbeds. Tommy thought his heart would burst, or worse, he'd wet his pants if so much as a stray breeze crossed his cheek while he frantically whispered his strange story to his new, if somewhat confused, confident.

#

CHAPTER 16

Karl entered the house the way most of the people in the area did, through the kitchen door. He often wondered why anyone bothered building living rooms on houses since everyone usually ended up in the kitchen. About the only person he could ever remember entertaining in the living room was Reverend Kent. Kitchens were usually the hearts of the home, and his was no exception, that is until Lyndsay died, now the house didn't have a heart.

The kitchen was empty. In the days when their daughter was still alive Karl could come home and always find his wife in the kitchen. If Lyndsay happened to be home chances were she'd be helping Sue prepare some special treat to surprise him. Sometimes he'd come home to find some of Lyndsay's friends sitting around the table laughing and joking with Sue. He missed those days most of all.

Moving through the house, Karl knew he'd find Sue in Lyndsay's bedroom. She spent just about every waking hour sitting in the old rocking chair that had belonged to his mother before being handed down to Lyndsay. Sue, he knew, was handling their daughter's death in her own way, just as he was handling it by driving around town treating old friends like criminals. He knew people were talking about him and the way he'd changed, but he couldn't help it. Until he talked to Alex Rogers earlier in the day he felt any one of those people could be Lyndsay's murderer. He promised Lyndsay, if only in a dream, that he would find the man responsible, and, by God, he would fulfill that promise, if it killed him.

The door to Lyndsay's room was closed, but, as Karl neared, he heard Sue talking. That was something else he got used to these last few days. She claimed Lyndsay visited with her just like before, and though it hurt him to see Sue in this mental state, he couldn't bear to take even that from his wife. Knocking lightly on the door before entering, he prepared himself for what he knew waited on the other side.

The scent of Lyndsay's perfume was the first thing that hit him. Sue had taken to spraying a little of it around the room, although she denied it, to give her delusions a little more reality. She claimed it lingered from Lyndsay herself, and was proof of their daughter's visits.

Sue turned as he entered the room, a sad smile curling the corners of her thin mouth, "Oh, if you'd only been a few minutes earlier you could have talked to Lyndsay. She just left, said she had to go meet Cindy. I don't know what they're going to do. You know how those two are when they get together. Why, they're inseparable, where one goes, the other isn't far behind. They're almost like sisters the way they argue, then make up like nothing had happened."

"Sue..." he started to tell her Cindy was dead. Instead he said, "I talked to the Chief earlier. They're finally going to release the...to send Lyndsay home for burial. Do you want me to talk to Reverend Kent alone, or would you like to go with me?"

He hoped she would go with him, but knew she wouldn't. To do that would be to admit her daughter was dead, so when she declined, he only nodded.

"Karl, do you think we'll really be with Lyndsay again someday? She said we would be, but I get scared sometimes. What if so much time has passed before I...before I go that Lyndsay has moved on, or doesn't remember me? What if I spend eternity looking and never find her? I couldn't stand that Karl, I really couldn't. Just the thought of it makes me crazy. Lyndsay tells me I'm being silly, that she could never forget us, but there are so many unknowns there. What if she has no choice?"

Startled by this conversation Karl sank down on the end of Lyndsay's bed. "Sue, honey, I'm sure Lyndsay knows what she's talking about. The love that we have for her, and her for us, will keep us together always."

Sue just nodded. A tear dropped from the tip of her nose leaving a dark circle on the front of her baby-blue satin blouse.

"I've got an idea, Sue. Let's go out for dinner. We need to get away from town for a while. Let's go over to the Boat House and have some of their delicious shrimp. You know how you love those great big shrimp they have."

"Oh Karl, I don't think that's a very good idea. What if Lyndsay comes, and I'm not here? She would think we didn't care anymore."

Karl was one step ahead; "We'll leave a note on her pillow, just like always, OK?"

Sue hesitated then smiled. "Well, I suppose that would be OK."

"Sure it will be, and I'll tell you what else we'll do, since Lyndsay loves those shrimp as much as you do, we'll bring some home for her too. How does that sound?"

Sue stood slowly, her back and legs stiff from sitting for so many hours in the rocker. "Karl Abbott, I love you very much. Not many women are as lucky as I am to have such a good man. I've had a perfect life, a beautiful daughter, and the best husband a woman could ever ask for."

Karl, not used to such a show of emotion, embraced his wife, patting her gently on the back. In his mind he'd been the lucky one. His eyes watered, and he fought to hold back the tears. He'd had everything any man could ever ask for, but in one night his Heaven turned into a living Hell.

#

Sandy stopped beneath a clump of fern to rest. He knew this respite would be short, and soon he would be forced to travel on through the forest. The being would allow no rest until he reached his destination. He moved slowly because of his missing leg, and the image of his destination could easily have been on the other side of the world, but he would keep going even if it killed him. He had no other choice.

#

Tommy saw Mr. Jenkins still working in his flowerbeds. When he saw Tommy looking in his direction Mr. Jenkins waved, motioning for the boy to come to him, but Tommy pretended not to notice his neighbor motioning for him as he hurried around the corner of the house. Tommy knew he was being rude, and if his mother had seen she would scold him, but Tommy just didn't feel like talking to anyone. He had to think.

He decided to go to the kennel and check Bruiser's water. That would give him something to do, and keep him away from Anna. The mood she was in sure wouldn't help his mood, and they'd end up fighting about something stupid, then both of them would feel bad.

Near the kennel Tommy finally looked up. Bruiser was staring at the forest, while his tail wagging happily. Tommy's heart began to pound triple time. His gaze followed the dogs and he easily spotted Lyndsay standing just within the tree line.

So, it had been Lyndsay he felt watching him when he told Chief Morman everything that happened. The way his day was going he should have known. Now not only was his mother mad at Chief Morman, but Lyndsay was probably mad at him. He envied Chief Morman, because when Mom was mad she wouldn't talk to you, Tommy had a bad feeling that he wasn't going to be that lucky.

For a long time Lyndsay just stood staring him. He felt his cheeks burn with guilt. Finally unable to stand the silence any longer he blurted out, "I had to tell him, it's the only way I could make him keep looking for your murderer instead of Cindy's!"

Lyndsay's eyes flashed, but she spoke softly, "You shouldn't have told, Tommy. I trusted you, and you told."

"You didn't tell me not to tell anyone, you just told me to help you, and now he'll help us." Tommy pleaded, his voice high with fear. Bruiser whined softly at his master's agitation.

"Don't be stupid, do you really think he believed a word you told him? Do you? All you accomplished was to make the demon even madder. How do you think I'll be able to protect you and your mother when the Indian knows you betrayed me?"

Nearly in tears, Tommy pleaded, "But I didn't betray you, honest. I was only trying to help. Please don't let the demon hurt my mom or me, please. I'll do anything I can to help, Lyndsay, just don't let anything happen to Mom."

"I don't know, Tommy. When she gets really mad, there isn't much I can do to stop her. Look at what she did to Cindy."

Curiosity momentarily overshadowed his fear, and Tommy blurted out, "If Cindy was your best friend, how come the demon-lady killed her?"

"Because she betrayed me. That's why I'm worried about you tattling on me, the Indian doesn't like it when people do bad things to me, like tattling."

"I didn't tattle!"

Lyndsay sighed, and it sounded like a breeze on a summer night blowing through the pine trees outside Tommy's bedroom window.

"I'm sorry Lyndsay, really. I just wanted to help. I didn't know what else to

do 'cause I can't go away from the house now. Mom won't let me out of her sight because of the demon killing your friend, ah, your used-to-be friend."

"Well, I'll see what I can do. Tommy, I overheard your mother and Chief Morman talking here in the forest earlier, and I wanted to ask you, do you know who Dee Clark is?"

Tommy thought for a moment the name sounded kind of familiar, but he couldn't place it, "I'm not sure. I think I heard her name before, but I don't know where. Why, do you think maybe she killed you?"

"No, it was definitely a man. This Dee woman has something to do with your father. Does that help?"

It did. "Yeah, now I remember! Once, just before Christmas, I went by Mom and Dad's bedroom, and the door was open a little, and I heard Dad talking to someone. I knew Mom was Christmas shopping, so I thought maybe he heard me in the hall and was talking to me, but, when I looked in the door, I saw he was talking on the phone. I remember he said, 'Dee honey, you know I wouldn't forget to get you a present.' I thought that was funny because I didn't know what deehoney was, but then he said, 'Look Dee, I told you I haven't had sex with her in months.' I didn't know her last name, and that's the only time I ever heard the name Dee."

"Did he say anything to you about it?"

"Nah, he never even knew I heard him. I forgot all about it until you just now reminded me."

"OK Tommy thanks."

"Will you talk to the demon and explain to her why I told Chief Morman?"

Lyndsay started to fade out. "Someone's coming, I've got to go."

"Wait, please!"

"Hi Tommy, what are you doing?"

"Oh, hi Mr. Jenkins. I just came out to give Bruiser some clean water." Tommy said, trying to hide his fear.

Ted nodded, looking toward the forest. "Ah huh. Who were you just talking to, Tommy?"

Flustered, Tommy quickly opened the kennel gate, and stepped through into the straw covered enclosure. "Ah, I was just talking to Bruiser."

"No, just a couple of minutes ago, when you were looking at the woods."

A ridiculous image of his nose growing longer with each lie flashed through Tommy's mind, and his hand darted upward to hide the telltale signs. "Yeah, I was, ah, just telling Bruiser that it sure would be nice to take a walk in the forest like we used to before Lyndsay was murdered. Wasn't I boy?" he asked the husky as though Mr. Jenkins would believe the animal, if not the boy.

Ted knew the boy was lying. He heard him say something about a demon, and he'd distinctly heard Tommy say, 'wait, please.' He decided to drop it but kept watching the forest. Something weird was going on all right, and the kid knew what.

#

CHAPTER 17

When Tony finally got back to his office, Sally handed him a stack of pink while You Were Out slips. She wasn't happy, complaining that with all the phone calls she hadn't even gotten to take a potty break, let alone have lunch. He apologized, and sent her off with an extra half-hour.

Most of the calls were from people worried about Karl Abbott, but Tony knew the only person who had reason to be concerned about Karl Abbott was Alex Rogers. Tony thought he should feel guilty about his earlier conversation with Karl because he'd done little to detour Karl's suspicions from Alex, in fact had probably fanned the flames by telling the grieving father he was having trouble confirming Alex's alibi for the time in question. With Karl hounding him, maybe Alex would be so busy he'd stay away from Anna. Besides, he admitted, he enjoyed watching Alex Rogers squirm. Every time he looked into Tommy's eyes he hated Alex a bit more. The emotional turmoil the kid was going through shouldn't happen to a grown man, let alone a nine-year-old kid. If he could find good reason to get Alex in custody the man would know exactly how it felt to have someone use their fist on him, and be unable to do anything about it. How could a man do that to his own child? The poor kid actually thought there were demons, not just the one in his father, but demons that sought out murderers, and took revenge on them. Tony could imagine a whole police force of demons cramming naughty girls onto treetops, and stuffing bad boys full of bugs.

He wanted to discuss Tommy's problem with Anna, but two things kept him from it, one, she was still mad at him, and, two, he didn't want Tommy pissed at him for betraying a confidence. He hoped Tommy was right, and Anna wouldn't stay mad long. He wanted to see her again, and was looking forward to Tommy's birthday party.

If she got that mad at him for suggesting Alex had been cheating on her, what would she do to him if he tried to hint that her only child had emotional, and perhaps even mental, problems? It was just one more thorn in his side thanks to Alex Rogers.

#

Anna watched through the kitchen window as their neighbor spoke to Tommy out by the kennel. Her earlier outburst embarrassed her, leaving her feeling especially bad for Tommy. With so much going on in his young life, the last thing he needed was his mother acting like a damn fool.

She phoned Tony, but he wasn't in, and she didn't want to leave a message with the irritated woman, who answered the phone at the police station, so she'd hung up thinking to call back later. He probably wouldn't want to talk to her after her out burst; it wasn't his fault she'd married a man who didn't know the meaning of the word loyalty. Besides, if she were honest with herself, hadn't she known all along that Alex was messing around on her? She hadn't cared because Alex wasn't pestering her for sex when he was drunk. She shivered thinking about those times when he'd wake her in the middle of the night smelling of stale beer. He'd want sex, and, if she wasn't in the mood, or turned off just by the smell of him, he didn't care. Then he'd keep pumping away for what seemed like hours, because he was so drunk he couldn't reach a climax. Never again, she vowed.

She made up her mind, Monday morning she was going to find an attorney and get a divorce. No sense putting it off any longer, Alex will never change, and even if he did by some miracle stop drinking, too much hurt had passed between them, and she could never forgive him for what he did to Tommy.

As she watched, Mr. Jenkins turned and walked back toward his own yard. She sensed loneliness in the man, and wondered if he and Betty had any family. She knew they'd never had children, but she didn't know if there were nieces and nephews around to fill some of the void, but if there were they'd never been to visit that she knew of.

Before Ted could escape into his house Anna hurried outside, to invite him and Betty to Tommy's birthday party on Saturday.

The small act of kindness made Anna feel a little bit better, and, when she returned home, she was humming to herself. All she had to do was make it up to Tommy and Tony. Tommy was easy, all she had to do was call and order pizza for supper. Tony, however, was another matter. She thought she shouldn't worry about it, so what if the man thought she was a bitch? Yet something inside didn't want this handsome man thinking badly of her. Why should she care? Unfortunately she did care, and that scared her. She didn't trust men, didn't want to get involved again, yet she couldn't relax until she'd made up her mind to call Tony the following day and apologize.

#

Betty was all smiles at supper, and it irked the shit out of Ted. "For Christ sakes Betty, it's only a kid's birthday party. She probably only invited us so she wouldn't be the only adult there. It doesn't mean anything."

"Oh, I know. I think I'll make some of my special Heavenly Hash. I think the kids would really like that, don't you?"

Pushing away from the table, Ted shook his head, "You're pathetic, do you know that? The woman told us not to bring anything. Nothing! Don't you know what nothing means? She said no food, no gift, no nothing!"

Pooh-poohing her husband, Betty said, "Of course we're going to take Tommy a gift. I think something that him and his dog both could use would be nice. He loves that animal, and they're together all the time. Any ideas?"

Leaving the kitchen, Ted said over his shoulder, "Yeah, matching muzzles, and while you're at it, get one for yourself."

Ted walked to the window and peeked out. There was a car in the Rogers driveway, and it took him a minute to realize it was the pizza delivery boy. He watched Anna move past the windows heading to the kitchen where he could see Tommy moving around. Probably getting out paper plates and napkins. The houses were far enough apart that he couldn't see details, but close enough that he could make out individuals. More than once he watched as Alex staggered into the house and slapped Anna around. It really pissed him off to see that bastard hitting Anna. He liked Anna, a lot, and she starred in the majority of his fantasies. On those nights when Betty let him out of her sight long enough to take a walk, he lingered beneath the trees near the road, and watched Anna's silhouette as she undressed for bed. When the weather was cold, he went for drives and often turned off the car lights before coasting to a stop across the road where he watched Anna's bedroom window, hoping for a glimpse. Last winter he even started hiding his binoculars under the front car seat.

With Alex finally gone, the last thing he wanted or needed was Morman hanging around. Morman would be there Saturday, and that was the main reason Ted agreed to go to the kid's party. He wanted to find out what was going on with the cop and Anna, and he wanted to find out what was going on with the people in town suddenly.

Tommy stood up, and went to the refrigerator, and took something out, then went back to the table and sat down. Tommy was definitely a weird kid, no doubt about that, and Ted wondered if was because his old man had bounced him off the wall one to many times. Ted knew Tommy was talking to someone out by the dog's kennel earlier, but the boy kept denying it, until Ted gave up asking. He said something about a demon. Maybe he'd been pretending, like playing Cowboys and Indians. No, the kid was talking to someone, but who? And why deny it? Maybe Tommy knows something about Lyndsay. Hell, he might even know something about her death. All the more reason to go to the kid's party.

#

"You're late, as usual," Jake snapped. He still hadn't forgiven Dee for sneaking out and leaving him sleeping on the office couch. She knew the rules, and if there were someone willing to take her place he would have fired her. Not many women as attractive as Dee would work for him though, but he wasn't going to let her off the book without some retaliation. Peggy had kicked him so hard it still hurt just to take a piss, but he didn't hurt so bad now that he couldn't make the little bitch pay. Tonight would be the night too, because Peggy had a meeting in the morning with the old biddies from church, so she'd go to bed early tonight.

Jake followed Dee into the office, enjoying the swing of her tight ass. He closed the office door behind them, and waited until she got her drawer out and started counting her money before he made his demands, "You're going to stay late tonight, to make up for all the time you've been late this week."

Dee, losing count of her money, glared at him. "What about Peggy?"

"Oh, don't you worry your sweet little ass about my wife," he smirked, rubbing his hand across her bottom.

Dee stepped away from his groping hand, disgust and anger dripping from her words, "Seems to me you'd be careful not to get caught with your pants down again so soon."

"That's the beauty of it, Peggy would never expect me to do it again so soon. Hell, after the kick she gave me she probably thinks it'll be a long time before the ol' stud's ready again. Lucky you, I heal fast."

So, she'd been right! She almost burst out laughing.

"Alex is supposed to come in tonight." Alex hadn't said he'd see her tonight, but Jake didn't have to know that. Besides sometimes Alex just stopped by without telling her first.

Jake laughed. "I doubt if Alex Rogers is going to be making too much trouble for anyone. Seems to me he's a man who better keep a low profile. Everyone around has been in here asking questions about your 'boyfriend,'" he spit out the last word with distaste. He never liked Alex, and he was glad the bastard was in trouble.

"Who? Who's been asking questions about Alex, besides Morman?"

Jake enjoyed seeing Dee squirm. "Karl Abbott for one, Capt. Robbins for another. Funny, isn't it, how good old Alex's fate hangs on my word. Be a real shame if he couldn't take you to Florida 'cause he's in the slammer. Know what I'm saying, darlin'?"

Dee could only nod. "Overtime."

The night was slow with only four customers all evening, which was lucky since the beer deliveryman still hadn't shown up, and they were running low again. Finally at midnight Jake locked the front doors. On slow nights he closed up rather than pay a barmaid to do nothing. Normally the girls would have liked this gesture, but with Jake they knew that just because the bar was closed didn't necessarily mean they got to go home.

"Come on," Jake snapped. "Quit dilly-dallying around. If you do your job right you can still get home early enough to bang Alex. Of course assuming he doesn't mind sloppy seconds."

He was still laughing a couple of minutes later when Dee finally walked into the office to find Jake stripped down to his boxer shorts. His huge hairy belly draped down over his crotch so that only the dingy gray legs of his shorts were visible, and Dee wondered, not for the first time, how such skinny legs could hold all that weight. Each time he laughed his pendulous breast jiggled and Dee thought if he wore a Wonder Bra he could make Dolly Parton jealous. The man was a stinking slob.

"You're disgusting," she told him making him laugh even harder

Jake's speed belied his bulk as his hand shot out, grabbing Dee's wrist and twisting until, with a cry of pain and disgust, she dropped to her knees in front of him.

"I'm still mad at you, you know. What you did last time wasn't very nice. You were a bad little girl, and now you're going to have to be punished."

When Dee shook her head, Jake gave her wrist a vicious jerk, until she saw things his way.

"All right you son-of-a-bitch, all right!"

"That's better, you naughty little girl. You know Mommy really hurt Dunkin when she kicked him, so I think you should give him a great big kiss to make him all better."

Dee glared up at him, "I wish someone would chop Dunkin off, and cram him down your throat!"

"Oh, but darlin', he'll be so much happier down your throat. Come on baby, show big Dunkin how much you love him," Jake laughed as she pulled Dee forward.

#

CHAPTER 18

The buzzing fit so well into her dream that it was ten minutes before Peggy finally pulled herself awake. With a moan she reached over and hit the off button on the clock. Seven-ten, no one should have to get up at such an ungodly hour. She wouldn't if it weren't to impress her friends and neighbors, and to make up for Jake and that sleazy bar of his. Thinking about Jake caused her to roll over and check the bed next to hers. Instantly she was up and pacing. The rotten bastard, he hadn't even been to bed yet.

His only salvation would be if he were sleeping downstairs on the couch, because he hadn't wanted to wake her when he got home. He knew she had to be up early. Nice thought, but Jake never had a nice thought in his life.

The bottom floor of the house was empty. Jake was messing with that bimbo again, and the stupid ass fell asleep again! Fuming as she grabbed her coat, Peggy had to smile. She had to give Dee credit because none of the other girls had balls enough to leave Jake sleeping like that for her to find. As mad as she'd been she had to bite her tongue to keep from laughing when he opened his eyes and saw her standing over him. Yeah, that face was almost as good as the one he'd made when she planted her size-nine boot right in Dunkin's eye. If he thought that was bad, just wait till he sees what I've got planned for him this time.

After slipping her trench coat on over her robe, Peggy hurried from the house. She wanted to get to the bar before Jake woke. Surprise was the only way to get that bastard.

Driving like a madman, Peggy zipped through every red light and stop sign in town. Luckily each intersection was deserted, an unusual event given the time of morning, or Peggy most likely would have ended up in either the hospital, or, considering her speed, the morgue. Jake's car was parked on the side of the building. Gotcha!

Slipping quietly through the back door, she stood quietly for a couple of seconds while her eyes adjusted to the bar's dim interior. On the way there an unsettling thought occurred to her. "What if Dee's still there?" Then decided so much the better. She'd give them both such a scare they'd never look at one another without crapping themselves.

Peggy wiped her hand on her coat, then gripped the butcher knife tighter as she moved towards the bar. There she picked up the ice bucket, filled it halfway with ice, and then topped it off with cold water. It was heavier than she thought it'd be, and she left a trail of water behind as she moved slowly towards the office door, trying not to cut herself with the knife she struggled not to drop. The front of her coat was soaked, as were her slippers, making her even madder.

Panting from anger as well as the weight of the bucket, Peggy stopped outside the office door, straining to hear any sign that the two 'love birds' were awake. Only silence greeted her. Rotten bastard! I should cut off your balls and cram them down your throat!

The office door was open a couple of inches, and Peggy nudged it with her hip sending it crashing into the wall behind. She hoisted the ice bucket and threw its contents toward the conch before the scene before her registered in her disbelieving mind.

#

Tony was just getting ready to head for the office when the radio in his squad car burst alive.

"Chief, you there? Come in," Sally's morning rough voice demanded.

"Yeah Sal, I'm here. What's up?"

Three minutes later Tony walked through the back door to Jake's 1—. 4 The Road Bar. Peggy was sitting on a stool at the end of the bar with half a bottle of Johnny Walker Red resting between her hands. Peggy never drank alcohol of any kind, so when she picked up the bottle and guzzled enough to knock a grown man on his ass, Tony knew it was going to be a long day.

Moving cautiously, yet with enough noise not to scare her, Tony quickly moved to the woman's side. "Mrs. Rhodes, are you all right?"

Squinting as though searching through a dense fog, Peggy leaned close enough to Tony that their noses almost touched. "Oh, it's you. I don't feel very well Chief, not well at all, but it's nice of you to ask."

Tony nodded. If she thought she felt bad now just wait until she started sobering up. "I'm going to check out the office now Mrs. Rhodes. Will you be all right while I'm gone?"

"I didn't do it, Chief. I thought about it, I was even going to threaten to do it, but I swear to God I didn't do it!"

"You stay right here Peggy. I'll be back in a minute."

Tony stood in the doorway taking in the scene before him. Jake Rhodes was lying naked on the couch, and there seemed to be water and ice all over the man as though someone had tried to wash away all the blood. On the floor near the door lay a butcher knife, and an ice bucket

.Looking down at Jake, Tony thought, Well it goes without saying Jake, you won't be diddling your barmaids any more. Tony shuddered to think what had become of the man's private parts. You should have kept them a little more private, Jake.

Tony decided to call his office from behind the bar where he could watch Peggy who was taking another long swallow from the now nearly empty whiskey bottle. Holding the receiver in one hand, Tony reached out and pulled the bottle from her hands, spilling what was left down the front of her coat. He needed to ask her some questions before she passed out, and from the looks of her, decided he'd better hurry.

Sally answered on the second ring. "Whitefields Police Department."

"Sal, its Tony. Get hold of Mike and Pete, and have them meet me at Jake's. Then call State and tell them we have another murder, but don't call them until the guys have a chance to get here. After you take care of that call Bill Padgett and tell him we're sending him another one."

"Who is it this time?"

"Jake Rhodes."

"Jesus, Tony, this is getting ridiculous. He wasn't killed the same way as the

Milner girl, was he?"

"No. Look Sally I'll fill you in as soon as I can, but right now I want you to call my men, then the State boys. I need Pete and Mike here A.S.A.P., OK?"

Sally wanted to know more, but when the Chief said he'd tell her later she knew not to press the point, instead she replied, "Right away Chief," then remembering whom all she had to call, added, "but do I have to call Bill? He's getting really crabby about all this, and he yells at me every time I have to call him."

"Sally, handle it."

Peggy's head was on the bar between her hands now, and Tony was afraid he'd missed his chance to talk to her, but when he touched her shoulder she looked up at him through red, puffy eyes.

"Mrs. Rhodes, can you tell me what happened?"

Peggy looked around the room, trying to place where she was, and then with a sigh said, "He didn't come home. When I got up this morning he wasn't in bed. I've almost caught him in the act before, and I thought I had him this time. I came down here." She shivered, and went on, "I was going to scare the hell out of him, out of them both. I was going to pretend that I was going to…to cut off his balls, but I didn't do it, I swear to God I didn't!"

"Peggy, there's water and ice all over the…ah, all over Jake."

She nodded, "I filled one of the bar buckets with ice and cold water. When I opened the door I didn't look, I just threw it where I knew the couch was. Isn't that what you're suppose to do to dogs in heat? Throw ice water on them?"

In spite of himself Tony laughed. "Is the butcher knife yours too?"

"Yeah, I dropped it when I threw the bucket of water. There isn't any blood on it 'cause I didn't do it."

"I know." He'd noted the knife was clean when he first saw it.

"Chief? Do you think that girl he has working for him did it? She left him naked and sleeping earlier in the week so I'd find him. I kicked him in the balls so hard I'm surprised they didn't end up in his throat."

Her eyes bulged in shock. "Oh God! You don't suppose that's where they're at, do you? Oh God, poor Jake, he should have listened to me. Some people are just so stupid, they never learn until it's too late."

"Would that be Dee Clark, Mrs. Rhodes?"

"What? Oh, ah, yeah, Dee, ah yeah, she's the one he's got working for him now." Peggy grabbed Tony's arm, pulling him close, "You know I never did hold it against the girls so much as I did Jake. They probably didn't want to, ah, you know, ah, sleep with him,

but if they didn't he fired them. I could never catch him at it though, but I heard the talk, just like everyone else in town." At the thought of the town Peggy cringed. "Oh God, everyone's going to know, aren't they? I'll never be able to look anyone in the face again."

"Sure you can, Peggy. You can make right what Jake was doing. You run the place, and make it respectable." He was relieved to hear the sirens on the towns other two squad cars coming nearer.

"Just one more question Peggy. What time did you find the body?"

"Huh? Oh, it must have been close to seven-thirty. I got up a little after seven, and then drove a hundred miles an hour to get here, so it had to be close to seven-thirty."

Tony looked at his watch, it was now nine forty-one, "Why did you wait so long before calling?"

Frowning Peggy said, "Did I? I don't remember. I don't remember calling anyone. Did I? I don't feel good."

Tony scratched his head. Maybe she hadn't placed the call. He assumed she had, because she was there, but if she hadn't called to report it, who had? Dee Clark?

Pete, after making arrangements for Doctor Klein to meet them at Peggy's house, left to take Peggy home. Mike was in Jake's office taking pictures for their files. The State Police sometimes had a way of being selfish with things like that. A few minutes later

Mike came out of the office. He was a tall lanky man, only a couple years younger than Tony's thirty-eight, with curly red hair that stuck up stubbornly any way it wanted to, and he was constantly running his fingers through it to keep it from sticking straight up. He was doing this now, as a small smile played across his lips.

"Any idea where they're at?"

Looking up from his notes, Tony asked, "Where who's at…oh, those! No idea at all, you?"

Mike shook his head. "Where did all the water come from?"

"Peggy threw it on him before she realized he was dead. Said she was going to break them up like you do with a couple of dogs." Tony laughed.

"Jesus, good thing he was already dead, the shock would've killed him." Mike said, running his fingers through his hair.

"No shit. You done with the pictures?"

"Yeah."

"All right then, let's have a quick look-see, before Robbins and his merry men get here. They have to be somewhere."

"Who? Oh, those!"

#

CHAPTER 19

When Tony finally crawled into bed that night he was exhausted. He didn't want to think about Jake Rhodes and his missing gonads. He especially didn't want to think about where he ended up finding them. Unfortunately that's all he could think about.

After making sure Jake's body was tucked in and on its way to Bill, Tony drove down the block to Dee Clark's apartment building. It was a little after eleven and he found himself thinking about Anna and Tommy, and that drew him to Alex. Alex Rogers and Dee Clark. Jake and Dee getting it on night after night, maybe Alex got tired of sharing what he considered his own personal nookie. Who had a better reason to want Jake dead? Dee was his alibi, and her word depended on what Jake said, so Alex actually had two good reasons for wanting the bar owner dead. Jake hadn't liked Alex either. Tony knew that the first time he mentioned Alex's name to Jake. Maybe Jake wasn't going to back up Dee's story, and Alex found out and killed him.

With everything else going on in town Jake's death seemed almost easy by comparison. When the shock wore off it would become funny, the town joke. "Ol' Jake never could keep his gonads out of the girls, ha, ha, ha."

Pulling up in front of the old apartment building Tony wondered if Alex was up there with Dee right now. Wishful thinking. Seemed like anytime Tony wanted to see Alex he was nowhere to be found.

Upstairs Tony knocked lightly on Dee's door and was surprised when it moved beneath his knuckles. Pushing slowly, Tony called out. The door opened partway then stopped. He pushed against it as he called her name again, but there still was no answer, and the door wouldn't budge.

Something was blocking it. Tony put his shoulder against the door, and pushing hard, finally managing to get an opening large enough to stick his head through.

Dee Clark was on the other side of the door, and she was looking up at Tony with bulging eyes. Her face was covered with blood, which seemed to be flowing from her mouth and nose. The thing that haunted Tony even now was the way she clawed at her throat, leaving long bloody flaps of skin in their wake.

Dee wore only panties, and a matching black lace bra, and Tony wondered again if Alex Rogers was in the apartment at this very moment. Perhaps hiding in the bedroom, or standing just out of sight, waiting for Tony to look the other way so he could slip away.

Dee searched for Tony above and behind her, and when she finally managed to make eye contact Tony wished she hadn't. He'd see those pleading, insane, accusing, eyes in his dreams for the rest of his life.

A strange animal sound filled the room, and Tony realized Dee was ripping the flesh from her own throat in a desperate attempt to fill her oxygen-deprived lungs. The world seemed to be moving in slow motion, as a long magenta painted nail sank out of sight into liquid flesh of the same hue.

A car born blared outside, and someone called for Tina to come home for lunch, while dust modes danced through bright slivers of golden sunlight caressing a naked thigh, and Tony was positive the whole world had suddenly gone mad. Forgive me Father for I have sinned…How many years since he'd been to church? Was it too late for him? Was it too late for Dee?

Reaching out from the darkest recesses of his soul Tony screamed again for Dee to move away from the door, but she either couldn't move, or was so far gone that his words failed to register. Then Dee started cramming her fist into her mouth, and, for a crazy moment, Tony almost giggled, because it looked as though she was trying to swallow her arm. Hey kid-o, don't put that in your mouth, you don't know where it's been, besides I got a new friend who'll make you a sandwich that'll taste a whole lot better!

He was trying frantically to push the door open enough to slip through when Dee began to convulse. She slammed backwards, ramming the door into Tony's head so hard that he literally saw an explosion of flaming red and white stars.

Clenching his teeth against the pain, Tony slammed against the door with an agonizing howl. He only had seconds if he was going to save the woman, and the need to save this one burned through him like napalm. Finally, an opening large enough to slip through and within moments he was through the opening and straddling Dee.

He rode her like a rodeo star while trying to pry her fist from her throat. Fear rose like bile in his throat, she was turning blue, and tears of blood leaked from her eyes, leaving crazy-quilt patterns on her cheeks.

Finally her arm was freed and he squeezed his thighs tighter, pinning her arms to her side while he used his fingers to pry open her mouth, searching for the obstacle blocking her breathing. He pried her jaw apart like an old-time lion tamer preparing to stick his head into

the lion's mouth. So much blood! He couldn't see the obstruction because of the blood, so he rammed his fingers as far down her throat as he could, hoping to dislodge the blockage. His fingers touched something big, and slippery, so big he couldn't get his fingers around it.

The Heimlich Maneuver wasn't any more successful, so he tried holding her around the waist with her head dangling towards the floor while he beat on her back. Panic filled him with cold dread, he was losing her and there didn't seem to be a damned thing he could do about it.

"Goddamned it Dee, don't you dare die! Spit it out!" He was screaming, not in control. He had to stay calm, had to think clearly. Yet he continued to swear, as his fist bludgeoned her back.

"No! Damned it, I'm not going to lose you, I'm not!" He dropped her to the carpet, unable to hold her lifeless weight any longer, and continued pounding on her back, with more and more fury! Goddamned you Dee, don't you dare die without telling me who did this to you! Come on bitch spit it out! Then as on command something plopped from her mouth, landing with a wet splat at his side.

A scream brought him out of his momentary stupor. A neighbor woman, her eyes wide with shock and accusation, stood in the doorway, her mouth covered with shaking hands as she stumbled away from the insanity in the Chief's eyes.

Only a few minutes passed since he first knocked on Dee's door, but to Tony it seemed like hours. Weakened and shaking he began CPR after screaming at the neighbor to "Stop standing there screaming like a fucking idiot, and call the paramedics!"

Alex Rogers was the only link to both Jake and Dee. As usual Alex wasn't to be found, and Tony searched every corner of Dee's apartment hoping to catch the bastard hiding in some dark shadow. Even if it turned out Alex was innocent, Tony vowed to make the man's life hell. He didn't think Alex was innocent though, because any man who would beat his wife and child was capable of anything.

Tony tossed and turned on the bed, sleep as elusive as an honest politician. What other link was there besides Alex Rogers? Cindy Milner, Jimmy Russo, Jake Rhodes, and Dee Clark? Cindy and Jimmy were linked to Lyndsay Abbott, but that didn't explain Jake and Dee. Alex Rogers was connected to Jake and Cindy, but as far Tony could tell, had no connection to Jimmy or Cindy, except for being the one to find Cindy's body, unless the pervert had been doing the Milner girl too.

Tommy! Not sleepy any more, Tony got his notebook from the living room and began taking notes. Little lists of names and dates, and suddenly his pulse beat a little more rapidly. Tommy Rogers found Lyndsay, Alex Rogers found Cindy. Tommy and Alex Rogers, father and son. Jake and Dee were both connected to Alex. Jimmy was Lyndsay's boyfriend, and, rumor had it, he was also seeing Cindy Milner and that's why Lyndsay ran out into a raging snowstorm. Except for Jimmy Russo, and his death could have been accidental, almost had to be, because as far as Tony knew there wasn't any way to murder someone with maggots.

Alex and Tommy Rogers were the only common denominator, and there was no way in hell a nine-year-old kid could be responsible.

Tony glanced at the clock next to his bed, but didn't really care what time it was. It was after midnight, but he couldn't wait, because to wait might mean losing another life. He needed to warn Anna, to make sure she didn't let Alex into the house again.

Much to his surprise Anna answered on the first ring.

"Anna, its Tony. I'm sorry to bother you this late, but I need to know if you've heard from Alex today?"

"No, and if he knows what's good for him I won't hear from him again, ever! Why, what's going on now?"

Warn her, no matter how it makes you sound! "Dee Clark, and Jake Rhodes were murdered today, Anna. I, ah, I need to talk to Alex, but I can't find him."

Anna was silent. Alex a drunken no-good two-timer, but a murderer? She thought of all the times he'd come home drunk and slap her and Tommy around. As much as she wanted to deny it, Anna had a feeling that Alex, drunk, was capable of anything. Truthfully how well did she really know Alex? Hadn't he already turned into a complete stranger, someone so totally different from the man she thought she'd married so many years ago?

"You think he murdered them," she stated flatly.

"I'm not saying that, Anna. I just want to talk to him. Do you have any idea where he might have gone?"

"Sometimes if he's with a client in another town he stays over night, then drives back the next morning. Since he's obviously not with Dee", she added bitterly, "I'd suggest calling him in the morning."

"OK, thanks. Anna, if he comes out there…."

"Don't even worry about it, that bastard will never get near me or my son again. Besides, if he tries to get in I've got a little surprise for him this time."

"I don't usually encourage people to have guns in their homes," he said, reading between the lines, "but in this case I'm glad you do. I won't even ask you if it's registered, but after all this is over I expect you to take care of that."

Anna laughed, but it contained little humor. "Yes, Sir! I'll take care of that, Sir!" Tony chuckled softly, and Anna remembered the reason she'd been unable to sleep earlier. "Ah, Tony, about yesterday? I want to apologize for treating you so badly. I know it wasn't your fault, and I'm sorry I was such a bitch to you."

"Don't mention it," but he was glad she had. He didn't want her mad at him for any reason, and somehow knowing she wasn't mad any more made him feel better than he had all day.

"Well I wouldn't blame you if you never talked to me again." Her voice, low and husky, sent shivers through him.

"I don't think you have to worry about that."

Anna felt herself relax, and thought that maybe she'd be able to get some sleep "I'm glad. You'll still come to Tommy's birthday party Saturday?"

"Wouldn't miss it. Keep your doors locked, and, if anything bothers you, give me a call at home, 555-8978."

"I will, Tony, thank you. Good night."

Tommy listened to the soft tone of his mother's voice and sighed. At least whomever Anna was talking to makes her happy, so it couldn't be Alex, Lyndsay, or the demon, although Tommy wasn't sure if ghosts and demons used telephones, but kind of doubted it.

He'd been lying awake in the dark for hours, listening for any sound that might indicate trouble coming. He was convinced that at any minute the demon was going to appear, to rip him and Anna to pieces, because he'd tattled to Chief Morman about Cindy's death. So far though the night was quiet, almost too quiet. That's why when the telephone rang minutes earlier; Tommy's heart had almost stopped beating. For just a moment he was sure it was the banshee scream of a wildly pissed off demon.

Rolling onto his side Tommy looked out his bedroom window at the stars shining brightly against a black velvet sky. He could see the moon tonight, and wondered why Bruiser hadn't started howling yet. A lump the size or a baseball settled in his stomach. I just want to be a little kid, he thought, blinking back heavy tears, which threatened escape. Like Chief Morman said he was, "not a worry in the world". God, if you could make everything like it was for Chief Morman when he was a kid I'll, um, I promise to say my prayers every night, and, ah, I'll even clean my room without Mom having to yell at me. He stared out the window several minutes, concentrating on his prayer, hoping God heard.

Rolling away from the window, Tommy closed his eyes and tried to sleep. After a while the soft murmur of his mother's voice carried him across the threshold to dreamland.

#

CHAPTER 20

Sue was confused and upset by Lyndsay's last statement. It wasn't something Lyndsay would normally say, no matter how upset she was with another person.

"Lyndsay, I don't want people killed. I couldn't stand to think innocent people died because of me. It's hard enough that I lost you, please don't add guilt to my grief."

"But Mama, it's their fault that you have grief, instead of a daughter, to keep you company. Daddy is out looking for my murderer, and when he finds him, he'll kill that man with his own bands. He'll do it because he loves me, and because he wants me to find peace."

"The Lord said, 'Vengeance is mine'."

"He also says, 'An eye for an eye.' Why wouldn't you want me avenged, Mother? Is that so much to ask?"

"Oh Lyndsay, baby, I do want you avenged. I want the man who murdered you to die a slow miserable death. It's what he deserves, but all the others you talk about, they haven't murdered anyone."

"They're all guilty, one way or another. I won't let anyone hurt the people I care about; I don't care who they are. If someone looks at you wrong they'll suffer the worse horrors they can imagine:"

Sue pushed back in the rocking chair, away from the venom in her daughter's voice. Lyndsay would never say the things that were being said.

"Who are you?" Sue asked, her voice weak and shaky with fear, "You're not my daughter, Lyndsay would never say the things you're saying."

Lyndsay smiled. "I guess being murdered changes your outlook on life, Mama."

#

Alex punched the strange pillow again, and flopped onto his other side on the lumpy mattress. He couldn't sleep, and had just about convinced himself to give up trying and head for home. If he left now he could be back in Whitefields in less than an hour, enough time to stop by Jake's for a couple of drinks before going home with Dee. He was surprised to find how attached to Dee he'd become.

He never expected to care for any woman other than Anna. *Anna, you don't realize what you're throwing away. I can't be as bad as you make me out to be or Dee wouldn't be so crazy about me.*

He looked forward to June when he and Dee would spend two glorious weeks basking in the sun. It would do him good to get away for a while. *Jesus, that sounds good. I wish we were leaving now.* He'd have time to sort out his feelings, think things through. *Who knows, maybe it's time to talk to Dee about getting a place together.*

It'd turned out to be a pretty good day after all. The commission on the million-dollar insurance policy he sold would go a long way toward renting a nice place for the two of them. *We can get some sharp new furniture and fix the place up real nice. Make Anna eat her heart out.* Maybe it was time to let the past rest. Anna didn't want anything to do with him anymore, and Tommy acted like he was scared to death most of the time when they were together, so why bother?

Monday maybe I'll get a hold of an attorney and file for divorce. End it once and for all.

Jumping from bed, Alex quickly threw his few belongings into the small overnight bag he always carried in the trunk of his car. He was excited, wanting to talk to Dee about his plans as soon as possible. *She'll be so excited!* She wouldn't admit it, but he knew she loved him. *What I need right now is a couple of beers, then Dee's loving embraces. No doubt about it, I'll sleep like a baby then.*

#

Ted Jenkins saw the light come on in Anna's bedroom and wondered if she, too, was having trouble sleeping. From this angle he couldn't see into her bedroom, to do that he'd have to walk to the front of the house, but he could see the light shining out onto the lawn from her window. Behind him Betty snored lightly. His mind made up he crept from the bedroom.

Outside the night was cool and still. He looked at the sky, amazed at how brightly the stars shone. Far off in the east a nearly full moon sought dominance in the crowded sky. It's a night for lovers, he thought glancing over his shoulder as he walked down the driveway.

From his vantage point he could see the ceiling in Anna's bedroom, but, unless she stood up and walked past the window, he couldn't see Anna herself. He imagined her laying across the bed gazing out at the sky above, knowing, as he did, that it was made for lovers.

She would be lonely, needing the love of a good man. She would stand and slowly move to the window, her nightgown gossamer in the light shining from behind. She would look down and spot him walking slowly down the driveway. A sad smile would cross her lips. She would think how lucky Betty was to have such a wonderful man and wish she could share that luck, if only for a couple of hours. He would stop, raising his head to look up at the stars overhead, and spot her standing there in the window. They would stare longingly at each other, neither of them moving. Then she would wave, beseechingly. He'd slowly raise his arm in response, and she'd motion for him to come to her. He'd hurry to the front door where she'd be anxiously waiting. The door would open, and they'd instantly be in each other's hungry embrace. Her lips would be soft, warm, and eager as they covered his mouth, neck, and chest. She'd pull at his shirt, ripping away the buttons. Then her hands would frantically work the belt from his waist. He could feel her large full breast pulsing through her shear gown.

The light went out in Anna's bedroom.

#

After making a slow tour of the town, Robbins pulled his cruiser to the curb and turned off the lights. Looks like Morman is in for the evening. Must be nice.

His surveillance was strictly unofficial. His boss wasn't happy with it, but what the hell, this was his town, his people, and if that asshole Morman wasn't going to do the job right then someone better. After Cindy was murdered he'd dropped in to see Rita, Cindy's mother. Him and Tina went back as far as first grade, even dated a few times in high school, although it never led to anything permanent. Rita was devastated. He could well imagine finding out your kid was skewered to a tree, Jesus! Rita told him that she felt Morman wasn't doing his Job. She thought that maybe the case was too much for the city boy. "I wish you were Chief, Doug. I know you'd get to the bottom of this." That's when he promised her he would look into the case personally, and, if Morman were jerking off instead of doing his Job, then maybe he, Robbins, would go for the Chief's Job.

#

CHAPTER 21

Only half-awake, Alex reached out and grabbed the ringing telephone. "Dee?"

Tony, taken back, said, "No Mr. Rogers, its Tony Morman. I need to talk to you."

"Christ Morman, it's practically the middle of the night. Haven't I already answered all the stupid questions you could possibly dream up?"

Bristling, Tony apologized, "Sorry it's too early for you, but this is important." It's after ten. Must be nice to be able to sleep this late on a weekday. Too bad I just spent the last forty minutes on the phone listening to Bill Padgett tell me what a bunch of sick perverted bastards we have living in Whitefields. If I'd known how you hate to be wakened early I would have called at seven.

"You have more questions about the Abbott girl?"

"No, Sir." Tony replied, almost choking on "sir."

Alex, suddenly wide-awake asked, "It's not Tommy is it? Has something happened to my son?"

Gritting his teeth to keep from telling Alex Rogers exactly what he thought about his concern for his son's welfare, instead he said as calmly as possible, "No Sir, as far as I know Tommy and Anna are both fine. This is another case. I'll be there in ten minutes." He hung up before Alex could reply.

"Great," Alex mumbled, dragging his legs off the bed. "Just what I need."

Tony's use of Anna's first name hadn't been missed either. Which I'm sure he did on purpose just to get me on the defensive. Alex wondered if Morman was making a move on Anna just to piss him off. Shit. He thought he'd finally gotten her out of his system but realized he still felt that old familiar tremor of jealously. Tremor hell, I'm feeling the whole earthquake. Least now I know why Morman is harassing me about every little thing that happens in this stupid town. With Alex out of the way Morman's path to Anna would be clear. Shit, maybe he's already done the nasty with my wife, and in my bed, and with my son in the bedroom across the hall! Well, the bastard's in for a fight, no one takes what's mine until I say so.

The day-old coffee was strong and cold as Alex poured it into a chipped mug and placed it in the microwave to heat. What, he wondered, was Morman up to if it wasn't about the Abbott girl. Maybe it had something to do with the other girl, the one in the tree, the one he was trying his damnedest to forget. He didn't want to think about her, but the memory was still too fresh, and more than once her pathetic image popped unbidden to mind.

Tony knocked at the door exactly ten minutes later, causing Alex to wonder if he'd been standing outside so he'd arrive at the exact time he'd stated.

Morman looked ragged, tired, and worried. Things weren't going well for the Chief, Alex thought gleefully. If I didn't dislike the man so much I might almost feel sorry for him. A little voice whispered, but then again, maybe Ann's responsible for Morman being so tired. Anna, in the mood, could wear out any normal male. Alex's stomach tightened with rage.

Tony followed Alex into the kitchen, waiting silently while Alex took a cup of nasty-looking coffee from the microwave. Without offering Tony, thank you for small favors, a cup, Alex sat at his cluttered kitchen table, waiting for Tony to make the first move. I've never wanted to kill any one as much as I do him. Thinks he's special because he's a cop.

Tony watched Alex closely. They were sizing each other up like a couple of rutting rams. Alex seemed calm and relaxed, not at all like someone who had just mutilated two people, but in his line of work Tony knew looks could be deceiving.

Clearing his throat, Tony began, "When was the last time you saw Dee Clark and Jake Rhodes?"

Alex's mouth dropped open in surprise. This most definitely was not what he'd been expecting. When he'd arrived at 1—4 The Road it had been locked up, but that hadn't surprised Alex, because he knew Jake often closed early if business was slow. Also Jake was still low on beer because the delivery guy hadn't shown up. Alex had been pissed though, when he got to Dee's apartment and she wasn't there. He'd thought about going back to the bar in case Jake was banging her again, but in the end he decided that Dee was a big girl, and if her job meant that much to her he wouldn't interfere. He'd made up his mind though that if he and Dee were going to be living together she'd have to tell Jake there'd be no more funny stuff, and if Jake didn't listen to her, then Alex would be more than happy to intervene.

"Dee Clark and Jake Rhodes? I asked you when you last saw them," Tony repeated.

"Oh, ah, I saw Dee yesterday morning, she was still sleeping when I left for Detroit.

I saw Jake the night before, when I stopped to pick Dee up from work. Why, what's happened?"

Ignoring the question, Tony continued, "I suppose there's someone who can vouch for you, that you actually were in Detroit yesterday?"

Alex paled, but his voice was firm as anger seeped back in, "Of course I've got witnesses, for Christ sake. I sold a million-dollar policy. Now will you please tell me what's going on?"

"In a minute. What time did you get back in town?"

"Around midnight. I stopped by the bar to pick up Dee, but it was already closed, so I drove by her apartment, but she wasn't there. I thought...." Alex stopped realizing that what he was about to say could very likely land him in a world of shit. Make him look guilty, but guilty of what?

Then Tony told him, in graphic detail.

Tony knew he was being cruelly descriptive, but he couldn't help but enjoy seeing the same kind of horror on Alex's face that he'd seen on Tommy's.

When Tony finally finished talking, Alex just sat there staring into space. He did manage one simple question, "what's happening here?"

Tony could only shake his head. "I wish to God I knew. If you're planning on
going out of town, let my office know."

Alex nodded. He couldn't believe it. Dee dead? How could that be? He was going to ask her to move in with him, so how could she be dead? Dead with Jake's balls crammed down her throat, for Christ sake! He sat at the table for a long time without realizing that Tony had gone, and his coffee was cold. Coffee? Hell he didn't need coffee; he needed a good stiff shot, and realized, with a start, that he'd been ready to head for 1—4 The Road. Jake's was the only bar in town. With that closed life was going to be a bitch.

"Shit! Shit! Shit!"

#

"Karl, I know you've been out looking for Lyndsay's killer, so what are you going to do if you find him?"

Karl looked up from his breakfast. "Who say's I'm looking for anyone?"

Pouring a cup of coffee, Sue sat at the table across from the man who's life she'd shared for twenty years. She knew him as well as she knew herself. If something was bothering Karl, Sue often knew it before he did. "Lyndsay told me. She also said that if, no when, you find him you're going to kill him. She said you'd do that for that for her."

He thought about the dreams of Lyndsay he'd been having, and simply said, "Yes."

"You would throw away your life when there are laws to take care of things like that? What about me? Where would that leave me? Not only would I have no daughter, I'd have no husband. Don't you care about what happens to me?"

"Laws?" Karl sputtered. "Laws that let murders out in just a matter of years? Laws that smart lawyers can get admitted murders out by plea-bargaining? Are those the laws you're talking about? I owe it to Lyndsay, 'An Eye For An Eye!' You owe it to her. What are you asking me to do woman? Do you expect me to stick my head in the sand and pretend it never happened? To let some sick bastard go so he can put some other girl's parent's through what we're going through? No! By God, I won't do it! When I find that bastard he's mine, and I'm going to make him suffer. I'm going to cut off his balls and cram them down his throat, and I'm going to laugh at his agony! And don't you dare try to stop me!"

Sue was more frightened than she'd ever been, "Karl, listen to me, please. Lyndsay, there's something wrong with her. She says things that aren't right, she's changed!"

Karl leapt to his feet, spilling coffee across the tablecloth. "What the hell do you expect? Of course she's changed. She was murdered! Don't you understand? How could anyone go through what our daughter went through and not be changed? How?" Karl slammed through the kitchen door leaving Sue to wonder why God chose to rip her world apart.

Sue sat at the table staring into space long after the roar of Karl's truck faded. She had to talk to Lyndsay, get her to make Karl stop before it was too late. Lyndsay was the only one who could make Karl change his mind once it was set. But could she convince Lyndsay? Her daughter was confused. *She needs me, and there's only one way I know of to help her now. I have to go to my daughter. Take her by the hand and lead her down the right path.*

Taking the breakfast dishes to the sink, Sue began by cleaning the kitchen. She didn't want anyone saying she had been a bad housekeeper. When the dishes were done and put away, and the kitchen spotless, Sue went through the rest of the house, cleaning until her fingers were raw. Once the inside of the house was spotless, she poured a fresh cup of coffee and went out into the afternoon sunshine.

The small vegetable garden looked good, and after pulling a light scattering of weeds from around the tender shoots, she was satisfied that in a month or so Karl would have all the fresh vegetables he needed.

The flowers were blooming in a wide array of colors and shapes. They would be fine without her constant fussing, perhaps they'd go a little wild, but that was all right, as long as they continued to grow after she was gone. The air around her was thick with their pungent aroma, and Sue enjoyed the sun-warmed afternoon as she surveyed the yard, etching every flower, leaf, and butterfly to memory. After a long while she moved slowly toward the house, it was time to go to Lyndsay.

#

Anna put the finishing touches on Tommy's birthday cake. It didn't seem possible to her that he was going to be ten years old already. Sometimes it seemed he should still be a baby. Other times it was hard to remember a time when he hadn't been there with her. She looked down at the cake and smiled. A blue-eyed Siberian Husky stared back from the top of the cake. Pretty good likeness, if I do say so myself. Tommy would love it.

Looking out the kitchen window, she saw Bruiser staring out toward the front of the house where she knew Tommy was riding his bike. The dog looked so sad and lonely not being able to run with Tommy that Anna decided to finish what she was doing and take Bruiser out front so he could at least be near Tommy. She felt a tiny pang of guilt as she walked around to the front of the house with Bruiser. She should be working on her book, but since the day Tommy found the body in the forest Anna hadn't been able to bring herself to make contact again with the little turtle. No matter how many times she told herself that she was being silly, that the turtle wasn't really Sandy, and her vision was just a coincidence, the thought of making her mind blank again scared her. What if? But that's silly, isn't it?

Tommy pedaled to the end of the long drive, and as Anna watched him, she thought she saw movement in the woods across the road. It looked as though someone was standing there among the trees watching as the boy rode back and forth in front of the house. You're being paranoid. For heavens sake it looks like an Indian. Tommy waved, catching Anna's attention, the bike swayed slightly, but Tommy was proud of his accomplishment. Waving back Anna strained to make out the shape. Something white and blurred. Didn't I see something like that before? Where?

Walking casually to the end of the drive where she could be closer to her son, Anna, despite telling herself she was having vision problems, continued to probe the shadows across the road. She was sure she'd seen the same white blur, or something similar to it, before. If only she could remember where, then maybe she'd understand where this feeling of terror was coming from.

Of course there's nothing there. What'd I expect, Sitting Bull in drag? There's probably a raccoon over there making Bruiser growl like that. Tommy pulled up beside her, a puzzled frown creasing his brow when he head the dog growl, and realized that Bruiser and Anna were both staring into the forest. Before Tommy could react Anna smiled, trying hard to keep her imagination in check, Tommy was having hard enough time of it without her adding to his nervousness. One last glance showed nothing more than green leaves and thick foliage. There's no one there, Indian or otherwise. Yet later, as she turned the corner of the house to put Bruiser back in his kennel, she ventured one last glance across the road and saw an Indian woman dressed in shimmering white buckskins staring back at her. Then there was nothing, and never had been, she told herself, except trees, birds, and spring flowers. *I'm a writer, I'm supposed to have a good imagination.* Nonetheless she shivered in the warm spring air, and made Tommy go inside with her.

#

Sally looked up from the report she was trying to read when Tony came through the front door. He looked like she felt. There wasn't a doubt in her mind that something bad was happening in Whitefields, and even if Captain Robbins' men weren't right calling the town Demon's Howler, Sally wouldn't be surprised to find out that the Devil himself had taken up residency.

Tony stopped a couple of feet in front of Sally's desk, as though fearful of her intent. By the look on her face he knew she had more bad news, but was reluctant to tell him. He was suddenly overwhelmed with a burning desire to escape to the logical madness of Detroit.

A heavy sigh filled the room when he said, "Now what?"

"Better get your coffee first," she replied maternally. When Tony first took the chief's job Sally wasn't too sure of the sullen young man. If truth were told she hadn't much cared for the way he seemed to brood all the time, and he never let anyone slip through the ironclad armor he'd built around himself. It's only been the past few months that he seemed to be letting people get close to him. Now with all this trouble Sally was afraid he was going to slip back into his untouchable shell again. She hoped that didn't happen because she'd always felt a little frightened of him before, without really knowing why. Sally was grateful when his personality changed, as she'd been ready to quit her job rather than put up with the stress of working with a man who seemed ready to come undone.

"Shit." Tony mumbled as he took her advice. He wasn't normally a drinking man, but thought how appealing several beers would be right now. He wondered if it would be possible for him to drink enough that he would just pass out, or if he'd throw it all up before he reached that stage. The way his luck was running lately, he'd throw it up before oblivion took over.

When Sally saw he was ready, she took a deep breath. "Sue Abbott's dead."

"Sue?"

"Yeah, you remember, the first girl's mother."

"Shit. How?" He was already trying to make a link to the other murders.

"Suicide."

"Sally, I wish you'd be a little more informative with your information. Why do I always have to pry information from you piece by piece?" he snapped.

Slightly offended, Sally retorted, "Well excuse me! You'd think that after all the time I've spent typing out your reports I'd know how to be more informative."

Tony shook his head as he apologized. "I'm sorry Sal, this whole business is getting to me. Forgive me?"

Mollified, Sally went on with her story. "Well it seems that Mrs. Knowles from the church decided to stop by and pay her respects, and see how Sue was doing. The door was open, and, when Sue didn't answer her knock, Jean, that's Mrs. Knowles, went on inside. She knew

Sue wouldn't go away and leave the house open, so she started looking. Said she had a bad feeling when she got to Lyndsay's room and the door was closed. Jean said she got a really weird feeling, and wanted to turn around and leave right then, but she couldn't.

Said she owed it to Sue 'cause they'd been friends since grade school, and so she went in. Sue was sitting in Lyndsay's rocking chair. Doc. Says she cut her own throat."

Tony could only stare at Sally, not sure that he heard her right, but when she made no move to correct her story he said, "OK, I give up, just how the hell does someone cut their own throat? Jesus! Is Doc. Sure? I mean wouldn't it be more likely that someone else cut her throat? I wanted to kill myself, I'd sure as hell find an easier way to do it, like pills or a gun. I just can't believe it."

"The knife was in her hand, and there was a note to Karl." Sally shrugged, the news related, her job was done.

"I want to see that note." Tony demanded.

Again Sally shrugged him off as she turned back to her typewriter. If Doc. Klein said it was a suicide, then it was a suicide, no questions asked, why couldn't the city boy accept it like everyone one else in town?

#

CHAPTER 22

Had Sandy pulled his head any further into his shell, he'd been looking where he came from instead of where he was going. After his previous encounter with a fox Sandy knew there was no such thing as too deep when you were about to become an entree. Whether the beast with the bad breath was actually the ol' red fox, or his mother's, brother's, cousin, didn't really matter, 'cause dead was dead no matter who did the chewing. Sandy just hoped all his limbs were tucked safely inside with his head.

Something strange started happening, and Sandy momentarily forgot about the fox, his instincts instead turning to hibernation as the air turned winter frigid, but then the fox yipped, and once again Sandy's attention focused on the impending threat. Strangely, though, he no longer heard, nor smelled the fox.

"Come on little one, it's time to go. You must hurry. Even for you the journey is taking too long. Go now and dawdle no longer."

Sandy peaked out, looking one way then another. The fox was definitely gone, as was the being that had spoken to him. Moving as fast as his three little legs could carry him, Sandy scurried on his way. He wanted to get as far as possible from the fox, but most importantly, he positively did not want to anger the god.

#

Somewhere in the black of night a dog howled, or maybe it was a wolf, or maybe a ghost. Cold sweat soaked through Tommy's pajamas, causing them to twist tightly around his thin legs. In his nightmare sometimes it was Lyndsay who chased him, other times the Indian. He ran as fast as he could, the pain in his side deepening with each stride, yet he had to keep going. Off to the left he saw a shadow figure pacing him, then it stopped in a thick stand of trees and waved, calling Tommy's name. It was his father, come to save him from ghosts and demons. Tears of relief flowed down Tommy's cheeks as he veered left into Alex's welcoming arms. Tommy pressed closer to his father, never in his life had he been so glad to see Alex, to be protected, as parents who loved them protected kids in some of his favorite movies.

Alex's fingernails dug into the tender flesh on Tommy's back as he hugged him closer. Tommy tried to pull away, but Dad was holding him too tight, and the pain was becoming unbearable.

Tommy could see little in the darkness, but he realized two things that made his flesh tighten. The flesh pressed beneath his hands was cold and rough, instead of warm and smooth like Alex's should be. He became aware, as well, that whatever had been tracking him through the midnight forest was no longer darting from shadow-to-shadow; the forest was deathly still, as though holding its breath.

In spite of his momentary disorientation and terror, Tommy finally managed to twist out of his father's embrace. As he turned to face his protector, Tommy realized he'd been holding his breath, and now it issued from his chest with a whooshing sound as his eyes locked with the flaming red glare of the demon.

Tommy looked down at the hands of the beast still outstretched as though willing him back into their cold embrace, and saw that the ends weren't adorned with fingernails, or even claws, but long sharp teeth. He knew the thing before him was the demon that possessed his father. He didn't know how he knew since all he'd ever seen of it before were the red glowing eyes, but it was Dad's demon, of that he was sure, he also knew he was dreaming. *I don't like this dream! Wake up! I'm dreaming, so wake up!*

Cold. Tommy's mind struggled to pull him from the depths of the nightmare. The window was open, he remembered, and a chilly breeze was caressing his sweat soaked pajamas causing him to shiver.

DEMON'S SORROW

He remembered kicking his blanket to the foot of the bed earlier as he prepared for sleep. Now he wanted that blanket desperately. The light tap-tap-tap of his teeth chattering disturbed him, the sound loud and unnerving in the night. Pulled from the depths of his nightmare, Tommy slowly opened his eyes and saw the blanket bunched up at the foot of the bed. He'd have to sit up to reach it, but that seemed like too much trouble since he was so sleepy he could hardly move. His eyes shut again.

Freezing! Nuts. His eyes opened, and in the bright moonlit room Tommy sighed. He couldn't go back to sleep; he was shivering too hard.

A hint of movement at the window. A shadow. Two red glowing dots searching. Imagination? An airplane? A star?

Tommy lay perfectly still, while the rapid-fire pulsation of his heart performed an exorcism on any lingering notions of sleep.

By moving only his eyes, Tommy was able to view the window without giving any indication that he was looking in that direction.

Ahhh! His heart dropped, he couldn't move now if he'd wanted to. Don't look; don't let it know you saw it! It's staring at me! Pretend I'm sleeping. Don't move. Play like the possum did when it thought Bruiser was going to hurt it. He couldn't stop shivering, fear adding to the cold to make his chattering teeth sound like gunfire. His mouth felt glued shut, and he desperately wanted to call Anna, but though his mouth opened, not so much as a whimper broke the silence.

Cold! Mom! Help! Gotta pee! Mom, it's gonna hurt me! M-o-o-o-m-m-m-y please!!

"Tommy?" Not a demon voice, which made it seem even worse.

Tears escaped Tommy's tightly sealed eyelids.

"Toooommyyy, Toooommyyy. Time to open your eyes, Son."

No! No! No!

"THOMAS ANDREW ROGERS! OPEN YOUR EYES THIS MINUTE! YOU LOOK AT ME WHEN I'M SPEAKING TO YOU, YOU LITTLE SHIT!"

Despite his mind screaming at him not to look, years of obedience demanded that Tommy obey. With a tiny whimper, he opened his eyes.

Instantly his mouth opened, and a long horrendous scream filled the night. Outside in his kennel, Bruiser howled and snarled as he repeatedly hurtled himself against the fencing that kept him from protecting his little master.

When Anna hit Tommy's bedroom door, she came through with so much force that the doorknob punctured the plasterboards wall. Nervously chewing her lip, Anna looked at the window; the moonlight shining into the room was bright enough that she didn't need to turn on the overhead light. In moments she had Tommy wrapped tightly against her breasts. His shivering alarmed her, he felt as though he were in the throes of a violent convolution.

"Shh! Honey, it's all right", Anna hugged him closer, fearing he'd vibrate right through her arms into the black void of night. "Shh, Tommy, it was just a nightmare, it's OK now, I'm here, you're safe. Tommy, come on honey, settle down. Shh!"

Tommy's body continued to shake uncontrollably as he tried to shake his head. "N-n-no!"

After several minutes, with Ann's help, Tommy managed to get himself under control. Then, pushing back against the headboard, he dared to look toward the bedroom window. He knew his father was out there somewhere, waiting to sneak into his room as soon as Anna went back to bed. No, not Dad, but his demon.

"You feeling better now, Tommy?"

Tommy's heart felt as if it were stuck in his throat.

"It...it was Dad, no, not Dad, his...his demon. It was outside my window, Mom! It was trying to get in!"

Taking his small cold hands in hers, Anna tried to comfort her son. "Honey, you were dreaming. We're on the second floor no one could look in your window. It's too high."

"Demons can float. They can float right up to the sky if they wanted to."

"All right," she said in a calm yet determined voice, "Tommy, this demon stuff is getting out of hand. I know it's my fault; I should have been more persistent when you were little. I want you to listen to me, OK? There is no such thing as demons. Your father isn't a demon, and there isn't one living inside him, either. When I said he could get his demon taken care of, it was just a figure of speech. I didn't mean there was a real demon. I meant that the alcohol made him do things that he wouldn't normally do. Do you understand? It was like the day I said you looked like you saw a ghost. I didn't mean that I thought you really saw a ghost, just that you looked like what I imagined someone who might see a ghost would look like. And demons aren't any more real than ghosts, and you know ghosts aren't real."

If ghosts aren't real, and demons aren't real, Tommy wondered what else in his world wasn't real. Well there are ghosts, so there must be demons, too. "Dad's demon was here!"

"You were dreaming!" Anna snapped, her frustration getting the best of her.

"Then how come Bruiser's being all weird? Was be having the same dream?" It wasn't much in the way of proof, but it was all he had, and if he couldn't convince his mother of the reality of the bogeyman, how could he protect her?

Anna suddenly realized that Bruiser was acting as if someone were out there. That's silly, there are no demons! The dog was probably carrying on because he heard Tommy screaming.

"He must have heard you screaming, and that upset him."

Calmly Tommy replied, "I'm not screaming anymore."

A sharp pounding at the kitchen door downstairs caused Tommy and Anna both to jump. Tommy grabbed Anna's arm as she began to rise from the bed. "Mom! Please don't let it in!"

"Tommy, there's someone knocking at the door. I hardly think that if there really were demons they'd have enough manners to knock, do you?"

Tommy reluctantly released her, but said, "OK, but take the gun with you, please"

"How'd you...?" Anna began, but was interrupted by another, more persistent knock. Nodding, she hurried out of the room. "All right, I'll take the gun."

Jumping from his bed Tommy hurried to watch Anna from his doorway. When she returned a couple of seconds later he nodded in relief. Anna held the dark metallic weapon in her hand. Glancing quickly at Tommy, she turned and hurried down the stairs.

Despite her belief that there were no such things as demons, Tommy's belief in them caused the small hairs on the back of Anna's arms to rise painfully. Don't be stupid, she chastised herself.

The gun was cold and heavy in her grip yet gave her a sense of confidence she knew she'd lack without the weapon. The gun had a slick reptilian feel to it, and yet it was comforting in hand, the way a snake could never be.

The pounding at the kitchen door was louder, more frantic, as though someone was being chased by the demon she didn't believe existed.

Anna flipped the switch for the kitchen light, and then moved cautiously across the white tile floor to the door. She could make out little more than a dark shape on the other side. Whoever was there stopped pounding on the door when Anna turned on the kitchen light, and now seemed content to wait patiently.

Holding the gun in front of her, Anna approached the door. "Who's there?" Her voice held strength she didn't possess, but for which she was thankful.

"Anna? It's me, Ted? Ted Jenkins from next door, are you all right?"

After hiding the gun behind her back, Anna pulled open the door. "Oh, Ted, I'm sorry we disturbed you. Tommy had a nightmare, and I guess Bruiser heard him. I'm sorry if his barking woke you."

"I wasn't sleeping. Insomnia. Bruiser did get my attention, but that's not why I'm here." Ted glanced nervously over his shoulder before he continued. "Can I come in, Anna?"

Anna stepped back to let Ted in, then closed and locked the door behind him.

Ted glanced at the gun, then at Anna, then out the kitchen window. "Someone was behind your house, Anna. I heard the dog barking, real crazy like, and I looked out to see what was making him carry on like that, because I know that other than howling sometimes he never barks. I saw someone…something…." He stopped, and stared silently into space, as though trying to make sense of what he'd seen.

"Ted? You saw someone? Where?"

"Huh? Oh, yeah, well you'll probably think I'm crazy, but I swear to you Anna, it looked like someone was looking in Tommy's bedroom window. I know it isn't possible, not unless he had a ladder, but I already checked, there isn't a ladder. As soon as he saw me he kind of…kind of…shit! It was like he was standing in an invisible elevator and it floated right down to the ground. I was already out on my deck then, and I came right over as soon as I saw him run around the other side of your house. I was afraid he'd get in, or something."

Anna was shaking so badly that she had to lean against the table for support, "Did you recognize him, Mr. Jenkins?"

From the doorway Tommy cried out, startling them both, "I told you it was Dad! His demon!"

"Tommy."

Tommy looked at Anna, then at Mr. Jenkins. "You saw him, didn't you, Mr. Jenkins? It was my dad, but it wasn't, isn't that right, Mr. Jenkins, isn't that what you saw?"

Ted didn't know what to say. It had looked like Alex Rogers out there, but there had been something wrong with the likeness. Alex Rogers? No, he didn't think so, more like something pretending to be Alex, but Ted wasn't about to admit that to anyone. Anna was the last person in the world he wanted worrying about his mental health. Anna was his dreams, his desire, and his reason for living. If he said or did anything to ruin his chances of making good on his fantasies, life wouldn't be worth living. He knew she was safe that's all that mattered. He could go home now, and spend the rest of the night, in the bathroom, remembering how the light played through the shear material of her nightgown, revealing nothing, yet suggesting a world of pleasure.

He knew they were waiting for him to say something, so he told a lie, hoping it would somehow make him appear saner than he felt, "I don't know who it was, didn't get to see him that well. I just wanted to check to make sure you were both all right. I better get home now, before Betty wakes up and finds me gone. She worries about me." He didn't want to talk about Betty, but lying made him ramble uncontrollably, "She always worries. I'm glad you have the gun, Anna. It makes me feel better knowing you can take care of yourself. If you need anything call, when I do sleep I don't sleep very soundly. Good night." He fumbled with the lock on the door as he chattered on knowing the only way he'd stop his foolish chitchat was to be gone from the witnesses of his lie.

Before he could slip through the door and disappear into the night Tommy stopped him, "Mr. Jenkins, please tell my mom who you really saw, please?"

"I'm not sure who I saw, Tommy, just a figure. Good night." He escaped through the kitchen door into the moon-dappled night. He looked hesitantly around before stepping off the deck and hurrying next door. *It's creepy out here at night. I never realized just how isolated we really are.*

"Mom?" Tommy pleaded.

Anna shook her head, "I don't know, Tommy, I just don't know." She draped her arm over his shoulder as she led him from the kitchen. He looked so defeated that it nearly broke her heart. *She would kill to protect her child, yet without knowing whom she was up against,* Anna felt angry, and frustrated, and helpless.

She led Tommy to his room. He didn't speak until she leaned down to kiss his forehead, then he whispered, "I know. Mom?"

"What, Honey?"

"How can I find out who killed Lyndsay? Even Chief Morman can't do it, so how can I? If I die will I go to heaven?"

Anna dropped to the bed beside him. *He sounded too grown-up, too full of responsibility, and defeat. Suddenly she saw before her, not a nine-year-old boy, but a very wise, very old little man.* "Don't you even think about that, you're going to live a very long time. Now go to sleep, and just think good thoughts, like about your party, and your new bike, OK?"

Sighing heavily, Tommy nodded, "I'll try. I love you, Mom."

CHAPTER 23

Karl stared into space as he rocked back and forth. The rocking chair still had blood on it, Sue's blood, but he didn't notice, or if he did, was beyond caring. The shot Doc Klein gave him hours ago was still working, and Karl's world seemed slightly off kilter. The things running through his head couldn't be right. No, the way he felt this was all just some weird sick nightmare and pretty soon he'd wake up in his chair in the living room. The television would be on and Sue and Lyndsay would be talking in excited hushed voices over some dumb thing on the X Files, the only program that neither would think of missing. He usually napped through the show, waking in time for the evening news. Sue or Lyndsay would fill him in on some of the important highlights of the night's show. He would listen, or pretend to, just to make them happy. He'd learned long ago that this was one program he didn't criticize. How he missed that stupid program.

Daddy?" Lyndsay said softly, pulling him from his thoughts.

Karl looked up slowly, the chair continued to rock back and forth, back and forth. "Hi, Baby. Have you seen your mother? I can't find her anywhere."

Lyndsay stood, moving to her father's side. The smell of blood was heavy in the air, but, when his daughter placed her hand on his shoulder, there was another odor, something unpleasant and rancid. He ignored it with the help of the drugs racing through his veins.

"Mom was with me, Dad, but the Indian came and took her away. I tried to stop her, but she's quick and sneaky. I'm sorry I couldn't help Mom, but she'll be waiting for us when we get there."

"Indian?" He remembered something about an Indian, but every time he almost grasped the thought it fluttered away.

"In your dream, Daddy, remember?"

Classy eyed, Karl looked up at Lyndsay. The stink surrounding her was so strong that even the shot wasn't keeping it completely out of his mind. He breathed through his mouth. *God, how I miss my daughter, and now with Sue gone too, what do I have to live for?*

"I want to be with you and your mother, Lyndsay. Can I do that, please?"

Lyndsay sighed, moving back to the bed where she drifted down onto the edge of the mattress. "I want us to be together, too, Daddy but I don't think the Indian will let us, not until I'm avenged." She started crying, and Karl thought his heart would rupture from grief.

"I'll find him Baby, for you I'll find him. I think it was…was Alex Rogers. When I've killed him, will you come for me?"

She studied him without speaking, as though weighing the truth of his words. Gradually a smile crawled across her face, and when she finally answered Karl remembered hearing the same excitement in her voice the year she turned ten and got the much-desired pony for her birthday. "Oh yes Daddy!"

#

Tony examined the Monopoly game he picked up for Tommy. He hoped it wasn't too old-fashioned in this age where every kid owned high-tech electronic equipment to play games on. He remembered spending many long hours playing Monopoly with his friends when he was a kid, and hoped Tommy would get some of the same pleasure out of it that he had. Besides, this was a game that could be played even when the power was out, which happened quite frequently in Whitefields.

He was tired, overly tired, and now he couldn't sleep. Every time he closed his eyes the dead cried out for justice. Whitefields was becoming a living nightmare.

He stopped out at the Abbott farm earlier, and tried to talk to Karl, but the man was so heavily sedated that most of the time he just looked through Tony as if he were a ghost. The note that Sue left for her husband was short and to the point. "Karl I'll love you always. I have to go to Lyndsay. She's confused and hurt, and I know in my heart she doesn't mean what she says. She needs my guidance. Please don't do it, or we may never be together again. I love you with all my heart and soul. Forever, Sue."

The note made Tony's skin crawl. It was obvious Sue wasn't in her right mind when she killed herself, yet some of the things she said could almost make sense if he forgot the fact that Lyndsay Abbott was dead. Lyndsay was linked to Jimmy and Cindy, but what about Dee and Jake? And what was Karl planning on doing that Sue begged him not to?

In the still of night the ringing phone sounded too loud and ominous. His stomach tightened, and he didn't want to answer it, because the only reason anyone would be calling this late was to report more bad news. This town was making Detroit look appealing. At least there he knew what was going on, where as in Whitefields nothing made sense anymore.

On the fourth ring Tony reluctantly picked up the handset. "Morman," he sighed heavily.

"Tony, it's Anna. I'm sorry for calling you so late, but something really strange just happened here, and I need to hear a friendly voice."

"I'll be right there."

"No, I don't need you to do that, I just wanted to talk to someone sane." She giggled nervously, trying to make light of the situation.

Tony leaned against the headboard, the fingers of his right hand making small circular motions at his temple where a throbbing headache seemed to originate. "You tell me what happened, then I'll decide whether or not to come over, OK?"

Twenty-five minutes later Tony was walking through Anna's front door. The headache now appeared to have no one place of origin but seemed instead to radiate from the whole frontal area of the brain. On the drive over he pictured little men running around in his brain screaming, "Melt down! Melt down! Abandon ship while you can!"

"I'm going to take a look around the house, and bring the dog in, if that's all right with you?"

Anna shrugged. "Sure. I thought about going out and getting him, but to be honest with you I was afraid to go outside by myself. Silly, huh?"

"No, not at all. As a matter of fact that was pretty sensible thinking on your part. Better to call me, that's I get paid for."

As he turned to go back outside Anna grabbed his arm. "Be careful, it's getting too weird."

#

Alex staggered into his house a little more than an hour before. He couldn't remember getting home from the shabby little bar out off 1-75, but that wasn't unusual. Many mornings he'd wake up not remembering where he'd been, or how he'd gotten home. Luckily he usually awoke in his own bed, or in bed with whichever lady he happened to be humping at the time. He often thought he must have a guardian angel watching over him, especially since some of the broads he'd been doing were married and he seemed to have a sixth sense about when their loving hubbies would return.

A loud thump echoed through his brain. Someone was in the house. Slowly his mind began to register, and, with a moan, he rolled over and tried to see the bedroom door, more accurately to focus on the person standing there watching him.

"Dee?" Part of his mind said it couldn't really be Dee standing there, because she choked to death on Jake's balls. Another part said that he was dreaming, while still another part said that this was all real and totally logical.

She moved across the room towards the bed, her hands working the buttons on the peach blouse that he got her last March for her birthday. By the time she reached the bed Dee was completely nude, and Alex was amazingly erect. He felt the bed sink beneath her weight as she slithered across it to his side. Her long magenta fingernails circled teasingly around his testicles, causing him to moan with desire.

Grabbing her by the arm, Alex pulled Dee to him, and kissed her with a passion he'd never felt before. His tongue played against her closed teeth, trying to gain the access she denied him. Instead she pushed herself up, and swung her long leg across his waist, straddling him. When she was positioned exactly over his throbbing member, she thrust herself upon him with such force that he cried out in momentary pain. She rode him as she would a fine Arabian, sitting tall and straight in the saddle, her head thrown back so her golden locks tickled the tops of his thighs. Alex jerked and shuddered, unable to contain the small cry of dismay, as his precious seed gushed into her pulsing sex. Too soon. It was a long time since he'd had sex so great that he couldn't control his climax, and now it was over and he was angry with himself. He started to pull away, but Dee was having none of it, as she clamped her legs tighter around his waist. She amazed him, it should have been at least half an hour before he got hard again, but she seemed to have some magic muscles hidden away, and within minutes she was riding high again, much to his pleasure and surprise.

He lost count of the times she was able to bring poor Mr. Happy back to life. If it weren't for the fact that he was so tired, and almost sober he might find the episode fun, but it wasn't fun any more. He was sore and tired, and he wasn't sure which hurt more, his head, stomach, or his penis. She sat up there without saying a word for what must have been hours, because he was sure the sky outside his window was taking on the first hint of daylight.

He tried to turn on his side, but immediately her legs tightened. "Enough, Baby. I can't handle any more."

Ignoring him she began working those special muscles of hers. "Dee, stop it now. I'm sore, and it really hurts."

When she made no attempt to stop Alex started getting mad. "Damn it Dee, I said enough. Now get the hell off of me."

Still she ignored him. The pain was enough to sober him completely, and, with a cry of agony, he swung out with his fist. She was quicker though, and had his wrist pinned before he made contact. His anger was full-blown as he reached up and grabbed her nipple. If she wanted pain, by God, he'd give her pain. Then she had his other wrist and slowly, with strength he never imagined, she pushed both his arms to the bed above his head, as she silently bent down to kiss him. He felt her tongue prying, trying to enter his mouth, and reluctantly he parted his clenched teeth. Her tongue felt cold and bloated as it probed deeper and deeper into his throat, causing him to gag. With all the force he could muster he shoved her away, then almost screamed when he realized she was off of him but part of her was still in his mouth. Jesus, I bit off her tongue!

Throwing his head off the edge of the bed, Alex threw-up on the floor. When he turned back to check on Dee she was gone. Gone? Of course she's gone, dumb ass, she wasn't ever here 'cause she's dead and you just had a wet dream that turned into a nightmare. Happy with this logic Alex looked around the room, just to make sure.

"Dee?" The house was silent. A dream, but what about the pain? My poor dick feels like it's going to fall off.

#

Alex crawled from the crumpled bed, and grabbed a couple old towels he saved just for this purpose. Then kneeling next to the bed began to clean up the mess on the floor.

Straining to see in the early gray light of morning the contents of his stomach looked lumpy, and very dark. There was an unpleasant, almost familiar odor, beyond the normal stink of puke. Something about that stench caused him to reach up and turn on the table lamp beside the bed.

"Jesus, what the hell did I eat last night?" Alex asked the empty room as he scooped the vile mass into a pile. With a cry of shocked disgust, he threw the towel to the floor, and backed away from the two blood red testicles. His hand instinctively dropping to cup the bruised bags dangling between his legs, his mind screamed NOT A NIGHTMARE!

Tony arrived forty-five minutes later. First Alex had tried reaching Morman at the station, only to be told by the snooty bitch that answered the phone that the Chief was out, and she didn't know where. It was shear luck that he then called Anna, because Morman just happened to be there. By that time Alex had himself in such a hysterical state that little else seemed relevant.

Tony stared at Alex in disbelief. In spite of his terror, Alex realized that Morman wasn't about to believe his story as long as he kept ranting like lunatic. So he forced himself to take a deep breath, hold it, exhale, and then start again.

Tony had hoped to get some helpful information from Alex, anything that would make sense of the bizarre deaths. Unfortunately that wasn't to be the case. What Alex said was no more logical that what had happened to Anna that night.

More to satisfy Alex than because he thought that anything useful would come of it, Tony inspected the pile of vomit on the floor. Though the odor was a bit overwhelming, the mound appeared to contain little in the way of solid substance. "Sorry, Alex, looks like a pile of regurgitated booze to me."

Alex stepped to Tony's side, then dropped to his knees and, to Tony's disgust, began searching through the vomit with his fingers.

"Jesus man," Tony snarled, backing away, "you better lay off the sauce for a while. Next thing you'll be calling to tell me there's little pink elephants in your refrigerator."

Alex jumped up, and, before Tony knew what was happening, unzipped his jeans, and dropped them to the floor. "What about this, huh? I told you Dee kept screwing me and wouldn't quit. Look at this! This is proof that Dee was here all night!"

Looking down at Alex's inflamed penis, Tony nodded. "It proves something all right. It proves that you'd better go see Doc Klein for a great big shot of penicillin. Don't know who you been 'doin', Buddy, but if I were you I'd sure as hell start practicing safe sex."

It was obvious that he wasn't going to tell him anything useful, so Tony left Alex mumbling about kinky sex with Dee, and how cold and slippery Jake's gonads felt in his mouth. The man was obviously suffering hallucinations caused by the huge quantity of booze he consumed daily. Detroit was looking better all the time.

#

CHAPTER 24

A cold wet nose against his cheek brought Tommy awake with a start, "Bruiser! How'd you get in here?" In reply the dog's huge tail whipped back and forth, knocking loudly against the wall. "All right, settle down before you knock the house apart. Come on, you gotta go potty"

The dog danced to the bedroom door, knocking a chair, a lamp, and two model cars to the floor in his excitement.

"OK, let me get my pants on." Pulling on his jeans, Tommy continued his one-sided conversation; "Mom must have let you in last night after dad's demon was here, huh? I'm surprised she went outside to get you. I sure wouldn't, at least not by myself. OK, come on." Tommy opened the bedroom door, and Bruiser raced down the stairs and was waiting anxiously at the kitchen door. As soon as Tommy opened the door the dog raced to the kennel and hiked his leg, spraying the large log propped in one corner. Tommy laughed at the silly expression on the dog's face it almost looked as though he was smiling.

As Tommy pulled the kennel gate closed, he told the dog, "You're silly, you know that?"

Bruiser uttered a Husky word or two and continued watering the log. His expression and lack of attention told Tommy that nothing was more important, nor more pleasurable at that moment than the task at hand.

Suddenly the lighthearted mood fled as Tommy's skin tightened. Turning to look over his shoulder, he searched the shadow-dappled forest. The shadows were impregnable in the early morning light, and so quiet that the very silence became a pressure against his ears. And, although he couldn't see anyone, Tommy knew he was being watched. With his eyes riveted to the forest, he took several backward steps, fearful of giving the watcher a chance to sneak up and grab him. When nothing happened after several more steps, he turned and ran to the house.

Tommy watched Bruiser from the kitchen window, but the dog showed no sign of sensing anything unusual. That should have made him feel better, but he feared the dog had gotten so use to Lyndsay's visits that he no longer forewarned her presence.

A little before nine Anna appeared. "Morning, birthday boy."

Tommy smiled, his cheeks turning a rosy hue. "Morning Mom. You let Bruiser in my room last night after I went to sleep?"

Anna took a sip of coffee before she said, "Chief Morman did."

"The Chief was here?" Tommy frowned, what had happened after he'd gone to sleep? Some protection be turned out to be, sleeping through something as important as Chief Morman's visit.

"I, ah, I thought it'd be a good idea to have him come out and take a look around, just to be on the safe side."

"Did something else happen?" Tommy was really feeling guilty, sleeping like a baby when he was supposed to be taking care of Anna.

Anna thought about the kiss that had been interrupted by Alex's phone call, and it was her turn to blush. "No, nothing happened. Tony, ah, the Chief just checked around outside to make sure no one was out there, then he brought Bruiser in the house so he could see that you were okay."

"Is the Chief still coming to my party today?" Tommy asked hopefully. Knowing the lawman was on duty last night lessened some of the guilt he was feeling. After all, the Chief's a grown man, and he has a gun, all he'd be able to do to protect his mother is scream loud. Screaming probably didn't have much effect on either a ghost, or a demon.

"As far as I know, unless something else comes up."

"Did you tell him it was Dad's demon outside last night?"

"I told him exactly what happened, what you said, and what Mr. Jenkins said. I'm pretty sure he'll be at your party today, too, because he wants to talk to Mr. Jenkins about what he saw, and I told Tony, ah,

Chief Morman that both Mr. and Mrs. Jenkins would be here. Why do you seem so anxious for him to be here?"

Tommy shrugged, trying to remain unconcerned, "I don't know, I just want lots of people to come so I'll get lots of presents. So, are you gonna let me open some of my presents now?"

"Hey, you're pretty good at that." Anna was pouring herself another cup of coffee, and looking out the window at Bruiser. The silly dog was dancing around in his kennel as though he saw Tommy hiding in the woods beyond.

"At what?"

"At changing the subject, that's what. And besides, what makes you think it's presents instead of present, as in only one present for Tommy this year?"

Tommy laughed, "'Cause I know you! You'd never get me just one lonely present. Can I open them now, huh? Please?"

"Sure. Why not."

"Tony? It's Anna. Is Alex OK?"

Tony wanted to say, "Nothing wrong with him that a shot of penicillin won't cure." Instead he said, "Yeah, he's fine, just a bit too much to drink. How about you, all quiet after I left?"

Anna chuckled, "I'm afraid the house could have blown away and I wouldn't have noticed. I died when I finally got to bed. OH! I shouldn't say that, too many people have already died. I just wanted to make sure you're still coming to Tommy's party. He keeps asking. I think he's taken a real liking to you, because it seems important to him that you be here."

"I wouldn't miss it, unless, God forbid, something else happens."

"Oh, I know what you mean. God, I hope you're here."

"Got to go Anna, got another call. See you later." He jabbed the button for the other call, "Morman."

"Chief Morman?"

"That's right, may I help you?"

"Sir, my name's Nancy, and I'm the secretary here at Porter Distributors. We've trying to locate one of our drivers all week, but haven't had any luck. I know he has one stop in your town at a place called, ah, here it is, a place called Jake's 1—4 The Road Bar? I've been trying to get hold of someone at the bar, but haven't had any luck reaching anyone. We really need to know if Steve made his delivery there on Monday. Would you have any idea how I can get a hold the owner?"

Tony had been taking notes as the woman spoke and asked, "Porter Distributors, did you say?"

She hesitated a moment then said, "That's right."

"And this driver, Steve…"

"Douglas, Steve Douglas."

Tony jotted down the name, as he offered an explanation for the missing driver, "Maybe he just quit, and didn't bother giving notice."

Soft laughter, "I certainly hope not, Chief Morman. Mr. Douglas has one of our trucks, and it was loaded to capacity. Deliveries were suppose to be made Monday and Tuesday, but I've checked with everyone on his route and, as far as we can determine, the last delivery he made was to a place called Neighbors in Lapeer. His next stop should have been in Whitefields around three o'clock Monday afternoon. I called the rest of his delivery points, but no one has seen him. I—4 The Road is the only stop I haven't been able to verify, so if you could please tell me how to reach Mr. Rhodes?"

"I'm afraid there's no way you can reach Jake, unless you know a real good medium. Mr. Rhodes is dead, but I'd like to ask you a few questions about this Steve, ah, Douglas."

#

"Mrs. Rhodes, its Chief Morman. I hate to bother you at a time like this, but I need to get into the bar, and wondered if I could stop by and pick up the key?"

"Why? Is there something else wrong?" Peggy asked, afraid of the answer, yet oddly curious at the same time.

"I don't know. Basically I just need to know if there were any beer deliveries made earlier this week."

"Oh, is that all", she said, slightly disappointed, "Well I can save you a trip anyhow. I know Jake was really pissed, because the delivery guy never showed up Monday, and Jake had to go pick up beer in Mt. Clements."

"Did the guy show up later?"

"No, he didn't. Is…do you think maybe that has something to do with Jake's, ah, Jake's murder?"

"I doubt it. The company that delivers the beer seems to have misplaced their driver, and this is where his next stop should have been. I'm checking anything out of the ordinary, Mrs. Rhodes. We'll find the person, or persons, responsible for your husband's death. How are you doing?"

"Pretty good. The women from the church have been very kind, and they're helping me cope. The worst time is late at night when I think I hear Jake come in, then lay there waiting for him to sneak into the bedroom, but of course he never does."

"I'm sorry."

"Oh, don't be sorry, it wasn't your fault. Jake wasn't exactly what you'd call a good Christian man, but still he didn't deserve to die like that. No one would. Only some kind of monster could do what's being done to the people in town. Reverend Kent says that the Devil's minions walk among us, and I'm beginning to believe him. I hear the State Police have a similar nickname for Whitefields.

"Well, Chief, if there's anything else I can do for you, please feel free to call."

#

Sandy reached out, snapping at the moth that practically landed on the tip of his nose, and only by sheer luck did he manage to catch the insect. His tough little jaws clamped tightly while he waited for the bug to die, because he didn't trust his reflexes, and was afraid the only tidbit he'd had to eat in days would fly away. He was beyond exhaustion, beyond sore. His tiny toenails were worn completely off, and nothing remained of his feet but a mass of bloody tissue, yet the being insisted he keep moving. He felt her presence and quickly gulped down the moth.

"This is your destiny, little one. This is where the past seven years have led you. Soon your life will belong to you and you alone, and never again will there be voices commanding you do their bidding. First you must fulfill quest. It is very important.

"The destiny of Whitefields has already been written, but it has two endings. One good, the other…well, just know that if the second ending happens you won't have to worry any longer about reaching the end of you pilgrimage, because there'll be none left to save. Now hurry on your way, please."

Sandy watched as the being drifted slowly away into the dense forest. He didn't understand her words, but the images she put into his head had him scurrying off before she's completely vanished.

#

Tommy balanced a bowl of potato salad in one hand, and in the other a large bowl of chips, as he hurried out into the sunshine. It was finally his birthday. He hoped that neither Lyndsay nor the Indian would make an appearance to ruin the party. All his friends from school were coming, even his best friend Billy, who was suppose to be grounded for two weeks. Billy's mom wasn't going to let him come, but Anna talked to her, and, to Tommy's surprise, she changed her mind. Tommy thought a two-week ground was pretty stiff punishment for Billy, because all he'd done was pull stupid Carrie's jeans down to her knees. It wasn't like anyone saw anything except the silly mermaid underpants she had on, but she'd screamed and cried so much that Billy got grounded. At least he gets to come to my party. Please God, please don't let Lyndsay or the Demon ruin the party!

Bruiser grumbled in his kennel, causing Tommy to look up and laugh as he put the bowls on the picnic table. "Oh, don't complain. You look really cute with that big ol' bow around your neck, and like Mom said, it matches your eyes."

Bruiser shook his bead violently, twisting the bow around so it hung beneath his chin. Tommy laughed even harder, and Bruiser turned away from him, moving to the side of the kennel that faced the forest. There he plopped his butt down and stared off into the woods, ignoring Tommy.

"Ah, don't pout Bruiser. I'll take it off just as soon as I can. We don't want to disappoint Mom, do we?"

Pretending he hadn't heard Tommy, Bruiser watched a flock of sparrows swarm from one maple to another. Tommy shrugged, knowing that as soon as the kids got here Bruiser would forget all about the humiliating blue bow.

Just as he was getting ready to hurry back into the kitchen to see what else he could do to help Anna, Tommy heard a car coming down the drive. A grin spread across his face when he saw Chief Morman emerge from his squad car. Morman was carrying a brightly wrapped package decorated with colorful clown faces.

"Hi!" Tommy called, pretending he didn't notice the gift.

"Hey, Guy, happy birthday." Morman replied, handing Tommy the present.

Tommy was flustered, as he always seemed to be when someone he didn't know well gave him a present, or a compliment. Shy and embarrassed he muttered a quick thank you, remembering to add the appropriate "Sir", before leading Tony around the house to the kitchen door.

Tony, his arm draped across Tommy's shoulders, said, "Why don't you call me Tony? Or, if that makes you uncomfortable, you can just call me Chief, OK?"

As they walked Tommy tried shaking the present without being obvious, but when Tony asked Tommy to call him either Tony or Chief, the gift was momentarily forgotten. To call Chief Morman 'Chief' made Tommy feel grown up already.

"Mom's in the kitchen, Sir, huh, I mean, Chief. Come on, but I have to warn you, she'll probably put you to work."

As promised, Anna soon had both of them carrying loads of dishes and bowls out to the picnic table. Tony enjoyed himself more than he could ever remember. He felt good, no great, almost like he was really a part of the family.

By the time the kids started arriving the yard resembled a small carnival. There were balloons everywhere, and horseshoes, croquet, badminton, and volley ball games littered the lawn. There was even a Pin The Tail On The Donkey game, which Tommy insisted was a baby game, but Anna enjoyed, tacked to the back of the garage.

Mr. and Mrs. Jenkins waited until the kids began arriving before coming over. Tommy figured they must have looked out their window and saw all the work Anna was making him and the Chief do, and decided to wait until it was all done before arriving. Tommy didn't blame them he would have stayed away until all the work was done too, given the chance.

Billy was the first kid to arrive, and Tommy couldn't wait to show him the new bike and the computer game that Mom got him.

This is going to be the best day of my life! Tommy thought. The only thing that could make it any better is if Carrie doesn't come. The doorbell rang, and there stood Carrie, her cheeks reddening as fast as her smile faded when she saw Billy at Tommy's side.

After the first hour Tommy stopped glancing nervously toward the forest. He figured that Lyndsay and the demon either thought it would be really tacky if they ruined his birthday party, or they were afraid of the Chief, as he hoped they'd be. Whatever the reason, they stayed away, and the party was still going strong when the sun went down, at which time Anna turned on the outside lights along with the Christmas tree lights she'd had Tommy drag down from the attic, and string in the trees around the house. He had to admit it really did look awesome with the twinkle lights glittering like captured stars among the tree branches.

Some of the parents began arriving to pick up their kids about eight, and even though Tommy was tired, he was sad that such a perfect day should have to end. This must be what Chief Morman meant about not having a care in the world, Tommy sighed. If only it could stay just like this forever.

The Chief left shortly after eight, thanking Tommy for inviting him to 'the best party I've ever been to.' Tommy beamed, remembering to thank him again for the Monopoly game.

Mr. and Mrs. Jenkins got ready to leave, and Tommy smiled happily as he thanked Mrs. Jenkins for the neat hash she brought, and for the dog grooming kit they gave him.

By nine it was just him and Billy, whose mother had, beyond belief, agreed to let spend the night! The boys played computer games until midnight then sat talking in Tommy's room about everything from Carrie's fishy underpants to frying ants with sunshine and a magnifying glass. Tommy didn't want to talk about Lyndsay, not even mention her name, fearing she'd somehow think she'd been summoned.

"So Man, how come your mom let Bruiser sleep in your room?" Billy asked as he rubbed Bruiser's ear. Billy was slightly taller than Tommy, and outweighed him by twenty-five pounds; he wasn't fat, just solidly built. His reddish brown hair was cut in a really neat style that Anna wouldn't let Tommy have. It was really short everywhere except for a little tail that hung down Billy's back, which some of the older boys called a 'homo-handle'.

Tommy shrugged. "I don't know, maybe 'cause it's my birthday."

"Oh. I thought that maybe it was because you found that girl in the forest. Like maybe your mom thought whoever murdered her was going to try and get you too."

Tommy didn't like the turn the conversation was taking and quickly turned it onto another topic that was almost as bad, but would, he hoped, get Billy's mind off of Lyndsay.

"Nah, I think it's because of my dad being such a butt-head."

Billy's hazel eyes widened, "Wow, how can you say that after be gave you that neat bike?"

Feeling guilty for sounding ungrateful put Tommy on the defensive. "Ah, he only got it for me to make up for throwing me into the wall. It you put all the good things Dad did in one pile, and all the bad things in another pile, the bad pile would reach to the moon, but the good pile wouldn't be any taller than...than your dick."

"Oh yeah? Bite me jerk. Mine's bigger than yours!"

"Is not!"

"Is too!"

"Bet! Come on, I'll prove it!"

"Hey! Stop it! Let go of my shorts, Homo! Get him Bruiser! Help!"

Anna opened the door after knocking once, "OK Boys, time to settle down. You want the neighbors to call the police and report a riot over here? What on earth are you doing anyhow?"

Red faced, both boys said at the same time, "Nothing."

Anna shook her head. "Well, I'm going to bed. It's after two, and it's been a long day. You can stay up for a little longer, as long as you keep it down, got it?"

After Anna pulled the door closed Billy whispered, "Your mom's really cool. No way would my mother let us stay up this late. And your mother never grounds you."

"I never do anything wrong," Tommy smirked.

"You ass-wipe! You just never get caught." Billy giggled. "How about hanging over the roof at school and peeking into the girl's shower, huh? How about the time you put chalk in the powdered creamer in the teacher's lounge? How about the time . .."

Giggling so hard he could hardly talk, Tommy said, "OK, OK! You win, I'm just lucky."

Billy was shushing him when something moved outside the bedroom window, catching his attention. "What was that?" He rose from the bed moving across to the open window. The night was black and still, and nothing moved in the darkness except the branches of the pine right outside.

Bruiser was rumbling deep in his throat, and Tommy felt a cold clammy sweat break out on his face. "Get away from there, Billy!"

Billy spun around. Tommy's voice sounded strange, like he was having trouble breathing. "What was it?"

Swallowing his fear, Tommy managed a weak, "I don't know. Let's go to bed before Mom comes back in. Close the window, and lock it, Billy, OK?"

Turning back to the window Billy did as his best friend asked, quickly scanning the yard where be thought, just for a moment, he saw someone, or something, run into the forest.

Billy jumped into the bed next to Tommy, "OK Man, what's going on? Who was that out there?"

Bruiser quieted and lay with his head resting on his front paws staring at the window. Tommy shook his head. "It wasn't anyone, Billy. Trust me, OK?"

"But…"

"Please! You're my best friend, you and Bruiser, and I don't want anything bad to happen to you. I'll tell you when it gets over, promise."

Billy shrugged. Normally he wouldn't let Tommy get away with something like this, but for some reason, his instincts told him to drop it, so he did.

"Want me to turn off the light, Tommy?"

Tommy glanced at the window. He knew whoever had been outside the window could see in really well if the light was on in the bedroom, but on or off didn't really matter with the things that came visiting him at night.

"Doesn't really matter, Billy. If you want it on, leave it, or turn if off, it's up to you 'cause it doesn't much matter either way."

"Great," Billy mumbled, leaving the light on.

#

Anna was exhausted, but couldn't sleep. She listened to the soft whispering from the boy's room, and it made her feel good. Tommy's party was a success, and it made her want to cry with joy while she watched him playing and having more fun than he'd had in ages, with his friends. He needed it, no, she thought, he deserved it. The poor kid had known nothing put fear his whole life, and it was time to end it. Time for Tommy to be like Tony said he was at that age, "not a care in the world."

After a few excited whispers the boys finally settled down, and Anna listened to the silence of the night. The only sounds surrounding them were the sounds of spring.

She yawned and stretched, snuggling deeper into the pillow. Thank you Lord for a perfect day, she thought as her eyes drifted closed.

"Anna."

Every nerve in her body came alive as her eyes sprung open. Trying to swallow with a throat that was dry as the Sahara, Anna turned her head toward the window. Nothing's there. *It was just my imagination, or the boys talking.*

Goose bumps tightened the skin on her legs to the point of actual pain. Her mouth stretched open in a silent scream, as she backed off the bed. Never before in her life was she so frightened she literally couldn't scream, and it was a feeling she never wanted to have again. Gasping for breath, unaware that she'd even been holding it she jerked open the bedroom door and fell into the hall.

Bruiser was howling in Tommy's room, and both boys, with Bruiser in the lead, burst from Tommy's room.

"Mom! Mom!" Tommy cried hurrying to help his mother. Wrapping his arms around her and pulling her close he appeared the adult and she the child.

"What is it, Mrs. Rogers? What happened?" Billy cried, looking nervously toward Anna's closed bedroom door, expecting it to crash open any moment and some horrible bogeyman to rush out and rip them all apart.

Bruiser was growling and scratching at Anna's door, trying to get in, when he suddenly froze and cocked his head, listening to the dense silence. Then, with a snarl, eighty-five pounds of black and white fur disappeared down the stairs. They beard him running through the house from the kitchen door in the back to the front door, and back, again and again. Anna was amazed that the loving docile animal was capable of making such a ferocious sound, and hoped that whoever was down there was smart enough to stay outside away from the crazed animal.

Tommy still had his arms around Anna, and Billy had moved in so he too could be wrapped in their protective embrace. They remained huddled together as Bruiser thundered through the downstairs.

After several minutes, which seemed a lot longer, Bruiser was suddenly quiet. They tried, but couldn't even hear the sound of his nails on the kitchen tile anymore. Tommy was getting scared what if something happened to Bruiser? Just as he started to rise to go check on him, the dog appeared at the top of the stairs. Bruiser looked at the three with their arms protectively encircling each other, then hurried to them. He happily licked and nudged until they found the strength to get to their feet.

Billy was still crying, demanding that Anna call his mother to come and get him. Anna hesitated; she didn't want Billy afraid to spend the night with Tommy. God only knew that Tommy didn't need any more stress in his life. No, she had to do something to put Billy's mind at ease.

"Mom?" Tommy asked, wondering what Anna was going to do about Billy.

Anna nodded, her mind made up, and she lied. If twisting the truth would keep Billy here with Tommy, then she'd lie until God struck her dead. "Billy, it's OK, really. I had a nightmare. I fell asleep, and I had a really stupid nightmare, and it scared me, then, when I woke up, I thought it was real. You've had nightmares like that, haven't you?"

Billy looked up through tear-soaked lashes. "If it was just a nightmare, then how come Bruiser got all weird and crazy like that?"

Thinking fast Anna replied, "He was probably sleeping too, and when I screamed I scared him, and he thought someone was trying to get in the house."

"Sure Billy, Bruiser's the best watchdog in the whole world. He'd never let anything, ah, anyone in the house. He'd tear them apart first. Bruiser wouldn't let anybody hurt us, huh boy?" Tommy ruffled the dog's fur.

Billy looked back at Anna. "A nightmare?"

"Yep. And I'll bet you thought only kids have nightmares."

Still not totally convinced, Billy asked Tommy, "What about what I saw at your window earlier?"

Tommy shrugged, "What did you see at the window?"

"You know darn well, 'cause you said I didn't want to know!"

Grinning, Tommy chided, "Gee Billy, can't you take a joke? You should know by now when I'm kidding."

After a little more persuasion Billy finally agreed to stay. He'd known Tommy since they were little kids, and Tommy was right, Billy did know him well enough to know when he was kidding, and he knew Tommy had not been kidding, but he didn't want to think about it anymore. He wanted to believe their story, to believe it hadn't happened, that he hadn't seen a face with red glowing eyes peeking in Tommy's window, that there hadn't been some thing, trying to look human, running into the forest. No, it was much better to believe Mrs. Rogers had a nightmare and screamed, which frightened Bruiser, although he didn't remember bearing her scream. Much better to pretend that Tommy had been teasing him about the thing at the window; otherwise he might never feel safe closing his eyes again.

#

CHAPTER 25

With a heavy sigh Tony nestled his head into the thick down pillow on his bed. He couldn't believe his good fortune. A whole day passed without someone dying or being murdered. Tommy's birthday party was a huge success and for the first time since he'd know him, the boy actually appeared to be having fun.

The memory of his afternoon with Anna made him feel warm all over. The only dark shadow the whole day was Ted Jenkins. The way he continually caught the man glaring at him made Tony wonder what was going on in the neighbor's mind. Was he a friend of Alex's and felt honor bound to watch over Anna? Or was he interested in her? That was silly, the man was old enough to be her father, so why the animosity?

Thankfully Alex showed enough common sense to stay away from the boy's party. That was the last thing Tommy needed, Tony was sure. The best thing that could happen to Anna and Tommy is if Alex Rogers disappeared from their lives.

Tony reached that place between sleep and waking when the telephone rang, causing him to jump. "Shit, I knew it was too good to be true."

"Morman."

"Tony?"

At the hushed sound of Anna's voice Tony sat up on the side of the bed, sleep now a distant memory.

"Anna, what is it? What's wrong?"

Anna hesitated she'd only called to hear his voice, which always ease her jangled nerves. She did such a good job of convincing Billy that everything was just dandy that she almost convinced herself. All she needed now was the strong reliable voice of Tony Morman to smooth away any rough edges she missed.

"I just…did I wake you?" she asked, just realizing it was after three in the morning. "I'm sorry, I didn't realize it was so late. I shouldn't have called."

"It's fine, Anna. I told you to call me anytime of the day or night, I meant it, now please tell me what happened out there."

Embarrassed at having called, Anna tried to shrug it off. "Nothing. I just, ah, I had a nightmare, and it scared the boys and me. They're fine now, back in bed, and I hope sleeping peacefully. I'm just being silly, Tony. I'm really sorry about calling so late. Why don't you go back to sleep? I'll talk to you tomorrow."

"Anna", he said sternly, "tell me what happened. There's no way I could possibly sleep now knowing something happened and you won't tell me."

Reluctantly Anna told him what happened.

She ended saying, "I had to have been dreaming, and my subconscious remembered Tommy's nightmare from last night."

"Maybe, but how do you explain Bruiser?"

"I scared him," she added weakly.

Tony thought for a moment then said, "So now the dog's psychic? You said you were so scared you couldn't scream, remember? So if you didn't scream, and you and the dog both ended up in the hall at the same time how did he know you were having a nightmare?"

"Doggy intuition?" she tried to joke, embarrassed and upset that she'd called him like a child afraid of the dark.

"Yeah right, and I'm Superman. Anna, I'm coming out."

"No, please, really Tony, everything is fine now, and just hearing your voice makes me feel better. If anything else happens I'll call you right away, and you can come running, or rather you can come flying, Superman. Deal?"

"I suppose, but you make sure you call me the minute anything, anything at all happens, promise?"

"Promise. Thanks Tony."

"For what?"

"Just for being there for me. Good night."

Tony lay staring at the ceiling for a long time after hanging up with Anna. His heart was beating so loud it was the only sound he heard in the silent bedroom.

She likes me, he kept thinking over and over feeling more like a schoolboy than ever.

\#

Anna fluffed her pillow without opening her eyes. If there were a face at her window she didn't want to see it again. She felt bad for waking Tony just because she'd had a nightmare. I'm such a baby, he'll probably think I'm one of those silly women who gets frightened at every little noise. At least he hadn't laughed at her, and that was something. If I'm going to be a woman alone I've got to learn to be more mature, and stop freaking out every time Tommy or I have a nightmare! She shivered, wishing she'd pulled the blanket over her, but it was folded across the end of the bed. All she had over her thin nightgown was just a sheet. She wanted to reach down and pull the blanket up, but the little girl hidden

deep within wouldn't let her muster up the courage to perform even that little act of bravery.

\#

"Tommy?" Billy whispered.

"Huh?"

"There's something spooky going on, isn't there?"

"Go to sleep, Billy."

"We're best friends, Tommy. You're not suppose to keep secrets from me."

"Go to sleep Billy because we are best friends."

\#

Ted stubbed out his cigarette. He'd been chain smoking ever since nine o'clock when they got home from Anna's. It pissed him off, because he'd been trying to quit smoking and had been down to five cigarettes a day. Now he'd have to start all over.

"Damn that cop," he hissed. He saw the way Morman and Anna kept looking at each other, and it made him want to throw up. Who the hell did Morman think he was anyhow? For Christ sake didn't he realize that Anna was still legally married to that asshole Alex? Maybe Morman got his jollies sniffing around married women.

Betty hadn't helped the situation either going on and on about how cute Anna and Morman were together. That's when Ted dragged out the hidden pack of Camels. Six hours later the pack held only two cigarettes. Just let Betty say one damn thing to me about it too. I dare her!

A little while ago the lights came on in the upstairs of the Rogers house, and he heard that crazy dog barking and snarling like a wild banshee. If he hadn't been so angry with Anna for making a fool out of herself over that stupid cop he might have gone over to see what was wrong as he had done the night before. Now he figured if she needed help she could just call Morman and let him come out in the middle of the night. Besides, after last night he wasn't too crazy about being outside with the weird shit going on over there.

He tried earlier to draw Anna into his fantasy only to have Morman keep appearing. Talk about a turn off, for Christ sake! That cop sure had a way of being where he wasn't wanted.

#

The house was dark except for a single low-wattage bulb glowing in Lyndsay's room, and that's where Karl, rocking slowly back and forth, and staring into space. How could someone's world be turned so totally upside down in such a short period of time?

He and Sue worked most of their lives together to have the beautiful life they shared with their daughter only to have it all ripped away like the delicate fluff of a dandelion on a spring breeze. He never realized just how easily all his hopes and dreams could be destroyed. One senseless act in a matter of moments could tumble years of hard work and love. One moment you have the world by the ass, the next moment your life is a sewer.

What was the point? Why bother to go on? Reverend Kent told him it was God's will, and that it wasn't our place to question God, but Karl just couldn't find it in his heart to forgive, not God, not the murderer, and not even Sue. How could she do this to him? How?

She couldn't have loved him as she claimed, or she wouldn't so easily have placed that butcher knife against her own throat to leave him without a second thought.

"Damn you Sue! Damn you to hell for leaving me like this! I meant nothing to you. How could you just up leave me? You said you loved me, you lied, you lied, you lied," he sobbed into the gloom.

He reached down to the floor beside the rocker and picked his twelve-gage shotgun. The barrel was cold and slippery, and the scent of oil was pleasant. He held it close and inhaled, and the oil blanketed the rancid odor of blood and death in the room. Memories of his childhood flashed through his mind. He remembered his first gun when he was ten. He'd felt so grown up walking through the woods with his father, looking for the deer that would mark his step into manhood. It all came back, and Karl wished he could go back to that time and be that child again.

"No more! I can't take anymore!" he shouted into the still night, as he placed the shotgun between his knees. He already removed his boots earlier, and now worked his big toe into the trigger hold.

"DADDY!"

Karl jumped three inches off the rocker, almost firing the gun in the process.

"Lyndsay?" Sue told him their daughter came to her in this room, but he hadn't believed her, thought it was just Sue's way of dealing with the terrible grief. Now here she was standing in front of him. Maybe Sue was crazy and that's why she killed herself. Now he was crazy too. Having his dead daughter appear to him in dreams, like she had yesterday when the drugs controlled his mind, was one thing, this was something else. The scent of her perfume cloaked him, as it overwhelmed the stench of suicide.

I must have sprayed it in the room, and just don't remember, just like Sue used to.

"Hi Dad, whatcha doing with that gun?"

"You're not really here, are you? I've lost my mind, and I'm imagining you. I want you with me so badly that I'm making all this up in my mind just like your mother did, right?"

Lyndsay laughed. "I'm here for you Daddy, just like I was for Mom. She told me you didn't believe her when she said I came visiting. Oh, I want to thank you too, for the shrimp. You remembered how much I loved them."

Resigned to the fact that he'd gone completely crazy, Karl decided to take advantage of the situation and enjoy his daughter's company. So what if she'd dead. Who knows, maybe I'm dead too. Maybe I really did pull the trigger and I'm sitting here with my brains splattered all over the wall behind me.

"But Lyndsay, you didn't eat the shrimp we brought you."

"Don't be silly Daddy," Lyndsay teased. "I'm a ghost, and everyone knows ghosts can't eat. But it was the thought that counted, and I really appreciated that."

Karl nodded. "OK, I'm game. You're a ghost, so your mother must be a ghost too, right? Tell her I want to talk to her."

Sadly Lyndsay shook her head. "I can't, Dad. Mom's not a ghost. She's completely gone. The Indian woman grabbed Mom as soon as she killed herself, and pulled her through that scary-looking tunnel she's always trying to force me into."

Karl was confused. He couldn't understand what Lyndsay said. Sue said she was going to kill herself so she could be with Lyndsay, to guide the girl. Now Lyndsay told him Sue's death was for nothing? How could that be? This was his delusion, so why wasn't it going his way? Karl squeezed his eyes together, trying to change the situation.

Lyndsay laughed, breaking into his thoughts. "I'm really here, Daddy. I can't leave until I'm avenged. The Indian says it's an ancient law here in Whitefields."

"Lyndsay, I'm sorry, but I don't have the slightest idea what you're talking about. What Indian?"

"Oh Daddy, you remember. The one in your dream, you know."

Karl shivered at the memory. He didn't want to think about that dream. "So you really are just a figment of my imagination. How else could you know about my dreams?"

Smiling she said, "You were easier to reach in your dreams. Mom was easy. She believed right away so I didn't have to resort to dream enlightening. I know you, you never believed anything you couldn't see, hear, taste, or feel so, well, the dream."

Karl was becoming angry. "Well I'll tell you right now young lady, I don't appreciate having my dreams messed with, and I'll thank you not to do it again!"

"Oh good, that must mean you don't plan on killing yourself with that old shotgun after all. I'm glad to hear that, because you really do have something more important to take care of for me, remember?"

"I remember. You're the one who can't remember. How am I suppose to avenge you when no one knows who's guilty?"

"I'd check Alex Rogers if I were you, like you told me yesterday."

Karl blinked. "Goddamn, I thought that bastard was the one, but I just couldn't be sure." Looking at his daughter he asked, "Are you sure? You definitely remember him as the one who…you know."

Lyndsay nodded slowly. Karl pushed from the rocker, shotgun in hand, and headed out of the room. "I'll get him for you, Honey. By God that man's as good as dead now!"

Lyndsay smiled as her father slammed through the kitchen door. "And if he's not the one it's OK too, 'cause I don't like the things he's done to my little friend Tommy, so either way Alex Rogers death will be a good thing."

Turning toward the back of the bedroom, Lyndsay smiled at a shadow slightly darker than the others in the room, "Right, Mother dear?"

#

CHAPTER 26

The front of 1—4 The Road swam in and out of focus as Alex stared at it. A nearly empty bottle of Black Velvet nestled between his legs. He'd been sitting there looking at the bar for hours, remembering. Some of his fondest memories were associated with the place. He could almost see Dee laughing and teasing one customer or another. All his friends came to Jake's, his only friends in this town. Many nights he'd meet Tom and Nick, and they'd drink so much that Alex would remember little, or nothing of the evening's festivities. If he woke the next morning in his own bed with his mouth tasting like the inside of a septic tank, and his head feeling as though it would explode at the slightest sound, Alex knew he'd had a good time the night before.

He was really going to miss the place. In ways it was more home to him than the house he'd shared with Anna and Tommy. He'd definitely had more fun here than he ever had at home. 1—4 The Road had offered him everything he needed, companionship, entertainment, and love.

He sighed heavily, his vision so blurred that he wasn't sure if the things he thought he saw were real or imagined. Dee stood in the dark doorway motioning for him to come in and join the fun. In his drunken state he could almost forget she was dead and would never again enjoy the nights of passion they so often shared. Although he was still so sore from the wild sex they'd enjoyed the night before that sexual pleasures were the farthest things from his mind as Dee continue to beckon.

"Oh Baby, I'm sure going to miss the hell out of you," he told the image. "You would have loved Florida. Shit, Dee, why'd you have to go and get yourself killed?"

Headlights suddenly swept across the front of the closed bar, erasing the carefully honed image of Dee from his eyes. Swearing at the intrusion,

Alex twisted in his seat to see who dared to interrupt his mourning. He didn't want company, unless it was one of the guys come to pay their own respect. That would be nice because he all of a sudden felt very lonely, and alone. By squinting against the glare of the headlights Alex could just make out the shape of a pickup truck. Tom has a truck, he thought hopefully. The truck pulled up close, the headlights shining right in Alex's face on the driver's side. Without warning the driver switched the beams from low to high, effectively blinding him.

Alex rolled down his window, and called out, "Hey, Man! Turn off the damned lights, you idiot, you tryin' to blind me?"

Whoever was in the truck ignored his plea as the door opened and a tall figure got out. Must be Tom. The figure reached back into the truck for something, and Alex hoped Tom brought a bottle too, as his own was now a dead soldier. Might not turn out to be such a bad night after all, a little reminiscing, a little companionship, and a lot of booze.

As the man stepped into the glow of the truck's headlights Alex instantly sobered. It wasn't Tom, and that was no bottle he was carrying!

"Jesus Christ!" Alex screamed, as he dropped the keys in his panic to start his car. The first shot took out the rear driver's side window, and, if Alex hadn't ducked, it would have taken off his head.

"What the hell's the matter with you Abbott? You are fucking nuts? Look at what you did to my damned car!"

Karl was about ten feet from Alex's car when he aimed and fired a second shot, taking out the rear passenger window. He didn't want to kill Alex, not yet, not this quickly. Alex Rogers had to suffer, suffer like Lyndsay had.

"Get out of the car, Rogers," Karl spoke softly, and Alex knew then that the man had finally gone over the edge.

Alex fumbled with the handle, and managed to fall out of the car onto the gravel drive when he finally got the door opened. Determined not to let Karl see that he was frightened, Alex pulled himself to his feet, carefully stepping around the shattered Black Velvet bottle that had tumbled from the car with him.

"Christ, Karl, what the hell's wrong with you? You're going to jail, man, you know that? Look what you did, you fucking jerk!" Although

Alex knew the last thing he wanted to do was to anger Karl, he couldn't stop his mouth from spitting out every insult that came to mind.

Without uttering a work Karl stepped closer until the barrel of the shotgun rested against the tip of Alex's nose. "You're probably right, Alex Rogers, I most certainly will go to jail, but not for shooting up your car. No, certainly not for shooting your car."

"Hey man, come on. Put the gun down," Alex said, wishing that he felt as confident as he sounded, "and we'll forget the whole thing, OK?"

"A little late for forgetting, wouldn't you say, Alex?"

Alex saw the glazed look in Karl's eyes, and knew that he was in ton of trouble. Karl was crazy; there was no doubt about that. The loss of his daughter, and then his wife had obviously sent Karl over the edge, and now for some insane reason he decided Alex was the enemy.

Alex had to reason with Karl, make him realize he was making big mistake. "Look Karl, ah Mr. Abbott, let's talk about this, OK? I mean really, why would you want to do this to me? What did I ever do to you?"

The muscles in Karl's jaws twitched. "You tortured and raped my daughter, I'd say that was reason enough, wouldn't you?"

Alex's mouth gaped. His chest tightened. He couldn't breath.

"Ain't you going to deny it, Rogers?" Karl asked coldly.

"Karl, I swear to God," Alex cried, his voice barely a whisper, "I never touched your daughter! Who…why? Why would you think that I…I swear you got the wrong guy!"

"You're the one."

Alex braced himself against his car to keep from falling.

"No! I never, ever even looked at your daughter. She was just a kid, for Christ sake. I…who told you it was me? Was it that cop?"

"Lyndsay."

"Huh?"

"Lyndsay told me it was you."

Karl was still holding the shotgun, but it was no longer kissing Alex's nose, instead it now rested heavily against his chest. Both hammers, Alex saw, were cocked and ready to fire.

"Karl, please! Listen to yourself! Lyndsay is dead, she didn't tell you anything, 'cause if she had she sure as hell wouldn't be telling you that I was the one that killed her. She'd know better. She would tell you who really killed her!"

"She did."

"No, by God, she did not!"

Karl swayed slightly when he replied, "She said I was to avenge her. I asked who done it, and she said 'Alex Rogers'. That pretty much sounds to me like she was saying that you were the one who picked her up that night then raped her, beat her, and left her all alone in a blizzard to freeze to death."

"Karl, please, listen to me. Dead people don't come back and talk to you. If Lyndsay really did talk to you, then you'd know that I didn't do what you said. I was with Dee Clark the night Lyndsay was killed."

"Ah-huh, and who's your witness? Dee Clark? Or, maybe it's Jake, huh? Doesn't it seem a little too coincidental that neither of them is around to deny your alibi? No matter how you look at it Alex Rogers, all fingers point to you. Not only for my Lyndsay's death, but for those two." He nodded toward the bar. "God says 'An Eye For An Eye,' and that's what my Lyndsay says too.

"You been nothing but a pain in the ass for everyone since the day you were born. Nothing but trouble for your parents, rest their souls, who never did a wrong thing to anyone. Then you turned your foul evil on your nice young wife and your sweet little boy. You're evil Alex Roger, always was.

"Lyndsay says you're the one. She wouldn't lie!"

Alex was near tears, the brave front as shattered as the Black velvet bottle beneath his feet. "Please Karl, for the love of God, you've got to believe me, I didn't do it!"

#

Anna looked down at her old Smith Corona typewriter. She knew every inch of the machine from the broken return bar to the slightly worn letter "e." It had been a friend for more years than she cared to remember, yet now she hesitated to even touch the keys. It wasn't so much the typewriter that frightened her as the memory of the last time she sat at that very spot and sent Sandy out into the world only to discover Tommy and Bruiser.

"Just do it! For Christ sake it's only a typewriter. It's not going to bite you."

She decided to try writing that morning, because Billy and Tommy were out front riding Tommy's new bike, and she knew even if her mind blanked out on her she wouldn't see Tommy in any trouble.

Lightly running her fingers across the keys sent an unwelcome chill up her spine.

"I can't do it, damn it! This is so stupid! I'm acting like a two-year-old."

Forcefully placing her fingers on the keys she held them in place. She sat that way for several minutes then shaking her head pushed away from the table.

It was a warm sunny day, and she heard Tommy and Billy laughing out front. Its too nice of a day to spend it sitting at a silly old typewriter.

Outside she held Bruiser's lead as she and the dog watched the boys ride up and down the driveway.

#

"Morman."

"Chief, this is Peggy Rhodes. I was just out to the bar, and I wondered if you knew of any reason for Alex Rogers' car to be there?"

Tony swallowed a mouthful of coffee, almost choking. "Rogers' car is at the bar? Did you see Alex?"

"No, just his car. I went out to get Jake's books, and noticed his car sitting out front.

Chief, ah, it looks like someone shot out the windows, and there was a broken whiskey bottle on the ground next to the driver's door. I don't know what's going on, but it looks like more trouble."

"All right, Mrs. Rhodes, I'll check it out. Thanks."

He slammed his fist down on the desk, "Shit."

Sally, hearing the commotion, poked her head around the corner, saw the look on Tony's face, and quickly popped back to her desk. Don't even ask, she told herself.

Tony stomped past, and she didn't look up when he said, "I'll either be back shortly or I'll call in. Shit."

As the door closed behind the Chief, Sally looked up. She used to really like her job, but now she dreaded leaving home in the morning. With all the weird things going on she wanted nothing more than to lock all her doors and windows and hide until things were back to normal.

The phone rang, and she toyed very seriously with not answering it, she just didn't want to hear anymore bad news. She longed for the peaceful little town that she loved so much.

#

Tony walked around the car slowly. Peggy was right about the windows being shot out, but who had done the shooting, and why? And where was Alex Rogers now? He'd been trying to reach Alex all morning, wanting to ask him if he'd been at Anna's the night before sneaking around outside.

He was excited when he found two spent twelve-gauge casings about ten or twelve feet from Alex's car. At last clues! A real honest-to—God clue. No body stuck on a tree, no ball-less man or, ball-choked woman. This time whoever done the shooting had left real, honest to God, clues.

"I can handle this." Tony smiled. "At least this is real! This is something I can touch, something I can figure out."

Reaching through his car window, Tony grabbed his mike. "Sally?"

After a couple seconds Sally answered.

"Sally, I want you to call Anna Rogers and find out if she's heard from or seen Alex today."

"You want me to get back to you, Chief?"

"No, I'll wait."

A couple of minutes later Sally reported back, "There's no answer out there, Chief. You want me to keep trying"

Tony's first reaction was to panic, but he thought it over a few seconds and decided that there was any number of possible reasons for Anna not to answer the telephone. "Yeah, keep trying. Anything else I need to know?"

"Bill called. He's sending the…people back for burial. Said to let you know, and if you have any questions to give him a call."

"OK, Sal, I'm going to be away from the car for a few minutes. I've got Alex Rogers' car here, and it's been shot up pretty good, but so far there's no sign of Alex. Call the guys, and tell them to stand by in case we have to conduct a search. Call me as soon as you reach Anna Rogers."

#

"No!" Tommy cried.

"Ah, come on Tommy. It's the middle of the day, what's going to happen to us?"

"Billy…."

"Come on, Tommy, don't be chicken shit, I only wanna see where you found the body. What's it going to hurt? Besides, everyone knows nothing can hurt you in the daylight. Please?"

"You don't know anything," Tommy snapped. He was tired of arguing with Billy about going into the forest. Without actually telling Billy everything that happened, which he doubted Billy would believe anyhow, he really couldn't come up with any good reason not to show his best friend the tree where he found Lyndsay.

"So then tell me. If I don't know anything then tell me, or show me where you found the body," Billy challenged.

With a heavy sigh Tommy tried again, "Billy, listen to me, and listen good. If I tell you why we can't go into the forest, and what has happened, then you'll be in danger, and I don't just mean you'll have nightmares either. I'm talking like dead danger, OK? If we go into the forest to that tree, and you see what I've seen, you'll think dying would be better!"

Billy laughed. "You talk good shit, Tommy. I'll bet you're great around a campfire. Tell you what, since you're too chicken to go into the forest, then I guess that I'll just have to go, and try to find the place by myself. I heard it was in some clearing with a big oak tree in the middle"

"You'll never find it, dip-shit."

"Bet?"

"Yeah, 'cause you wouldn't even know where to start looking, and it's a mighty big forest."

Smugly Billy announced, "It's somewhere between here and town, so all I have to do is start walking in that direction." He pointed west toward town.

As Billy started toward the path that led into the woods, Tommy panicked. He couldn't let Billy go into the woods alone. The demon was sure to get him if he did. Maybe if Tommy went with him she wouldn't hurt Billy, maybe. Then again she might get both of them. Shit!

Tommy started running toward the kennel, calling over his shoulder as he went, "All right, but wait until I get Bruiser."

Billy waited patiently, and, when Tommy finally reached his side, Billy felt a brief twinge of guilt as he looked at Tommy's pale face.

Tommy said, "Mom always says, 'be careful what you wish for, you might get it.'"

Billy was having trouble keeping up with Tommy because Bruiser seemed really anxious to start running, and Tommy was moving fast to keep the dog under control. Billy thought about what Tommy just said, and asked, "What's that supposed to mean?"

"Think about it," Tommy shouted over his shoulder.

Billy thought about it, and it still didn't make sense, and that made him mad, so he turned on Tommy. "I think it means you're afraid."

Tommy stopped, yanking hard on the leash to bring Bruiser to his side, and faced Billy. "I am afraid, and before this day is over you're going be afraid too. Just don't forget, I tried to stop you."

Billy hesitated, chewing his lip, then said, "Just come on, and stop trying to scare me, 'cause you're wasting your time. You think you can scare me, so you can laugh, but it ain't gonna work, so let's go."

#

Betty turned from the kitchen window. "It's good to see Tommy able to go into the forest again. The way that boy loves those woods I was afraid finding that body would ruin it for him."

Ted looked up from the Detroit News, a frown creasing his forehead. "What are you talking about?"

As she wiped her bands on her apron, Betty nodded toward the window. "Tommy, and his friend, Billy are going exploring in the forest."

Ted mumbled under his breath.

Betty clucked her tongue, "My, aren't you in a dandy mood this morning? I swear you've become the biggest grump I've ever known."

"Well your constant bitching and nagging doesn't help. I'm going for a walk," Ted stated as he slammed the newspaper down on the table and crashed through the screen door.

"See if you can find a better attitude while you're out there." Sue called after him. She was sick of his rotten attitude.

Ted ignored her as he headed toward the path into the woods. The Rogers kid was up to something, and Ted wanted to know what. At least now maybe he'd find out if the kid had been talking to someone the other day, someone that stayed hidden in the trees, or whether the brat was just plain loony. Probably the latter, although there is something strange going on. Not only in town, but around the Rogers house as well.

He knew he saw someone outside the kid's bedroom window the other night. He saw that someone drift, or float to the ground before disappearing into the shadows. He'd been stymied as to how the peeping Tom had gotten up to the kid's window, because he checked and hadn't found a ladder. Then last night he figured it out. There must have been a rope. Whoever it was just climbed up and looked in the window, then slid down to the ground, flipped the rope, and brought it down with him. Just because Ted hadn't actually seen the person bring down a rope didn't mean he hadn't.

Whoever was in the woods that the kid had been talking to must have been the same person outside the window, and probably the same person who set the dog off last night. Maybe it's the same person who was killing people in town.

The forest was thick, but, since it was still so early in the season, Ted could see quite a distance into the forest through the immature leaves. Everywhere around him birds chirped, and frogs sang. White and pink flowering trees, and yellow buttercups added a warm glow to the thick vegetation. Ted smiled at the sights, and sounds of spring. He'd forgotten how beautiful and peaceful the forest could be.

Far off in the distance he heard voices, and hurried to catch up. He wanted to stay far enough away not to be seen, close enough to see, and hear what was going on. He hoped the dog didn't sense him, and give him away, but if he got caught he'd just tell the kids it was a free country, and he could walk wherever he wanted.

A huge green frog jumped across the path, startling Ted, "Shit."

He picked up his pace, and could soon make out some of what the boys were saying. He slowed down a bit, keeping far enough back not to be seen. Once Bruiser looked over his shoulder, and Ted could have sworn the big dog looked right at him, but Bruise chose to ignore their stalker.

#

"Are you sure you remember how to get there?" Billy asked, his voice slightly whiny. It felt like they'd been walking for miles and he wondered if Tommy was really taking him to the place he'd found the body, or just trying to psyche him out. Billy didn't like the way he felt either, like someone was watching him. The back of his neck prickled, making him want to look over his shoulder, but he couldn't because he was afraid of what he might see. Tommy had done a job on him, but there was no way he'd admit it to his friend.

"Of course I'm sure. I come here all the time, usually not so far in, but I know where we are. It's not too much farther." He looked hopefully at Billy. "We can turn back now, it's not too late."

Billy hesitated a second, then bravely as he could, said, "Just go on pecker-head. I want to see the tree."

"Jesus, Billy, it's only a tree. I mean they took Lyndsay away already. What do you think you'll see there? Her…her ghost?"

Billy shrugged, "Maybe if we look around where the body was we'll find something, you know, maybe something the killer dropped."

"You're an idiot, pecker-breath. The cops all ready searched all over the forest, and they didn't find anything."

"Yeah? Well maybe we'll look better, shit-eater."

"Fart-smeller."

"Kumquat."

Bruiser froze. They stumbled to a halt, nearly tripping over each other in their attempt not to step on the dog. They listened intently, but didn't hear anything unusual, so slowly began moving again, Bruiser reluctantly leading the way.

"How much farther," Billy whispered, his voice sounding spooky to him, and he wished he hadn't said anything.

"Just around the next corner," Tommy whispered back. "You sure you want to go on?"

Billy swallowed his fear, and nodded. Yeah, he was sure. No matter how scared he was, he knew if he and Tommy could find something that the police overlooked, something that would tell who the murderer was they would be heroes. Man, that would really be awesome, 'cause if they were heroes then Bryan the Bully wouldn't dare beat them up, and steal their lunch money anymore 'cause they would be the bravest guys in school.

Suddenly Tommy stopped, and Billy looked around. They were standing at the edge of a large clearing. Off to one side was a four-trunk clump of white birch. Billy let his gaze travel slowly to the large oak dominating the center of the clearing. So, that was the tree. He was disappointed. It didn't look any different than the thousands of other oak trees in the forest. There wasn't any scary gnarled knots that looked like faces, or any deformed branches that looked like long twisted arms with long clawed hands at the end. Looking upward, Billy noticed several birds, and a squirrel happily darting among the thick branches,

"This is it?" he asked, disappointment dripping from his voice like venom.

Tommy shrugged. "What did you expect? The tree from Poltergeist?"

Bruiser whined, tugging at his leash. He wanted to circle around to the other side of the tree, but Tommy held him back. It was bad enough being in the clearing, he sure didn't want to go around to the other side of the tree. Without warning Bruiser raised his head, and began howling.

"SHIT!" both boys screamed at once.

"Bruiser, stop it!" Tommy yelled. The dog stopped howling, but kept pulling on the leash.

"Come on Billy, let's go, now. You've seen the tree, so let's go back to the house before Mom finds out we're here."

With Bruiser quieted Billy regained some of his courage. He hadn't come this far to turn back without seeing everything the forest had to show "Where was she laying?"

The only way Tommy was going to get Billy out of the woods was to tell him what he wanted to know, so he pointed to the left of the tree and said, "On the other side."

"Cool, let's go see."

Billy moved slowly around the clearing, Tommy's earlier remark about finding Lyndsay's ghost fresh in his memory had him keeping his distance from the tree, not that he believed in ghosts, but, well just in case. He searched the ground for the elusive missed "clue", as he walked.

Tommy stayed where he was, holding Bruiser's leash with both hands to keep the dog from following Billy. Let the weenie-dick wander around the tree if he wanted to, Tommy wasn't getting any closer. He decided to cover the ground near the path instead, that way if Billy wanted to know what he was doing he could say that if the police had missed something they had a better chance of finding it if they split up, like they always did in the movies.

Billy kicked at a clump of leaves, having spotted something-shiny red beneath them. Excitedly, he bent down and pulled out a leaf smeared with something that looked to Billy like dark red paint. Amazingly, it was still wet, and when he touched it, his finger felt sticky. Without realizing it, he'd worked his way around the clearing to the backside of the tree, and when he looked up to call out his find to Tommy, he saw it.

At first his brain didn't accept what his eyes relayed. When his brain finally accepted it, his mouth wouldn't work, and instead of a scream all that came out was a hoarse whimper.

Bruiser jerked so hard on the leash Tommy thought the dog was going to yank his arm right out of the socket. Looking up to reprimand the dog, Tommy saw Billy across the clearing. Tommy almost laughed at his friend's silly expression until he realized it was the face of terror that stared back at him.

"Billy?" Tommy whispered. "Ah SHIT, Billy!" he yelled. Whatever was over there he sure as hell didn't want to see it, been there, done that, but Billy acted like he was froze, or something, and the only way to get to Billy was to go on the back side of the oak. Is it Lyndsay? Or the Indian? If it was Lyndsay, he was pretty sure she wouldn't hurt him, but if it were the demon they'd be lucky if the three of them didn't end up in that weird black fuzzy tunnel.

Reluctantly Tommy started toward Billy, calling out as he went, "Is it Lyndsay, Billy? Is it the dead girl? What do you see? What's there?"

He refused to look until he was standing right in front of Billy. Bruiser was howling again, and tugging at his leash. Swallowing hard, Tommy slowly turned his head to see who was waiting for him, Lyndsay or the demon.

When Ted heard the dog start to howl, and Tommy scream, he hurried into the clearing. Both boys and the dog were looking at something on the far side of a big oak tree in the clearing. Ted hurried to the boys, and, when he saw what they were looking at, grabbed each by the arm, yanking them roughly back across the clearing to the path.

"Jesus H. Christ," Ted muttered, over and over.

Back at the Rogers house Ted didn't bother knocking, but pushed both boys into the kitchen. Anna came in from another part of the house, to see what all the commotion was about.

Bile rose in her throat when she saw the look on the two young faces. "What…what's the matter? What is it? What happened, Ted? Tommy? Billy? What happened?"

Ted ignored the frantic questions. The boys were no longer his main concern, now there were more important things to be taken care of.

Ted, still ignoring Anna, went to the phone and called the Whitefields Police Station.

#

As Robbins drove past the bar, he was surprised to see not only Rogers' car still there, but Morman's car as well.

He thought briefly about pulling in, but decided against it, he didn't want Morman to know he'd been following, not only him, but Alex Rogers, also. Last night Doug had followed Alex until he pulled into 1—4 The Road's parking, but when it became apparent that Alex wasn't going to be leaving anytime soon, Robbins got bored and decided to find out what Morman was up to instead. Now it looked as though he should have hung around the bar a little longer, especially since it appeared Morman never left his house after he got home from the birthday party for the Rogers kid.

When Tony came scurrying around the corner of the bar, Robbins pulled away. He knew he'd find out later from Bea, or Art, every gory detail, and most likely a whole lot more.

#

"Chief? Come in Chief."

Morman came back to the squad car, reached in, and grabbed the mike. "Yeah Sal, what have you got?"

"Chief, you better get out to the Rogers place, quick."

Tony's heart dropped, "What is it, Sally?"

The mike was silent for several seconds, and then Sally said, "Body in the woods. Same place as the Abbott girl."

His heart was pounding hard, almost painfully as Tony asked, "Who it is?"

"Ah, Ted Jenkins said he thinks its Alex Rogers, but can't be one hundred percent positive, because of the condition of the body."

"Son-of-a-bitch." He wondered how he could feel so happy, and so scared at the same time. "Sally…"

"Hold on a minute, Chief," she interrupted, and Tony could hear the sound of muffled voices, as though she'd covered the mike with her hand while having a conversation with someone.

After a couple of minutes Sally came back across the radio, "Ah, Chief, um, Karl Abbott just came in to give himself up."

"Wha…?"

Karl's voice came over the mike. "Chief, I killed Alex Rogers out in the forest, just like he killed my Lyndsay. I'm giving myself up."

Tony's mind was whirling, has everybody in town suddenly gone psycho? When he regained his senses he said, "Sally, call the guys, and have them meet me at the Rogers place."

"What about Karl, Tony?"

"Christ, I don't know." He sighed, the pain behind his eyes throbbing with every beat of his heart. "Put him in a cell, and call Doc. Klein to come check him out. I'll see him when I can. Read him his rights first, though."

"Me? I can't…"

"Just do it, Sally."

#

CHAPTER 27

Anna was done crying, for now. The police had finished cleaning up, Billy's mother came and whisked him away, and Tommy was finally asleep. Tony told her he'd try to come back later, but all Anna wanted to do was go to sleep and never wake up.

Alex dead, it still didn't seem real. Sure they hadn't gotten along for sometime, and he was living apart from them, but he had been her husband, and Tommy's father, and a part of her would always love the good part of Alex Rogers, if for no other reason than that he was Tommy's father.

She looked up as Tommy stepped into her room, "I thought you were asleep, Honey."

Tommy sat on the corner of the bed, his eyes red and puffed closed from crying. He looked so very fragile and so very, very young.

"I didn't know, Mom. I didn't know she would kill him. Maybe I could have done something to stop her. I should have tried, but I didn't. I…I didn't care about him, only you, and Bruiser, and myself. It's my fault he's dead. I should have told her to leave him alone too, but I didn't even think about him."

Anna patted the mattress beside her, and waited for her son to scoot to her side. When he was safely tucked within her embrace, Anna said, "Baby, you are not in any way responsible for your father's death. You heard Chief Morman say Mr. Abbott admitted that he'd killed Alex. Mr. Abbott is suffering a lot of grief, because his only child was brutally murdered, then Mrs. Abbott killed herself. It was more than he could take, and he went kind of crazy. His mind snapped, and he lashed out at anyone that he could. It was just bad luck that he ran into your father.

If he had seen someone else first, he probably would have killed him or her instead. Do you understand what I'm saying, Honey?"

Tommy huddled closer to Anna's side. "Mr. Abbott said Lyndsay told him that dad was her murderer."

Anna brushed a lock of deep-brown hair out of Tommy's eyes. "Tommy, Lyndsay is dead. She didn't really tell Mr. Abbott anything, except in his imagination. Dead people don't come back for the dead to point a finger at their murder. If they did there would be a lot less murders, and that would be good, but that's not real, only wishful thinking."

Tommy glanced toward the open window. The night was black and still, and he could imagine that the window was an opening into another world. He wondered if the Indian demon was out there watching and listening to see if he would reveal her secret.

Gathering his courage he said, "She did come back, Mom. She was the girl who wanted me to have you find her, the one you called "my little friend". When you wouldn't come, she said she'd have to show me, because that was the only way I'd be able to convince you. Then she came to my bedroom again the next night, and told me I had to meet her in the forest in the morning, or more people were going to die. She said someone had already died, and I guess that was her boyfriend. She keeps coming to me, because she said that I have to help her find the man who murdered her, because she can't remember, and the Indian demon will keep killing people until she was, ah, was avenged.

"But if Dad…did kill her, then she should be gone now, because she said when the person who killed her was dead she could go wherever dead people go. Do you, ah, do you think Dad killed her, Mom?"

Anna felt like she was drifting somewhere just inside the edges of an endless nightmare. Tommy sounded so positive of what he was saying, so calm and casual, the way he would have said "Mom, I saw Billy today," only he was saying, "Mom, a dead girl keeps visiting me, and she says I have to help find her murderer." Her head throbbed, she needed to sleep, or maybe she was already asleep and the solution was to wake up.

"Honey, who's the Indian?"

Glancing quickly toward the window, Tommy whispered, "She's a demon who's killing people to make Lyndsay remember so she can be avenged."

"Tommy, I don't understand, it doesn't make any sense."

Tommy shrugged. "Who said demons have to make sense?"

"But…I…Jesus I have a headache."

"It's all true, Mom, and, if Dad did kill Lyndsay then it's all over, 'cause that's an eye for an eye, right?"

I'm not crazy; it's the rest of the world. She almost giggled, but caught herself. If she started, she'd never stop.

"If your father killed her, then I suppose she would be avenged, but Tommy I don't know that your father killed her, and no one else knows that either, and even if he did, we'll probably never know now."

"Lyndsay knows."

"Lyndsay knows," Anna repeated in a whisper. "Let's get some sleep now, we'll talk about this tomorrow. Do you want to sleep here with me?"

"Can Bruiser come in too?"

"Sure, let him in," she said, nodding at the huge bundle of fur sleeping in the hall outside her room.

"Come on Bruiser, it's OK."

"I love you, Tommy."

Throwing his arms around his mother's neck, Tommy mumbled into her hair, "I love you too, Mom, and we'll protect you always."

#

Ted's grip on the fantasy was slipping away. Come back, Anna. Then Anna's firm nude body was gone, and the bloody hunk of mangled flesh that had once been Alex Rogers reappeared.

"Shit!" Dropping his bare legs to the side of the bed, Ted reached over, grabbed the glass on the night table, and drained the last couple of inches of the scotch in one gulp.

It hadn't been hard convincing Betty to spend a few days with her sister in Lansing until the craziness was over. She protested slightly at first saying that maybe she should go next door, to see if Anna and the boy needed any help, but Ted assured her Morman would be there if Anna needed anything.

Betty left looking happier than he'd seen her look in years.

Now that Alex was dead Ted didn't have to worry about him coming around unexpectedly, but that still left the cop.

"Damn that Morman."

As late as it was Ted didn't think Tony would come back tonight. Anna probably told him not to bother. She's only being nice to him because she's nice to everyone, and he's taking it the wrong way. Stupid cop, too bad someone doesn't put a bullet or two into his head.

Not normally a drinking man, Ted was doing a fine job on the bottle of scotch. He hoped eventually it would do such a good job of numbing his senses that he'd stop seeing Alex Rogers' stinking corpse every time he closed his eyes.

Ted staggered naked across the bedroom floor to open the window. There was a light on in Anna's bedroom. The light seemed as a candle in the lonely night, and Ted shivered expectantly. *She's waiting for me. I can make her forget. I'll spend the night making love to her so she'll sleep like a baby.* He giggled drunkenly, as he picked up the bottle and refilled his glass.

Turning back to the window, Ted stepped closer so the curtains gently caressed his aroused flesh. With his eyes closed he could believe it was Anna gently running her long slender fingers up and down his fevered skin.

Ted moaned, and his glassy eyes moved, like a moth to the flame, back at the beckoning light across the way. *She's waiting.*

Lifting his glass in salute, he drained the amber liquid. The light went out next door, and he smiled.

"I'll help you forget, Darling. I've got just what you need." His groin tightened in anticipation.

#

Tony looked at the clock. He called Anna earlier, but she was going to bed, and said she would talk to him in the morning. He felt a little better knowing Tommy and Bruiser were sleeping with her; he was also a little envious. He wanted to be there with them, to hold them protectively against the nightmares that would surely visit.

As bad as he felt for Anna, and especially poor Tommy who had the misfortune of finding his father, Tony couldn't deny the tiny voice that silently thanked Karl Abbott. Tommy Rogers would probably suffer emotional problems the rest of his life after all the shit the kid's been through the past couple of months.

As for Karl Abbott, Tony doubted he would ever stand trail for murder. Karl was in his own little world now, one he shared with his dead daughter, and there wasn't a court in the country that would convict him.

The thing that nagged at Tony was how to be certain that Alex was guilty of, at least, some of the murders. Alex was the only person with any possible motive. Alex had good reason to kill Dee and Jake, jealously was high on the list of reasons to murder another person, and he nearly admitted he'd been jealous the night they were murdered. He'd caught himself, but Tony read the unspoken words when Rogers cut himself off in mid sentence. Alex had said that he'd gone by the bar, but it was closed, so he went to Dee's apartment, but she wasn't there, then he said, "I thought…" realized what he was about to say, and stopped. Tony knew what he'd thought, and he'd been right, Dee and Jake had been together, however, the big question is did Alex go back to the bar and catch them in the act, or not?

The boyfriend, Jimmy, and the Milner girl, well those deaths most likely never would be solved.

Karl was talking to himself again out in the back cell, or talking to his dead daughter, Tony wasn't sure which, not that there was much difference. Karl's voice rose in anger then became whiny as he pleaded for something his dead daughter obviously wasn't willing to give. Poor man, he's gone completely insane.

Tony looked down at his report, on the desk. He hated the endless hours-spent doing the mandatory reports. When he was done, Sally would type it up for him, as she did for the other three officers. He supposed he should consider himself lucky since he only had to worry about his own paper work.

Another hour passed before Tony finally finished the paperwork and, flexing his fingers realized he hadn't heard anything from Karl in some time. Maybe he'd finally fallen asleep, and if so, Tony hoped it was a dreamless sleep.

He moved quietly down the hall, not wanting to awaken Karl, but wanting to check on him before trying to get some sleep himself on the lumpy cot in his office.

"Ah Karl, Jesus man! What'd you want to go and do that for?" Tony asked the dead man, who still clutched the plastic fork embedded in his right eye. He noticed a sweet odor in the cell, like perfume, but dismissed the thought as he unlocked the cell door.

#

Anna was hurrying through the forest. It was night, and the moon hadn't risen yet, the only light coming from the stars shining brightly above. She hurried faster, not knowing where she was, going only that it was important that she get there as soon as possible before something bad happened.

Up ahead the path forked, and she stopped. Which way? I'm dreaming, so it doesn't matter which way I go because it'll be the right way. She turned left, and started down the overgrown trail.

"No, Anna, this way," a voice whispered urgently.

Anna stopped again. OK, so I'm not even perfect in my dreams. It was silly to argue with a dream, so she retraced her steps until she came to the fork in the trail, and with a mental shrug took the right path.

"Hurry. You must hurry, Anna."

Anna quickened her pace, but in her haste caught her foot on a protruding tree root. Unable to regain her balance in the thick foliage, she hit the ground with a teeth-clanking thud. Fire burned through her elbow where she'd skinned it on a rock hidden beneath a clump of feathery ferns.

"Ouch! Hey, damn it, this is a dream, it's not suppose to hurt!"

"Hurry!" The persistent voice demanded.

#

Bruiser was on the floor next to Tommy's side of the bed. His head had been resting on his front paws, but now he raised it, and looked toward the window. After a moment's hesitation, he stood up and looked at Tommy before moving around the bed to check on Anna.

He heard something outside, something so soft he wasn't certain he'd heard it at all. It wasn't either of the "others", because he always sensed their presence before they appeared.

Moving silently to the window, he stood on his hind legs, his front feet resting on the windowsill so he could see out into the dark yard.

The lawn was empty, but another sound, this one near the back of the house, caused him to drop to the floor and hurry out of the room. He stood in the hall, undecided whether to go downstairs, or stay in the bedroom where he could protect his people. He whined softly, then starting deep in his chest, a rumble emerged through his bared teeth. Someone was trying to get in the house, but if he went downstairs to protect against the intruder, the "others" might come through the bedroom window.

He growled loudly and hurried back to Anna's side. She continued sleeping, and Bruiser became increasingly agitated, finally he stuck his wet nose in her face. Still she didn't respond, and Bruiser stopped whining and listened to the sounds from the intruder. He growled louder.

"You're almost there Anna, hurry!"

Anna stopped on the path. Something was trying to call her back. She turned around and started hurrying back the way she'd come.

"No! You have to stay with me! Don't go, Anna, come back before it's too late!"

#

Anna fought against the dream-words as she slowly opened her eyes. Bruiser stuck his cold nose against her face again, and the shock brought her fully awake.

"Shh, Bruiser. What's the matter, Boy? You have to go out?"

The dog looked toward the bedroom door, and growled low in his chest, and Anna knew, this was no I-have-to-go-potty situation. Reaching beneath the bed, she pulled the gun out of the shoebox where she had it hid.

Slipping quietly from the bed, so she wouldn't wake her son, Anna moved to the bedroom door. Bruiser started to follow her, but she whispered to him, "No. Stay. Stay with Tommy."

She pulled the bedroom door closed behind her. If something happened to her, at least Bruiser would still be protecting Tommy.

Someone was moving around in the kitchen. Someone was in her house! She took the stairs two-at-a-time as she carefully avoided the steps that creaked.

Holding the gun in shaking hands, Anna stepped around the corner, and almost fired at the hulking figure slumped against the refrigerator.

"Oh my God! Jesus, Mr. Jenkins, I almost shot you."

Ted turned the color of paste when he saw the gun in Anna's hands. He'd forgotten about the gun.

"I…I'm sorry, Anna. I just…just wanted to make sure you were all right." He swayed slightly as he spoke, and Anna caught the all to familiar stink of whiskey on his breath.

Looking over Ted's shoulder at the back door, Anna asked, "How did you get in?"

Ted pushed himself away from the refrigerator, and took a hesitant step towards Anna. "I was worried about you, over here all alone. I knew you'd be scared, and lonely. Betty has gone away for a few days, and I didn't want you to be scared."

Anna stepped around Ted, intent on checking the back door, "I know I locked the door." At the same time she noticed the broken glass on the floor, Ted grabbed her arm, yanking the gun from her hand.

He pulled her close, pressing his face so close to hers that she thought she'd gag from the stench of his breath as he murmured, "I know you want me as much as I want you, and now is our chance. Betty's gone, and Alex," he laughed cruelly, "well Alex won't be bothering anyone again."

Feeling her chest swell as she took a deep breath to scream, Ted clamped his hand across her mouth, and hissed, "I don't think you want to wake the boy."

His hand dropped to her breast, and he squeezed hard as he ground his bony hips against her. Bile rose up in her throat, and she swallowed hard to keep it down. She had to keep her wits, had to think about Tommy asleep upstairs.

"Please Mr., ah, Ted, you don't want to do this. You've just had too much to drink. Why don't you go home, and we'll pretend this never happened. Please?"

"Anna…love the sound of your name…Anna. I love to hear you say my name too, go on say it."

"T-t-Ted…Ted, please stop, you're scaring me!"

Ted dropped the gun down to her abdomen, and rubbed it slowly up and down, dropping lower with each stroke. "No", he whispered, "you're not afraid of me, look at your nipples, see the way they're pressing against your nightie, you want me, you want me to make love to you! We've waited too long for this moment, and you know you want it as badly as I do. Tell me you want me, Anna. Tell me to give it to you now! Beg me for it, just like you always do."

Ted wrapped his leg around hers, knocking her to the floor. This isn't happening!

As he ripped at her nightgown with one hand, he held the gun against her chin with the other. "Tell me how much you want me, Anna. Tell me how you've always dreamed about me ramming it to you."

"Please…God. Ted, please, don't…." Anna wanted to bite, scream, and claw, but what she wanted most was to get the gun away from Ted, and blow his head off!

Ted was trying unsuccessfully to kiss Anna when his attention was drawn towards the doorway she'd come through earlier. She tried to see what he was looking at, knowing, but hoping with all her heart she was wrong.

Ted had seen the boy out of the corner of his eye, but, when he looked up, the kid wasn't even looking at him. He was looking behind him, back towards the kitchen door. Tommy looked down at Ted once, then back at the door, his eyes wide with fear. Whatever was there Ted was sure he didn't want to see. *Probably just that cop, and the most he'll do is throw me in jail until I sober up, and Anna won't press charges. She's too nice, and she likes me.*

The kid made a choking sound, and backed away just as something that felt like a sledgehammer hit Ted in the back of the head.

Anna screamed as blood and brains splattered her face. She couldn't see what Tommy was looking at, hadn't expected anything to happen to Ted, and when his head exploded all over her, she was so shocked she was momentarily paralyzed.

Tommy took a step forward, then stopped. He spoke to someone Anna couldn't see, and the weight of Ted's body prevented her from moving once the paralysis wore off.

"Was he the one? Are you done now? You made Mr. Abbott kill my dad for nothing!" Tommy screamed, as he ran past Anna, and out the kitchen door into the night beyond.

"Tommy! Come back!" Anna screamed, fighting to free herself from the bloody corpse weighing her down.

By the time she managed to crawl out from under Ted, Tommy had disappeared into the blackness. Upstairs Bruiser was howling, and digging at the bedroom door. She decided to free the dog, as he'd be able to find Tommy faster than she could. She took the stairs two, and three at a time, no longer concerned over which steps squeaked. As soon as she threw open the bedroom door, Bruiser streaked past, knocking Anna into the wall.

"Go to him, Bruiser! Go to Tommy! Oh my baby! SOMEONE HELP ME!"

#

Tony was in the back cell with Doc Klein when the phone began ringing. At first he thought about letting it ring. What could be more important than taking care of Karl Abbott? But something told him this was no ordinary call, and he hurried to the front office as the telephone rang for the fifth time.

Before he could say a word Anna was sobbing out something about Tommy being in the woods, and what sounded like, Ted Jenkins all over her kitchen floor.

"Stay right there, Anna. Don't leave the house…Anna? Goddamn it…"

Tony slammed the phone down, and yelled instructions at the doctor, who was still in the back with Karl, as he ran out of the building.

Ted Jenkins dead, Tommy running around in the forest and now Anna was out looking for him. "Shit! Shit! Shit!"

#

Anna swept the flashlight beam across the path. Which way would Tommy have gone? She listened for any sound either Tommy, or Bruiser might make, but there was nothing beyond the sound of frogs, crickets, and night birds.

The night was as black as the nightmares that Bruiser had waken her from.

"TOMMY!"

Maybe she could "tune" Tommy in, the way she did the day she found him in the forest through Sandy's eyes.

She closed her eyes, trying to relax her muscles, as she breathed in through her nose, and out through her mouth.

Tommy.

Behind her closed eyelids, she thought she saw movement. She concentrated harder, and, yes, something was there, something moving through the forest. With her eyes still closed, Anna began moving through the woods, using her inner eye as her guide. Hesitantly at first, then with greater confidence, Anna moved forward, as the vision showed her the way.

"Hurry Anna, hurry," a voice whispered inside her head. Anna opened her eyes, and began to run.

Tommy ran after the Indian. She was keeping just out of sight so all he saw of her was a glimpse of something white, flickering through the trees, every so often. Several times he'd thought he'd lost her, but suddenly he'd see the white shape hovering around the next bend in the path. He knew now where she was leading him, but he didn't care. He wanted to kill her, to rip her apart for killing his father for nothing. His anger raged through him as a blinding red heat.

Abruptly something slammed into the back of the legs hitting him hard enough to send him sprawling. Ready to fight to the end, Tommy rolled over and stared into Bruiser's ice-blue eyes. Tommy covered his face to keep the dog from licking it off. Bruiser whined happily, as his tail pulverized the ferns near by.

Swearing, he pushed the dog away. The demon-bitch would be long gone, he thought, but when he looked over his shoulder she was still there, hovering just up the path, as though she were waiting for him. That thought caused him to hesitate, but not for long, and he pushed himself to his feet determined to see this thing through. Bruiser, had other idea though, and kept grabbing Tommy's pajama bottoms, and once pulled them so low that the boy tripped, but didn't fall, as he pulled them back up. Nothing was going to stop him, not now, not when he was so close.

He screamed at the flicker of white up ahead, "An Eye For An Eye! Remember, Bitch?" And he kept thinking, Revenge!

Tommy was in the clearing before he realized he'd traveled so far. He stopped, and looked around, and saw Lyndsay standing next to the oak tree. He moved determinedly forward, fear of the ghost no longer an option.

"Where is she?"

Lyndsay smiled. "Very good Tommy. I'm glad you realize how badly revenge can eat at you. It grabs you, and devours you, until you taste the sweetness of it."

Ignoring Lyndsay, Tommy searched the clearing and repeated the question, "Where is she, Lyndsay?"

"Oh, I'm sure she's lurking around here somewhere, she always is."

A dark shadow near the clump of white birch moved, and Tommy jerked his head in that direction. "Come on out, you bitch!"

Lyndsay laughed. "That's not who you think it is."

Tommy squinted, but couldn't make out anything about the dark shadows other than a vague idea of movement. "OK, so who is it?"

"Just some friends."

Bruiser, standing at Tommy's side, growled at the dark movement. Tommy started to move toward them, but Bruiser grabbed his pant leg, and dug his feet into the ground so the boy couldn't move unless he wanted to lose his pajama bottoms, and, mad or not, he wasn't ready to be that open with Lyndsay.

#

Anna knew the voice she was following wasn't Tommy's, but it seemed important that she keep going. The voice told her that if she was going to save Tommy she had to 'seek the little one you call Sandy'.

#

Tony stood at the edge of the forest and called to Anna, and then Tommy, but got no reply so he was unsure which direction to go.

He broke every speed law getting here from town, but wasn't quick enough to keep from losing Anna in the forest.

Anna's normally spotless kitchen resembled a slaughterhouse, and, if she hadn't told him the bloody remains belonged to her next-door neighbor, Tony would have had no idea that the headless corpse belonged to.

Ted hadn't simply been beheaded; his head was gone, splattered over the kitchen floor, ceiling, and walls like a psycho's idea of modern art. It looked like someone had stuck a cannon in Jenkins mouth and pulled the trigger.

Tony moved forward on the path, never sure if he should take one of the many branches that led away from the main trail, or not. He followed his instincts, and they told him to just keep going. He'd know when to veer off the main trail, to the path that led to the clearing. That was the logical place to start since lately the clearing seemed to be a popular place to find bodies. He prayed that he wouldn't find another corpse, especially Anna, or Tommy, there tonight.

#

"Tommy, do you like me?"

"Huh?" Tommy was fuming mad, how could Lyndsay ask him such a stupid question?

"I like you. You're fun to be with. That's why I helped your mother when that nasty man tried to rape her."

"You?"

"Yeah. I told you I'd take care of you and your mom, and I did, just like I promised."

"You killed Mr. Jenkins?"

"Yep."

Tommy swallowed hard, "But I saw the demon." Lyndsay couldn't be the one killing people, she just couldn't. He'd trusted her, believed in her.

Lyndsay floated above the forest floor, "No you didn't, you saw what I wanted you to see. Think about it, Tommy, all you really saw was something white. You thought I was the demon, so to you that's who I was."

"My…my dad?"

"Especially your dad. 'If you took all the bad things Dad did, and put them in a pile they'd reach to the moon, and if you put all the good things he did in another pile, that pile would only be as tall as', Billy's dick. I didn't like him 'cause he hurt you, and your mom. He used to beat your mom all the time, and once he…he threw you into a wall, yes, into a bedroom wall. He was a bad man Tommy. He liked to hurt people, so I had my dad take care of him for you."

Tommy had trouble catching his breath. "It was you outside my bedroom window, wasn't it? I thought it was the demon, but it was you, and my dad isn't the one who killed you? You killed my dad, and he never even did anything to you?"

Lyndsay shrugged. "Well I didn't know that, did I?"

"What about that other girl, and your boyfriend, and those people at the bar Dad used to go to? What about your mother? Did you kill all of them?"

"Don't be silly, Tommy, I'm a ghost, I couldn't even get out of the forest without your help, so how could I kill anyone?"

#

Sandy looked down the trail he'd been traveling, and knew the woman was coming, the one who thought of him as Sandy-Anna. He waited, hoping she would hurry so his quest would finally end. He was tired, more tired even than when the weather turned cold, and he buried himself in the mud until the warm winds stirred his soul awake. He became excited when he heard branches snapping in the distance. She was near!

#

Robbins pulled up behind Morman's squad car and turned off his engine. His instincts told him things were coming to a head tonight, and for whatever reason, he had to be there.

Earlier he saw Doc. Klein go into the police station. That was interesting, but, when shortly after, Morman came running out of the station like a man with his britches on fire, Doug knew his hours of surveillance were about to pay off. It took only a couple of minutes to find out from Doc. that Karl Abbott had killed himself with a plastic fork, and that Morman was going to the Rogers' place because the kid was lost in the woods, and his mother had gone in looking for him. After catching a glimpse of Morman's flashlight in the trees, Robbins got out of the car intending to follow. Lights blazed in the Rogers house, and the back door was standing open. Doug glanced at the light from Morman's flashlight, calculated the direction he was headed, and knew he was going to the clearing. He knew the forest like most people knew the inside of their homes. He would follow Morman, but first he wanted to take a peek in the house. Instead of going into the kitchen, he stopped on the deck, the stink of blood overpowering in the still night air.

#

Bruiser stood in front of Tommy, his muscles taunt, and ready to lunge if the "other" came towards the boy. This one was putting off different vibrations than he was used to from her. She was dangerous; a threat to Tommy, and Bruiser was ready to die to protect his little master.

#

Tony's heart beat against his ribs like a caged animal trying to escape. He kept thinking of the story Tommy told him. It was nonsense, of course, yet…what if? No, there are no such things as ghosts and demons. Still, if it were true he'd know how the Milner girl got crammed on that tree, and how Russo strangled on bugs. The thought of Lyndsay Abbott roaming around taking revenge on everyone she thought wronged her made him break into a cold sweat.

He came to a fork in the trail and stopped. Which way? He was confused, because he felt a need to go in both directions at once.

"Come on instincts, don't fail me now. Which way?"

Suddenly he knew. Tommy was at the end of one path, at the clearing, Anna the other. Tommy, he felt, needed him more, and if Lyndsay really existed, that's where she'd be too. There was grave danger in the clearing tonight, and Tony felt it prickle his skin like a wool suit. Turning right, Tony hurried down the path where Lyndsay Abbott and Tommy waited.

#

Anna saw herself through Sandy's eyes as she hurried down the path. She was shocked by her appearance. Her hair was matted with the same gore that soaked the front of her white satin nightgown. There were scratches on her face, and bare arms from the thick vegetation that tried to bar her way.

"Hello, Sandy," she said softly, bending down to address the small creature captured in the flashlight beam.

Sandy, wanting to finish his task as quickly as possible, turned, and slowly moved down the path. What he'd come for was just a little ways ahead, and time was running out.

#

"You lied to me, Lyndsay. I trusted you. How could you do it? How could you kill all those people? How could you be so bad when I believed you? I'll bet you even remember who really killed you too, don't you?"

Lyndsay drifted a little closer to Tommy. Bruiser growled a warning, and she stopped. Frowning she said, "What's the matter with you, Bruiser?"

Throwing his arms around the dog's neck Tommy snapped, "He knows you're bad!"

"I'm not bad." She laughed. "Tommy, I'm just finishing it. Haven't you ever felt like killing someone?"

Tommy blushed knowing Lyndsay would sneak into his head and steal his memories. "Ah ha! I knew it." Lyndsay squealed as she clapped her hands together like a little kid. "The school bully, Bryan. He beat you up, and stole your lunch money, and you wanted to beat him to death! You wanted him dead, Tommy! I knew it, you're just like me!"

Furious at the theft of his thought, Tommy screamed, "I'm not like you! I didn't kill him, I just thought about it!"

"I didn't start this, don't tell me you never heard that an evil thought is the same as an evil deed. So you are just as guilty as me." She giggled. "I guess if I go to Hell, you go to Hell, too."

"I will not, 'cause I didn't do anything!"

"That's not the way I see it, and that's not the way Reverend Kent sees it either. Seems to me you've got only one chance of keeping out of Hell, and I know I'd do anything not to have to spend eternity in that bad, nasty place, looking at the devil, and all those scary demons every day. And, you know how they love to torture people over, and over, and you can never escape, no matter how bad they hurt you. You can't even die, cause you're already dead!"

Tommy buried his face in Bruiser's fur. It couldn't be true. He couldn't really be damned just because he'd thought about killing Bryan. Tortured, forever and ever!

Blinking away tears, he asked, "How? How can I not go to Hell?"

"Don't cry, Tommy, I'm your friend, you know that. Didn't I save your mom from that nasty man? Didn't I make sure your father would never hurt her again? Didn't I keep the demon from hurting you, and your mother?

"I like you Tommy. I like being with you, and Bruiser. We have fun talking about things. You could stay here with me, and we'd never have to worry about going to Hell."

Tommy looked up at Lyndsay, and as he plucked a chunk of Husky fur from his tear-streaked cheek, said, "I can't stay here, Lyndsay. I'd starve to death, and besides, I'm just a kid, why would you want me to stay with you?"

"I told you why, Tommy. I like you. You're like the little brother I never had, and I always wanted a little brother. Someone to take places, to play with, to teach things to, we'd have fun, Tommy. Just think, you'd never have to be afraid again, because nothing could hurt you. You'd never be hungry, or cold, or scared, ever again."

"You mean like you're not scared of the demon?"

"I'm not afraid of her. She's just a nuisance, but I'm not afraid of her. She can't touch me."

"What…what would I have to do?"

Smiling, Lyndsay floated a little closer and whispered, "Be like me."

Tommy's eyes bulged. "You mean a ghost? You mean dead?"

"You'd be able to protect your mother then, just like I did. No one could stop you. You'd always be there for her, just like you told her you would be."

"I'd have to die," he said it slowly, listening to the words as they rolled off his tongue.

"No more school, no bullies beating you up, no more being sick with the flu, no more nightmares. Just think about it Tommy, you'd never have to do anything you didn't want to again, ever."

"I'd have to die."

Bruiser whined, pressing his body closer to the boy. Something was happening, and he didn't like it. Something bad was happening to the boy. Bruiser raised his head, and howled long and low, and the sound filled the forest like the cry of a lost soul.

#

Tony froze when he heard the dog howl. The blood coursing through his veins turned to ice water. Was he too late to save Tommy? Then relief melted his veins of ice, when he heard Tommy's voice close by. But the boy sounded strange, and Tony began running a dangerous race through the black forest.

#

Anna nearly fainted when she heard, far off in the distance, a mournful howl break the silence. Bruiser!

Sandy looked back over his shell. The woman had stopped following him. He looked back down the trail and, yes, there it was just a few paces ahead.

She had to follow! They were almost there, so close to the end. She must not leave now, not when they were so very close.

Anna looked back at Sandy. The turtle was moving slowly down the trail again. Indecision assaulted her, forward, or back to Tommy? Bruiser's song floated to her again on wings of despair. She was being stupid, Bruiser didn't howl like that without a good reason, something was wrong with Tommy! She spun around, and began retracing her steps.

"No Anna, you must stay with Sandy! If you want to save your son you must go forward."

Swearing with frustration, Anna turned and hurried after the turtle, and almost stepped on him when she didn't find him in the beam of her flashlight. He'd stopped, and she thought he was waiting for her, until she realized he was sitting on something. His tiny head was stretched so far out that if she plucked his scrawny neck muscles it'd probably sound like a string on a harp. He looked up at Anna then down at the object he was sitting on, then he moved off the mound and jabbed at it with his tiny beak shaped mouth.

"What the...?" She reached down and picked up a dirt-encrusted mound. It appeared to be the decayed remains of some small animal, yet there was something familiar about it, and, after beating out the dried earth, Anna realized she was holding a woman's fuzzy house slipper.

Sandy moved a short distance down the path, and once again began his funny little head dance to get Anna's attention. She was stymied about the significance of the slipper, but hurried to see what else Sandy had for her. When she saw what he had to offer this time, she reached down with a numb mind and picked it up. Turning with a scream, she ran.

#

Stepping silently behind a tree just to the right of the trail, Tony saw Tommy and Bruiser standing in the center of the clearing near the oak tree. Tommy was talking to someone standing out of sight behind the tree. Bruiser was still howling like crazy, but Tommy didn't seem to notice.

With his gun drawn, Tony stepped into the clearing. He wanted to sneak up on whoever it was Tommy was talking to, but Bruiser saw him and began to growl.

Tommy spun around, fear etched on his face.

"It's OK Tommy, it's me, Chief Morman. Are you all right?"

"Chief?" He'd expected to see the demon, not the Chief, but his relief quickly turned to fear for the cop's life.

Moving slowly toward the boy, so as not to alarm him or the dog, Tony tried to see around the tree. "Who were you talking to Tommy?"

Tommy looked back at Lyndsay, who was shaking her head violently, warning him not to reveal her presence. "It's, ah, it's on one, Sir. There's no one here."

Moving to Tommy's side, Tony put his hand on the boy's shoulder. "It's all right now, Tommy. I'm here, and no one is going to hurt you. I'll protect you."

Lyndsay drifted around to the far side of the tree, or at least that's where Tommy thought she'd gone. He hoped she didn't hurt Chief Morman.

Looking up at the lawman, Tommy said, "Mr. Jenkins is dead. He's in our kitchen. He was trying to hurt Mom."

Nodding, Tony started slowly around the tree. "I know Tommy, I saw him. How did he die? Did you see who killed him?"

"I don't know. His head just exploded," 'Tommy admitted.

Tony stopped, and looked back at the boy, "A person's head doesn't just explode, Tommy, not like that."

Tommy watched the other side of the tree, waiting for Lyndsay to appear. "They must, 'cause his did."

Tony disappeared, and Tommy held his breath until the Chief reappeared on the backside of the tree.

"Who were you talking to, Tommy? I know there was someone here, I heard you talking to them."

"No one. There isn't anyone here, Sir."

Tony stood in front of Tommy, the gun still in his hand. "I like you Tommy. I think of you as I would my own son, if I had a son. It would really make me feel bad if you felt you had to lie to me. I really think you should tell me the truth now, son."

Tommy took a step away from Chief Morman. Something in the tone of voice scared Tommy. Bruiser didn't like it either, because he growled and bared his teeth as he stepped between them.

#

"Tommy!" Anna screamed, breaking into the clearing. "Oh, thank God you're all right." She threw herself at the boy knocking him to the ground.

Bruiser turned and lunged, grabbing Morman's wrist in his powerful jaws. Surprised by the attack, Tony dropped the gun as he fell to the ground beneath the weight of the dog. Tommy, pinned beneath his mother, could see very little of what was going on in the clearing. Why had Bruiser attacked Chief Morman? Why was his mother laying on him? Where was Lyndsay? Worse, where was the demon?

Finally Tommy felt his mother's weight shift off him, and he scurried to his knees? "Mom? What's going on? Bruiser, stop it!"

Anna reached out and grabbed Tony's gun before he could collect himself enough to realize it was on the ground beside him.

Tony, free of Bruiser, rose to his knees, and repeated Tommy's questions, when he saw his revolver pointing at his chest. "Anna? What's going on?"

Bruiser hurried to Tommy, licked the boy's face, and sat in front of him. Whether as a warning to the Chief, or to keep Tommy where he was, wasn't clear, but no one tried to make him move.

Anna, her hand shaking, lowered Tony's gun to her side. In her other hand she held her small nine-millimeter weapon, pointed at Morman's chest.

"Mom?"

"You," Anna managed to say, her voice shaking. "You how could you?"

Tony held his hands out in surrender. "Anna, I don't know what you're talking about."

"Mom?" Tommy asked again, his voice small and confused. What on earth had possessed his mother to point her gun at the Chief of Police, for Pete's sake? The Chief would probably throw her in jail then he'd be alone with no one except Lyndsay to keep him company.

Anna reached to the ground, carefully making sure her gun never wavered from the center of Tony's chest, and picked up the objects she'd dropped when she threw Tommy to the ground.

"Recognize this?" She showed Tony the dirty, torn slipper.

Tony shrugged his face pale and confused in the dingy moonlight. "No, should I?"

"No? Well I'm sure you recognize this", she snapped, holding something small and shiny in front of his face.

Tommy wished he could see what his mother had in her hand. Something shiny was all he could make out. So what did a hunk of rat fur, and a small shiny thing mean that Anna would threaten a policeman with a gun? This wasn't looking good. Maybe the Chief would forgive her for getting mad at him, like he had before.

Tony looked down at the badge then back up at Anna. "It's a badge? Anna, it's not mine. I have mine right here in my pocket. I don't believe this! How could you think I would do such a thing?"

"Yes, Mrs. Rogers, how could you think such a thing about our Chief of Police?" Robbins stepped into the clearing, startling them all.

"Robbins, what the hell are you doing here?" Morman demanded.

"Looks to me like I'm the one standing on the right end of a gun barrel," Doug moved into the clearing as he spoke, keeping an eye on Tony, Anna, and Bruiser who'd started growling again. Tommy also noticed that the big man's hand was resting on the butt of his holstered gun, and the strap that kept the gun secure was unsnapped. Now Tommy had another worry, what if Captain Robbins planned to shot Mom because she was pointing her gun at Chief Morman!

"What have you got there, Mrs. Rogers?"

Anna looked at the badge in her outstretched hand. A lawman's badge, not necessarily Morman's, but any lawmen. Could it be? Had she made a fatal mistake?

Stepping closer, Robbins motioned for Anna to hand him the badge. "Give it to me Mrs. Rogers. It's evidence."

Tony started to move, but Robbins pulled his gun out, and now he too was pointing a gun at Chief Morman!

"Stay right where you are, Morman. I'd hate to have to kill you before you have a chance to stand trail."

"It's not my badge, Robbins."

"Oh? I've been watching you, Morman. Been following you around town for days now. I find it particularly interesting that you've been investigating every murder so far except Lyndsay Abbott's. I asked myself why? Know what I came up with, Morman? You don't know how Cindy, or Jimmy, or Dee, or Jake died, but I'd bet years pay that you know exactly how the Abbott girl died.

"Don't listen to him, Anna. It's probably his badge!"

"Nice try, Chief, but our badges aren't even similar. Mrs. Rogers, put down the gun. It's his badge. You know, Tony, when you were checking around town about everyone's whereabouts on the night of January 18th, I got curious about something, so I did a little investigating of my own. There was one other person out on the roads that night. You were working the station by yourself, but at least a dozen people saw you cruising the roads in the storm. They didn't think anything about it; you were just doing your job, right? Well I got to thinking, if you were manning the station alone, you should have been there in case someone called in for help, that's procedure, isn't it, Chief?"

Tommy caught movement behind, and to the right of the two lawmen, then more movement just to the left of that.

Then Lyndsay came from behind the tree, and floated to a stop right in front of Chief Morman. She had changed completely, no longer resembling the beautiful girl Tommy knew, but the decaying corpse he'd discovered behind the oak tree.

No one moved, except Lyndsay, who cocked her head from side to side as she examined Tony. Her actions reminded Tommy of Bruiser when the dog was quizzical about something. Lyndsay did something then that Tommy would have laughed about, she sniffed the Chief, but he never got the chance.

A loud scream tore the night, and in an instant Lyndsay was on Tony. "YOU! I REMEMBER IT WAS YOU!"

Tommy heard Tony screaming that it was an accident, he didn't mean for it to happen, and he kept repeating that he was sorry, until the sound of his pleas faded completely, and only the sound of the demon ripping his flesh was heard in the still night.

Anna's temporary paralysis broke with a scream. Tommy was standing beside her, his mouth open in horrified fascination as he watched Lyndsay destroy the man who he had called friend. Anna grabbed her son's arm and roughly pulled him to her, burying his face against her chest.

The scent of blood stirred Bruiser's primitive instincts, and free of Tommy's grip, the dog charged the nearest possible threat, Captain Robbins. Before Doug realized what was about to happen, Bruiser hit him in the chest, knocking him to the ground. Stunned by the impact, Robbins didn't respond fast enough and found himself pinned beneath eighty-five pounds of quivering muscle. Doug was staring into the biggest, whitest fangs he'd ever seen.

Tommy fought to free himself from Anna's protective grip when he heard the dog attack, and Robbins startled shout.

"BRUISER! NO!" Tommy screamed, and, to Doug's surprise, and obvious relief, the blue eyes disappeared, as the dog obediently returned to Tommy's side.

Doug, still leery of Bruiser, moved cautiously to Anna and Tommy, taking them in his arms to protect them from the horror in front of them.

He'd heard the old stories, everyone in town knew them, but never did he imagine there to be any truth to them.

"It is done," a voice behind them said, causing Anna to cry out, as she and Tommy both jerked from Robbins' embrace to face this new horror.

Turning as one the trio saw the woman at the same time.

Anna gasped. This was the same woman she'd seen watching Tommy the day he got his new bike. The beauty of the creature left Anna breathless. There was such peace and love in the being's black eyes that she instantly felt at ease, despite the carnage behind her.

If this was Tommy's demon then her son definitely had a strange sense of what was evil. The horror and grief over Tony's betrayal, and death, drained away, leaving only a sense of peace. Later, she knew the truth of Tony's deed would rip her heart apart. Just knowing that she cared for a man who could rape a young girl, and leave her to freeze to death, would haunt her the rest of her life, but for now those thoughts were shrouded, hidden beneath a veil of tranquility.

Anna glanced down at Tommy. Her son seemed as much in awe of the creature as she herself. He looked as though he couldn't believe this was the same being he'd been so frightened of, and as she watched, a strange Mona Lisa smile tugged his lips. When she looked up at Doug, she almost burst out laughing. His eyes bulged, and his mouth hung open in shocked surprise, but then he too smiled serenely.

"It was Lyndsay all the time," Tommy said, his tranquil smile turning sorrowful.

"Oh, you mustn't be too hard on her. Tommy, she isn't the monster you think."

"But she killed all those people!"

Shaking her head, the woman said, "It wasn't really Lyndsay who murdered those people, it was the demon that her anger grew into."

"No," Tommy argued, "she killed my dad! He didn't even do anything to her, and she killed him."

Smiling softly, the Indian said, "The creature you see there, Tommy, that is not Lyndsay Abbott. The sweet lost girl you first met in the forest is the real Lyndsay. Inside each and every one of us lives a demon. Sometimes we can catch a small glimpse of it when it shows itself as anger, or greed, or jealousy, or hate. All the bad feelings you feel are your demon trying to get out. In life this girl was a loving daughter, a devoted and loyal friend, and a faithful girlfriend. She never had an evil intent in her life. Then to die such a violent senseless death freed the demon within. Even your own Bible says, 'An Eye For An Eye.' It is just and right that she have her revenge."

Tommy glanced at Lyndsay, and what was left of Chief Morman and tried not to throw-up. Two people he learned to believe in and they both were totally different than he'd perceived them. How could he ever trust anyone again, how?

Would he know that when he looked into a face that it wasn't just a mask hiding another, completely different, person?

Then another thought struck him, a thought so horrifying that even the sight of Morman's remains seemed insignificant, "Lyndsay will go to Hell now, for killing all those people."

The Indian smiled, "No, Tommy, she won't. Hell is a place in the mind of man. You helped save her soul by bringing the guilty one to her, even though you didn't know he was coming. Each person who died by her hand had his or her own demon to deal with, whether it was guilt, greed, or lust. They killed themselves, because if they were able to control their own demon, Lyndsay could never have touched them."

Shaking his head, Tommy argued, "What about her mom and dad? Were they bad people too?"

The Indian looked toward the shadows that Tommy noticed earlier. "No, her parents were extremely good people. Their demon was grief, and a love so deep they refused to be parted from each other, and their daughter, even if it meant to be together in death."

"But Lyndsay didn't kill my husband, her father did," Anna argued, trying, as Tommy had, to expel every cloud of doubt.

"Yes," the demon nodded sadly. "I hoped this would end sooner. I am forbidden to interfere in the acts of man, except in the most obscure manner. This is sacred ground, this place you call Whitefields. The Ancient Ones were here long before even my own people came and it was they who laid down the law.

"I was the last person murdered here, until Lyndsay, now she will join me as guardian. Have you never wondered at the lack of crime in this place? Lyndsay's murder called me back, and I, with Lyndsay at my side, will return again, if need arises. It is the law."

"Called you back from where?" Tommy asked wide-eyed.

"A very beautiful place, Tommy. Imagine if you can a place so beautiful that the very sight of it takes your breath away."

Tommy thought for a moment, "You mean like Disneyland?"

"Even better," the demon laughed, and because she saw that Tommy doubted there was anyplace more beautiful than the amusement park, added, "You shall see, Tommy. Many, many years from now, when it is time, Lyndsay and I shall personally escort you there. That is my promise to you.

Now, Lyndsay and I must leave you, but," for the first time the woman addressed Doug, "be warned, and remind your people of the horror that awaits them should they transgress."

Tommy turned to look back at Lyndsay who was about to disappear from his life as quickly as she first appeared. He would miss her, even though he spent the past couple of weeks dreading her appearance, he knew it wasn't her he feared, but the unknown, and was surprised to see the beautiful, golden goddess he'd first seen across the stream. Her hair danced with fiery sparks of gold, and there was such a radiant smile on her face that Tommy wanted to run to her, to hug her, and never let her leave him again.

Lyndsay floated across the distance, and Tommy knew this was the way he'd always remember her. "I love you Tommy. You were a true friend when I needed one the most. Someday, when the time has come, and the Lady comes for you, I'll be there with her to show you the way. Thank you for all you've done for me, and I'm truly sorry for the bad side of my soul that caused you pain."

Tommy moved closer to Lyndsay. "I...I don't know how to feel about you Lyndsay. I mean because of Dad and all. I know the Indian lady said it wasn't your fault, but still...you know what I mean? I don't want to be mad at you, because I, ah, I kind of lo...ah, like you too, but, well it's kind of like how I felt about Dad. Part of me loved him, but part of me hated him too, 'cause he did those bad things to Mom, and me. You lied to me, and I don't know if I can ever trust you again, but I...I'll try, OK?"

Lyndsay smiled sadly, "I understand."

"Will you be OK," he nodded toward the Indian and the swirling black tunnel behind her, "with her?"

Lyndsay laughed her special-wind-through-the-trees laugh for him. "Oh yes, Tommy! What she said is true, and Mom and Dad will be there with me, and I've got so much to make up to them, but you'll see, Thomas, someday you'll see. Good-bye, for now. Good-bye, Bruiser, I'll see you again too, Boy."

Anna pulled Tommy close as Lyndsay floated to the Indian's side, and together they moved into the swirling tunnel, and in the dawning light, Tommy watched as several dark shadows quickly scurried after them. "Bye Dad".

"One thing, before you leave!" Anna suddenly called out, stopping the spectral procession, "What would have happened if Tony hadn't been found out?"

"Then your nightmares would have become your reality."

CHAPTER 28

January 18, 2065

Thomas laid the journal in his lap, and sighed wistfully as he stared into the dancing flames in the fireplace. A bitter winter wind beat relentlessly against the windows. The first major snowfall of the winter began at dusk. This storm would be talked about for years to come as one of the worst storms to hit Whitefields since the storm of 2000. Thomas rose from his chair and walked slowly to the window, and saw but a blanket of white.

Those who knew the signs were tucked safely into their nice warm homes. No one would venture from that safe haven unless his or her life or a loved one's life depended on it.

Thomas moved to the stack of seasoned logs beside the hearth, and tossed another one onto the fire. His bones ached from the cold, and no matter how warm he got the den he still felt the bitter wind seeping into his every joint.

On the book shelves lining the walls on both sides of the fireplace were row after row of books, some were Anna's, some of them his, and some of them written by other authors interested in life after death, all of them well worn.

His first book was labeled "fiction," but he knew the truth. It told of a couple of weeks in the life of a young boy, filled with death, and terror, and miracles. He knew no one would ever believe him, just as they hadn't believed his mother, or Captain Robbins, all those years ago.

Anna finished the Sandy The Three-Legged Turtle series she'd been working on, and then began a new series about a boy and his blue-eyed

Siberian Husky. The books were a huge success, and the original of every one was stacked like dominoes on the top two shelves, left of the fireplace.

Eventually Anna learned to trust again, and a couple of years later Tommy had the immense pleasure of walking his mother down the aisle, as she became Mrs. Douglas Robbins. Anna and her new husband lived in the house Tommy grew up in until they died within a couple of weeks of each other, just two months shy of their fiftieth wedding anniversary. Anna died of cancer, and Doug followed his beloved when his heart, without warning, just stopped beating. Thomas was sure that Doug, as Lyndsay's parents had all those years earlier, preferred being with his beloved in death, than being alone in life. Thomas grieved, not because they'd died, but because he'd miss them. He was happy that they were together, and he celebrated their fiftieth wedding anniversary alone.

Bruiser lived to the ripe old age of sixteen, and, although Tommy spent less and less time with the dog as he grew older, the special bond between them lasted until the day Tommy found Bruiser dead in his kennel. Tommy cried harder that day than he'd ever cried before or since, but even then he knew Bruiser was with Lyndsay, waiting for him.

The missing deliveryman was located the following week in a seedy motel room on the outskirts of Detroit with an even seedier woman. He was fired from his job instantly, but didn't much care. He and his companion drank over half the beer from the truck, and somehow, in a drunken stupor he hurt his back so severely that he was unable to work again and spent his remaining years, which weren't that many, drinking his Social Security Disability checks away.

Thomas pulled his cardigan together against the cold, as he dropped back into his chair. It was going to be a very long night, and, if the storm were as bad as he felt it was going to be, it would be an even longer day tomorrow. The only good thing about the storm was Ms. Philips; the crabby nurse Doc. Jenkins sent over three times a week to torture him, wouldn't be able to come out until the roads were cleared, and in Whitefields that could take several days.

Picking up his glass of ginger brandy, Thomas popped two more arthritis pills, the only good thing Ms. Crabby Ass brought with her, into his mouth. The pain was so severe these days he could hardly hold onto his glass. The pills weren't much help, but he was afraid to not take them fearing the pain became so bad it drove him insane.

Settling back into his comfortable chair, Thomas again picked up the journal. Ah, to be that young and innocent again! He loved to read the words he wrote so long ago. There seemed something almost magical about them, and if he tried really hard, he almost seemed to transport himself back in time to the night Lyndsay said good-bye. Such a beautiful girl, if only he'd been older....

The windowpanes rattled, and way off in the distance an animal howled.

Thomas, engrossed in his story, at first didn't hear the eerie song, then, when it finally registered, he dropped his glass of brandy to the floor, spilling the golden liquid across the rich blue carpet.

The dog howled again, closer this time, and Thomas' heart began a rapid drum-roll inside his gaunt chest.

"Bruiser?" With effort Thomas forced himself from the chair, and, hunched over

in unbearable pain, moved out of the den to the massive oak doors at the front of the house.

The front door seemed impossibly far away and instead of getting closer with each step that he took seemed to drift farther away.

The storm raged outside and for several heart stopping moments it was the only sound Thomas heard. Then the howling continued, growing in volume until it was so loud the old man had to stop and look around to see if the animal hadn't somehow managed to magically appear in the room with him, but the entrance hall was empty.

A searing pain dropped Thomas to his knees, and his cramped fingers clawed the emancipated flesh over his heart, as though to squeeze the pain from his body. But the pain wouldn't be denied. He wouldn't be able to make it to the door after all, and Thomas cried out in anger at his body's betrayal.

"Tommy."

Thomas looked up, and there standing over him was the beautiful Indian lady from his childhood. In her blinding radiance, it took him a moment for his failing eyes to search out her companions. On her right side stood Lyndsay, beautiful golden-hair goddess whom he never stopped loving, and on her left was Bruiser, his tail wagging so hard Thomas could feel the wind it caused.

Thomas smiled, his eyes filling with tears; they hadn't forgotten their promise.

"It's time Thomas. Time to leave the body, and come with us. Just as we promised, Tommy."

Bruiser walked over to the old man laying helpless on the cold tile floor, and began licking the wrinkles from his face, and Tommy reached up with strong young arms, and pulled the dog close and buried his face in Bruiser's warm, thick fur.

"Bruiser, oh, God how I've missed you, Boy!" Tommy breathed deeply of the dog's fur, the scent better than any expensive perfume he'd ever smelled. Bruiser licked Tommy again, then, backing away, grumbled a few special husky words, which made Tommy howl with laughter. "I know exactly what you mean old friend!"

The two women smiled silently as the boy and his dog rolled around the floor together in total bliss. Tommy seemed unaware of 'Thomas' withered husk laying a few feet away.

Finally Tommy stopped rollicking with the dog, but remained on his knees with his arms wrapped tightly around Bruisers' neck. His eyes filled with tears as he looked up at the women. "I've waited a very long time for you to keep your promise. I thought you'd forgotten me. I've missed you Lyndsay, and know what? You're even more beautiful than I remember, if that's possible.

"One thing though, how old am I? I hope I'm not the ten-year-old child you befriended back then, Lyndsay. I know too much to be a that young again!"

Lyndsay laughed at the boy, and asked, "What age do you want to be, Tommy?"

With a glint in his eye, Tom smiled, "Oh, I think eighteen should be just about right, wouldn't you say, Lyndsay? Of course, unless you prefer your men younger, or," he nodded at his discarded shell, "maybe you like more mature men?"

Linking her arm with his, Lyndsay looked up into his sparkling eyes, and smiled. "Why Tom, shame on you. I happen to think eighteen is a perfect age, especially on you!"

With Bruiser in the lead the little group walked out into the worse storm to hit the area since the winter of 2000.

Would you like to see your manuscript become a book?

If you are interested in becoming a PublishAmerica author, please submit your manuscript for possible publication to us at:

acquisitions@publishamerica.com

You may also mail in your manuscript to:

**PublishAmerica
PO Box 151
Frederick, MD 21705**

www.publishamerica.com

PublishAmerica

CPSIA information can be obtained at www.ICGtesting.com
224700LV00001B/96/P